Born in England and raised in Canada, Natalie recently founded the independent bookstore Archetype Books in Oakville, Ontario, where she lives with her family and two rescue dogs. A lifelong devotee of all things Jane Austen, *The Jane Austen Society* is her first published novel.

The Jane Austen Society

Natalie Jenner

ORION

An Orion paperback

First published in Great Britain in 2020 by Orion Fiction
This paperback edition published in 2021 by Orion Fiction,
an imprint of The Orion Publishing Group Ltd
Carmelite House, 50 Victoria Embankment
London EC4Y 0DZ

An Hachette UK Company

1 3 5 7 9 10 8 6 4 2

A CIP catalogue record for this book is
available from the British Library.

ISBN (Mass Market Paperback) 978 1 4091 9412 5
ISBN (eBook) 978 1 4091 9413 2

Typeset by Input Data Services Ltd, Somerset
Printed and bound in Great Britain by Clays Ltd, Elcograf S.p.A.

MIX
Paper from
responsible sources
FSC® C104740

www.orionbooks.co.uk

For my husband

Who shall inherit England?
The business people who run her
Or the people who understand her?

— LIONEL TRILLING

The
Jane
Austen
Society

Chapter One

Chawton, Hampshire
June 1932

$\mathscr{H}$e lay back on the low stone wall, knees pulled up, and stretched out his spine against the rock. The birdsong pierced the early-morning air in little shrieks that hammered at his very skull. Lying there, still, face turned flat upwards to the sky, he could feel death all around him in the small church graveyard. He must have looked like an effigy himself, resting on top of the wall, as if carved into permanent silence, abreast a silent tomb. He had never left his small village to see the great cathedrals of his country, but he knew from books how the sculpted ancient rulers lay just like this, atop their elevated shrines, for lower men like himself to gaze at centuries later in awe.

It was haying season, and he had left his wagon in the lane, right where it met the kissing gate and the farm fields at the end of old Gosport Road. Huge bundles of hay had already been piled up high on the back of the wagon, waiting for transport to the horse and dairy farms that dotted the outer vicinity of the village, stretching in a row from Alton to East Tisted. As he lay there, he could feel the back of his shirt damp from sweat, even though the sun was pale and barely trying; at just nine in the morning, he had already been hard at work in the fields for several hours.

The multitude of finches, robins and tits suddenly quieted down as if on command, and he closed his eyes. His dog had been on guard until that moment, looking out over the mossy stone wall at the sheep that dotted the fields below, just past the hidden ha-ha that marked the perimeter of the estate. But as the farmer's laboured breath became deep and rhythmic with sleep, the dog took his own cue and lay down beneath his master in the cool dirt of the graveyard.

'Excuse me.'

He jolted awake at the voice now resonant above him. A lady's voice. An American voice.

Sitting up, he swung his legs down from the stone wall to stand before her. He looked at her face quickly, glanced at the rest of her, then just as quickly looked away.

She appeared to be quite young, no older than her early twenties. She wore a wide-brimmed straw hat with an indigo-blue ribbon tied about it that matched the deep blue of her tailored dress. She looked quite tall, almost the same height as him, until he realised she was wearing the highest pair of heels he had ever seen. In one hand she held a small pamphlet, in the other a black clutch purse – and around her neck hung a tiny cross on a short silver chain.

'I'm so sorry to disturb you, but you're the first person I've met all morning. And I'm quite lost, you see.'

As a lifelong resident of Chawton, population 377, the man was not surprised. He was always one of the first villagers up and about in the morning, right behind the milkman, Dr Gray on his more pressing rounds, and the postman doing his pickup from the local office.

'You see,' she repeated, starting to adjust to his natural

reticence, 'I came down for the day from London – I took the train out here from Winchester to see the home of the writer Jane Austen. But I can't find it, and I saw this little parish church from the road and decided to have a look around. To find some trace of her if I could.'

The man looked behind his right shoulder at the church, the same church he had attended all his life, made of local flint and red sandstone and sheltered by beech and elm trees. It had been rebuilt a few generations ago – nothing notable was left inside of Jane Austen or her immediate family.

He turned and looked back now over his left shoulder, at the small stile at the rear of the churchyard, through which one could just glimpse towering yew hedges clipped into circular cones. Even as a boy, they had looked to him like nothing so much as extremely large salt and pepper cellars. The hedges ran along the south terrace garden of an imposing Elizabethan house set on an incline, with a gabled tiled roof, red brick-work, and a three-storey Tudor porch covered in vines.

'The big house is back there,' he said abruptly, 'just past the church. The Great House it's called. Where the Knight family lives. Miss Austen's mother and sister's graves are right here – do you see, miss, alongside the church wall?'

Her face lit up in gratitude, both for the information and for his slow warming to the conversation.

'Oh my goodness, I had no idea . . .'

Then her eyes began to well up. She was the most striking human being he had ever met, like a model in a hair or soap advertisement in the papers. As the tears started, the colour of her eyes crystallised into something he had never before seen, a shade of blue almost like violet, while the tears caught on rows of inky-black lashes, blacker even than her hair.

Looking away, he tried to step around her carefully, his dog, Rider, now nipping about at his muddy boots. He walked over until he was standing next to the two large slabs of stone that stood upright in the ground. She followed him, the heels of her black pumps sticking a bit in the graveyard dirt, and he watched as she silently mouthed the words carved onto the twin tombstones.

Backing away, he fiddled about to find his cap from his pocket. Brushing back the lock of light blond hair that tended to fall across his brow as he worked, he tucked it up under the rim of the cap as he pulled it forward and down over his eyes. He wanted to be away from her now, from the strange emotion being stirred up in her by the unadorned graves of simple women dead these past one hundred years.

Off he wandered to wait with Rider by the main lychgate to the churchyard. After several minutes, she finally appeared from around the corner of the church, this time stopping to read the inscription of every stone she passed, as if hoping to discover even more slumbering souls of note. Every so often, she would teeter a bit as her heel caught the edge of a stone, and she would grimace just so slightly at her own clumsiness. But her eyes never left the graves below.

She stopped at the lychgate next to him and looked back with a contented sigh. She was smiling now and more composed – so composed that he finally picked up the whiff of money in both her poise and her manners.

'I'm so sorry about that, I just wasn't prepared. You see, I came all this way to find the cottage, where she wrote the books – the little table, the creaking door,' she added, but to no visible reaction. 'I couldn't find out much about any of this while in London – thank you so much for telling me.'

He held the lychgate open for her and they started to walk back towards the main road together.

'I can take you to her house if you'd like – it's barely a mile or so up the lane. I've done my morning haying for the farm, before it gets too hot, so I've time to spare.'

She smiled, a great big white winning smile, the kind of smile he could only imagine being American. 'That is awfully kind of you, thank you. You know, I was assuming people came all the time, like this, like me – do they?'

He shrugged as he kept his pace slow to meet hers along the half-mile gravel drive that led down to the road from the Great House.

'Often enough, I guess. Nothing really much to see, though. It's just workers' flats now, at the cottage – tenants in all the rooms.'

He turned to see her face tighten in disappointment. As if to cheer her up, before he even knew what had come over him, he asked her about the books.

'I'm not even sure I can answer that,' she replied, as he pointed the way back down the country lane, opposite the end where his wagon sat with its load temporarily forgotten. 'I just feel, when I read her, when I reread her – which I do, more than any other author – it's as if she is inside my head. Like music. My father first read the books to me when I was very young – he died when I was twelve – and I hear his voice, too, when I read her. Nothing made him laugh out loud, nothing, the way those books did.'

He listened to her rambling on, then shook his head as if in disbelief.

'You haven't read her then?' the woman asked, a disbelieving light in her own eyes meeting his.

'Can't say I've too much interest. Stick to Haggard and the like. Adventure stories, you know. Suppose you might judge me for that.'

'I would never judge anyone for what they read.' She caught

the ironic look on his face and added, with another broad smile, 'Although I guess I just did.'

'All the same, I never understood how a bunch of books about girls looking for husbands could be on par with the great writers. Tolstoy and such.'

She looked at him with new interest. 'You've read Tolstoy?'

'Used to – I was going to be sent up to study, during the war, but both my brothers got called to fight. I stayed back here, to help out.'

'Do you all work the farm together then?'

He looked away. 'No, miss. They're both dead now. The war.'

He liked to say the words like that, like a clean cut, sharp and deep and irrevocable. As if trying to stave off any further conversation. But he had the feeling that with her this approach might only invite more questions, so he quickly continued, 'By the way, see those two roads, where they meet – you came in from Winchester, from the left, yeah? Well, stick along here to the right – that's now the main road to London – and you come into Chawton proper. That there's the cottage up ahead.'

'Oh, that's really awfully kind of you. Thank you. But you must read the books. You must. I mean, you live here – how can you not?'

He wasn't used to this kind of emotional persuasion – he just wanted to get back to his wagon of hay and be gone.

'Just promise me, please, Mr . . . ?'

'Adam. The name's Adam.'

'Mary Anne,' she replied, extending her hand to shake his goodbye. 'Start with *Pride and Prejudice* of course. And then *Emma* – she's my favourite. So bold, yet so wonderfully oblivious. Please?'

He shrugged again, tipped his cap at her, and started to walk off down the lane. He dared to look back only once, from just past the pond where the two roads met. He saw her still standing there, tall and slender in her midnight blue, staring at the red-brick cottage, at its bricked-up window and the white front door opening straight onto the lane.

⌒

When Adam Berwick had finished up the rest of his day's work, he left the now-empty wagon back by the kissing gate and trudged along the main road until he reached the tiny terrace cottage that had been his home for the past handful of years.

The family had once been much larger, his father and mother and all three boys, of whom he was by far the youngest. They had owned a small farm, proudly held on to through four generations of his father's family. This legacy had required all the Berwick men to take on hard manual labour, starting very young. And he had loved it: the repetition, the unvarying cycle of the seasons, the going-straight-to-bed with no time to talk.

But Adam had also been an attentive and diligent student, teaching himself to read when barely five years old from the books his father left lying around the house, then reading every single thing he could get his hands on. He would visit the larger town of Alton with his mother every chance he could get. His favourite moment, even more than the sweet shop and the single large jawbreaker she would occasionally buy for him, was the chance to look at the children's books at the library and find something new to borrow. Because – and he still did not understand how people like his brothers could not see this – inside the pages of each and every book was a whole other world.

He could disappear inside that world whenever he needed to – whenever he felt the outside world, and other people,

pressing in on him – a pressure from social contact and expectations that was surely routine for everyone else, but
affected him much more intensely and inexplicably. But he
could also experience things from other people's point of view
and learn their lessons alongside them, and – most important to
him – discover the key to living a happy life. He had a feeling
that, outside his rough farming family, people were existing
on a very different plane, with their emotions and their
desires telegraphed along lines never-ending, vibrating in as-
yet-unknown ears, creating little frictions and little sparks.
His own life was full of little friction, and even fewer sparks.

Winning the scholarship to college had been the one exciting moment in his young life, only to be just as quickly taken
away from him when his brothers were sent to war. He had
been both too young to fight and, according to his mother,
too grown-up now for what she called aimless study. The war
had changed everything, and not just for his family – although
everyone in the village acknowledged that the Berwicks had
been harder hit than most, with both older boys killed in battle
in the Aegean Sea in 1918 and the father less than a year later
by the Spanish flu. There was a solicitude now, for his mother
and for him, a deep community caring that had, at times, been
all that had buoyed them from the deepest despair.

But as much as they were kept from falling into the abyss,
they remained forever teetering on the brink. Neither he nor
his mother, despite their different temperaments, seemed to
possess energy for anything more than submission to life – the
idea that they might have to fight their way out of their lot
was beyond them. So, only a few years after the war, between
the debts and the grief and his mother's constant complain-
ing, they had sold the farm back to the Knight family at a significant discount. Over the generations, various Berwicks had
worked at the Knight estate as household staff or servants, his

own mother and grandmother among them, and now Adam, too, would join their employment by gathering the hay each summer, and tilling the fields, and planting a few rotating crops of wheat and hops and barley.

Eventually, the Knight family, like so many others in the village, began to suffer financial troubles of their own. Adam felt that they were all tied together, very much interdependent, and that the sale of the farm to the Knights, and the employment for him, were part of a larger community effort to sustain and survive.

He was surviving on the teetering brink – at least, he acted as if he were. But inside him, in the place that only books could touch, there remained both a deep unknowing and the deepest, most trenchant pain. Adam knew that part of his brain had shut down from all the pain, in a bizarre effort to protect itself, and his mother was even worse, for she appeared to be merely waiting to die, while constantly warning him how bad things would be without her. In the meantime, she was simply going through the motions of mothering him – having his toast and tea ready in the morning, and then, as now, his supper kept warm for him at the end of the day.

They would sit there alone together at the kitchen table, just as they were doing now, and he would tell her about his work, and she would tell him about whom she had run into in the village, or in Alton if it was her midweek shopping day. They talked about anything and everything, except the past.

But today he didn't tell her about the young woman from America. He wasn't sure what he wanted to say. For one thing, his mother was always on him to find a wife, and this stranger to town was so beyond him in her beauty as to be almost otherworldly. His mother was also one of the villagers for whom the connection to Jane Austen remained more an irritation than anything else. She saved her most bitter complaints for the tourists and gawkers who, often enough, did descend on the small village, demanding information, demanding to see something, demanding that life here be just like in the books. As if the villagers' little lives were somehow unreal, and the real thing – the only thing – that mattered, and the only thing that ever would, had happened over a hundred years ago.

He was becoming quite worried for Mr Darcy.

It seemed to Adam that once a man notices a woman's eyes to be fine, and tries to eavesdrop on her conversations, and finds himself overly affected by her bad opinion of him, then such a man is on the path to something uncharted, whether he admits it to himself or not. Adam did not know much about women (although his mother kept telling him it did not take much), but he wondered if, in the history of life, as well as in literature, a man had ever fallen into such obvious lust as fast as Mr Darcy, and not done anything about it except to inadvertently, and so successfully, push it away.

He appreciated more than ever that their small two-up, two-down terrace cottage, which sat next to a laneway leading back from the main Winchester road, gave him his own bedroom and space to read. In his sparse room with its gabled ceiling was the plain twin bed – one half of a set – that he had slept in since his boyhood. A single oak armoire and an antique dresser stood in opposite corners of the room. And he had his shelf of books that had once belonged to his father – adventure novels, the boys' treasury, and the greats, like Conan Doyle and Alexandre Dumas and H. G. Wells. But now, next to his bed, lay a fairly thick hardcover book with a laminated cover, from the library, showing two women in bonnets whispering to each other, while a man in the background stood imperiously next to a garden urn.

He had discreetly slipped it across the counter at the lending library only two days earlier.

It was going fast.

But as much as it amused him, the book also confused him. For one thing, he wondered at the father character; he did not think it reflected well on Mr Bennet to spend all his leisure time barricaded in his study or indulging his humour at the expense of everyone else. Mrs Bennet was much more easily understood, but something about the Bennet household was still amiss, in a way that he did not recall encountering before in literature. Not among a big family at least. He had read books about orphans, and treachery among friends, and fathers sent off to debtors' prison – but the biggest plots always turned on an act of revenge or greed or a missing will.

The Bennets, for all intents and purposes, simply didn't like each other. He had not been expecting this at all from a lady writer with a commitment to happy endings. Yet, sadly, it felt more real to him than anything else he had ever read.

Finishing the chapter where Darcy shows his estate to the woman who once so robustly spurned his marriage proposal, Adam finally started to drift off to sleep. He recalled the recent visitor to his own town, the tiny cross on a chain, the white winning smile: tokens of the faith and hope so sadly missing from his own life. He could not conceive of the willingness to travel so far for something so whimsical – yet an unguarded happiness had also radiated from within the visitor, real happiness, the kind he had always searched for in books.

Reading Jane Austen was making him identify with Darcy and the thunderclap power of physical attraction that flies in the face of one's usual judgement. It was helping him understand how even someone without much means or agency might demand to be treated. How we can act the fool and no one around us will necessarily clue us in.

He would surely never see the American woman again. But maybe reading Jane Austen could help him gain even a small degree of her contented state.

Maybe reading Austen could give him the key.

Chapter Two

Chawton, Hampshire
October 1943

$\mathcal{D}$r Gray sat alone at the desk in his office, a small room off the larger front parlour that acted as his examining room. He stared miserably at the X-ray film before him. Both of Charles Stone's legs had been so severely crushed, the good doctor could not imagine any degree of function being regained over time.

He held the X-ray back up to the golden October light streaming in from the side window and squinted at it one last time, even though he knew there was nothing more to see — nothing that would make any of this one jot easier to relay.

Having grown up in Chawton, Dr Gray had moved to London during the Great War for medical school and training, returning to the village in 1930 to take over old Dr Simpson's practise. Over the past thirteen years, he had welcomed into the world as many patients as he had seen out. He knew every family's history and their doom — the ones where madness skipped a generation, or asthma did not. He knew which patients one could tell the cold hard truth to — and which ones fared better not knowing. Charlie Stone would do better not knowing, at least for now. He would keep from the edges of despair that way, until the march of time and increasing poverty took precedence over his pride.

Dr Gray put his fingers to his temples and pushed in hard. Before him on the blotter pad rested a series of medicine bottles. He stared absent-mindedly at one of them, then pushed himself up from the arms of his wooden swivel chair with resolution. It was mid-afternoon, and normally the time that his nurse and housekeeper would be bringing him his tea. But he needed some air, needed to clear his brain and find some respite from all the cares that piled up before him every day. He was the general practitioner for the village of Chawton, but also its confidant, father figure and resident ghost – someone who knew more about the future, and the past, than anyone else.

He left his rose-covered thatched cottage through the green front door that was always open to patients and led straight out onto the street. Like all the former worker cottages, the house was so close to the main road that it practically half heaved itself onto it. His nurse, Harriet Peckham, tried to keep the front bay window's lace curtains drawn as much as possible during patient visits, but the small beady eyes of the town had proven themselves even smaller still by a willingness to peer through the eyelet pattern and thin crack where the panels tried to meet.

He started down the lane and saw the Alton taxi pulling up at the junction where Winchester Road split in two, and where the old pond had only recently been drained. Three ducks could still on occasion be spotted meandering about the roads, searching for their lost paradise. But right now Dr Gray was watching three middle-aged women instead, as they stepped out of the cab amidst a flurry of hats and handbags, landing right in front of the old Jane Austen cottage.

Despite the war now stretching across the Atlantic, women of a certain age still saw fit to travel to Chawton to see where Austen had lived. Dr Gray had always marvelled at their female spirit in coming to pay homage to the great writer. Something had been freed in them by the war; some essential fear that the world had tried to drum into them had collapsed in the face of an even greater enemy. He wondered if the future, just as the cinema foretold, belonged to these women. Chattering, gathering, travelling women, full of vigour and mission, going after what they wanted, big or small. Just like Bette Davis in *Jezebel* or Greer Garson in his favourite film, *Random Harvest*.

Dr Gray permitted himself one night a week to indulge a passion he had shared with his late wife: a bus trip into the neighbouring town of Alton to see the newest film release. The rest of his free time he spent trying to distract himself from thinking about Jennie. But now, when the cinema lights dimmed, and the couples slouched against each other even farther still, he allowed himself to picture his beloved wife and their own nights out at the cinema together. She had always wanted to see the 'weepies', those woman-centred films starring such actresses as Katharine Hepburn and Barbara Stanwyck, and he would sometimes put up a little fuss, a little push for a Western or a gangster film – but he always ended up enjoying her choices as much as she did. Sometimes they would even skip the bus after and walk the half-hour home in the moonlight instead, talking over the film they had just seen. He couldn't wait to hear what she had to say.

He had always loved her most for her mind – and he was smart enough to know that she was much smarter than him. She had been one of the few women at his college and had spent equal time in the library and in the lab. Her sharp mathematical mind could have been a real asset to the war effort, but this was one of many things about her that he would never know.

She had died four years earlier from a simple fall down the stairs leading to their bedroom, hitting her head in the absolute worst way, on the one jutting part of the lowest stair that he had always meant to fix. The internal bleeding was swift and acute, and he had been completely unable to save her.

A doctor who can't save his own wife achieves an unfortunate degree of notoriety to add to the grief and self-recrimination. No one was ever going to be harder on him than himself, but his professional pride often caused him to wonder if the other villagers might not blame him, too.

As he passed the trio of women chatting excitedly in front of the little white gate to the Austen cottage, he tipped his hat at them. He was not one of the villagers who considered them a nuisance to be wished away. Every person who made their village a site of pilgrimage was keeping alive the legacy and the aura of Austen, and as a lifelong fan himself, he appreciated that the villagers were involuntary caretakers of something much bigger than they could guess at.

He was turning onto the old Gosport Road that led to the Great House and neighbouring Knight estate when he saw a fellow member of the school board approaching him from that same direction.

They tipped their hats at each other, then the other man started in at a clip, 'Glad I ran into you Benjamin. Having a problem again at the school.'

Dr Gray sighed. 'The new teacher?'

The other man nodded. 'Yes, young Miss Lewis, as you surmised. She has those boys on a steady diet of lady authors from as far back as the 1700s. Can't make her see reason.' He paused. 'Thought she might listen to you.'

'Because why?'

'Well, for one thing, you're the closest in age to her.'

'Not by much.'

'And besides, you seem to have a pretty good grasp of her, um, teaching methods.'

Dr Gray's eyes narrowed imperceptibly. 'I've been the doctor here for many years now and would like to think I have a pretty good understanding of everyone in the village. It doesn't necessarily follow that I have any particular influence over them.'

'Just give it a try, hmm? That's a good man.'

Dr Gray did not think he could persuade Adeline Lewis of anything. He did know that his fellow school board trustees – all male, all well into their fifties and beyond – were a little afraid of the young woman only one term into her first teaching job. Adeline was very confident in her lesson plans and highly resistant to anyone trying to manage her. She also physically matched most of the men for height – which was not difficult to do, since only Dr Gray was anywhere close to six feet tall. But perhaps most unnerving of all, Adeline Lewis was attractive, in a way that sneaked up on all of them, until they started to forget what they had come to say. She would stare straight in the eyes of the various board members, always ready to speak her mind, always up for a fight, and they each inevitably gave in to her. Dr Gray shook his head in remonstrance whenever one of them opened their monthly board meetings with yet another tale of capitulation.

'Well,' he replied tentatively, looking around as if hoping to see someone lying injured in the street and in need of his medical services instead, 'I suppose I could stop in there now.'

'There's a fellow.' The other man smiled. 'You're sure we're not keeping you from anything?'

Dr Gray shook his head. 'No, just out for a walk to clear my head.'

The other man tipped his hat again and continued on his way, cheerfully calling back, 'Doubt having to set Miss Lewis straight will help with any of that . . .'

Dr Gray hesitated, turned to look back at his colleague, then forged on ahead until he reached the old Victorian schoolhouse across the road from the village cricket pitch. He supposed class would be ending right about now, at 3:30 P.M. Sure enough, when he strolled into the vacated senior classroom, he found Adeline Lewis standing at the board, chalk in hand, half writing and half gesturing to a young girl sitting at the teacher's desk as if she belonged there. Dr Gray noticed a copy of Virginia Woolf in the student's hands.

Marriage as a Social Contract to Avoid Poverty was being written in bright white letters across both sides of the chalkboard.

Dr Gray sighed again, and Adeline must have heard him, because she whirled about.

'You've been sent to scold me,' she said with a smile – but it was the smile of the knowing, not the vanquished, and he felt his jaw automatically tighten.

'Not to scold; to understand. A steady diet of women writers, Adeline, really – for a room full of adolescent boys?'

Adeline looked down at the girl sitting at the desk, who had closed her Virginia Woolf and was now watching the two adults with unabashed interest.

'Not just boys – Dr Gray, you know Miss Stone.'

Dr Gray nodded. 'How are you, Evie? How's your father?'

Evie's father was the one whose X-ray Dr Gray had just been worrying over. Charlie Stone had been critically injured in a tractor accident a few months earlier, and Dr Gray knew how catastrophic this had been for the family, both financially and emotionally. He also knew that the father would never be returning to physical work again, even though Dr Gray did not have the heart to communicate that yet to his patient in no uncertain terms. Most worryingly, Dr Gray wondered how the large clan with five children under fifteen would manage going forward without the income of their sole provider. He had heard talk among the adults at the farm of pulling the oldest child, Evie, out of school for servant work, and this was just one of many secrets he had to keep.

'He's doing a lot of reading,' Evie spoke up. 'Miss Lewis gave him a list of books to cheer him, and he's working through it from the library, one by one.'

Dr Gray cocked one eyebrow at Miss Lewis as if stumbling upon evidence helpful to his cause. 'I'd like to see such a list sometime, if I may.'

'Hardly,' replied Adeline with a slight frostiness to her tone. 'I am judged enough around here for my choices.'

Evie continued to watch the two adults, having sensed a strange shift in mood between them, as if they had forgotten she was sitting there. Dr Gray was usually so gentlemanly with the ladies – along with his salt-and-pepper hair, intense brown eyes and broad shoulders, it was his manner as well as his vocation that kept him an object of interest and, young Evie suspected, lust among the village women. But with Adeline he always seemed, as now, both flustered and on the defensive. At the same time, Adeline was showing none of those same ladies' usual deference towards him, which Evie suspected was irritating Dr Gray even more.

'Well, let's ask Miss Evie, then, shall we?' Adeline was saying, and Evie popped out of her reverie to see both adults turn towards her.

But she had no interest in getting in the middle of any of it, being fully on Miss Lewis's side when it came to her teaching methods. Instead Evie grabbed her book bag from a nearby desk and, with a quick nod and a goodbye, scurried off along the old oak floorboards of the classroom.

'Ah, to be fourteen again and without composure,' said Dr Gray with a laugh when Evie was far enough away.

'Oh, Evie Stone is composed enough all right. She just doesn't feel like tangling with the likes of you.'

Adeline came around to the front of her desk and leaned back against it, arms crossed, the piece of chalk still clasped in her fingers. She was wearing a straight brown skirt to her knees, with a cream-coloured blouse open a few buttons from her neck that accentuated her tawny complexion, and the same stacked-heel, laced-up brown Oxfords that Dr Gray noticed on all the young working women of late.

'Look, we're doing critical and thematic analysis of the text, Dr Gray – what, so if they're all off seeking treasure or fending away pirates, that's more relevant? Understanding social mores through the lens of literature is just as important for young men as it is for young ladies. Or don't you think it important at all?'

Dr Gray took off his hat, and she watched silently, head tilted to one side, as he tousled his hair and then sat down in one of the extra-small desk seats in front of her.

'What?' he asked as she stared at him.

'You look so small, sitting there. You always look so tall.'

'I'm not that much taller than you, I believe.'

'No . . . but it *feels* like you are.'

'Can't you add some Trollope at least, some good old *Doctor Thorne* or the like?'

'You and your Trollope.' She now crossed her legs at their ankles as if she had all the time in the world to debate him, while still watching him curiously. 'Listen, we know you love Austen as much as I do. I do talk about the Napoleonic Wars and abolition and all that.'

'I'm sure you do.' He grinned. 'I am sure you cover it all.

You are nothing if not thorough in your lesson planning. But the other board members—'

'And you . . .'

'No, I agree only to an extent – but mostly because I don't want you to lose your job. When we hired you for this opening, I was pleased that you could stay close to home and help out with your mother. Pleased that one of Chawton's own, so to speak, was going to have a part in moulding our youngest minds.'

'Dr Gray, why so formal? Just tell me what you want me to do. You know I'll always do it. Eventually,' she added with a playful smile.

He was looking at her as she spoke, trying to do something with the dawning consciousness that she was mocking him in some way. Or, at the very least, daring him. He often felt that way around Adeline – it was most unnerving.

'Hey, Addy!' a young man's voice boomed down the classroom corridor.

Dr Gray turned in his seat to see Samuel Grover, another of the village youth, striding happily towards them in full uniform.

'Hey, Dr Gray, how are you?' The young man joined Adeline at the desk, put his arm about her waist, and gave her a lingering kiss on the cheek.

As the village doctor, Dr Benjamin Gray had cared for both Samuel and Adeline for many years now, watching them grow up together, both brown-haired and brown-eyed and quick to laugh, little mirrors of each other. They had done their parents proud since then, Samuel training in his father's footsteps to be a solicitor, Adeline receiving her teaching diploma. But Dr Gray had had no idea that they were now officially a couple.

He stood up rather abruptly, grabbing his hat. 'Well, I should be going. Miss Lewis, Samuel – I mean, Officer Grover.'

Dr Gray headed back towards the main school door and Adeline ran after him.

'I'm sorry, wait, I'm sure we weren't finished,' she called out, catching hold of the back of his coat sleeve to slow him down.

He looked down at her hand on his sleeve and noticed for the first time her engagement ring, a small solitaire garnet stone.

'I didn't know,' he said quickly. 'I should have congratulated you both. Please give my best to Samuel.'

'Dr Gray, is everything okay? I really will think about what you said – I probably have gone a little overboard lately. Drunk with power, as they say.' She offered him a wide happy smile, and he saw for the first time how very happy she was, too.

'When is the date?' He twisted the hat still in his hands.

'We're in no hurry.'

'You are both still so young, after all.'

'Not too young for Samuel to be sent off to fight for king and country. But, yes, still quite young, as you are always reminding me. It's all right – it'll be something to live for,' she said with a grin.

'I'm sure it will, for you both. Well, best be getting on.' He put on his hat and started back down the road that led into town.

Just as predicted, the exchange with Adeline Lewis had done nothing to clear his head.

Chapter Three

London, England
September 1945

The main room on the lower level of Sotheby's was packed, the bamboo-sided chairs with intricate needle-pointed seating having been supplemented on this occasion by extra ones from the other rooms downstairs. Still, many in the crowd found themselves having to stand with their backs to the mirror-panelled walls, reflecting all the people in the room many times over. This only contributed to the air of excitement that buzzed throughout the room as the auction-house director ascended the podium.

'We have before us today the contents of Godmersham Park, ancestral home of the Knight family, seated in the heart of Kent. Famous family and visitors over the years include several generations of the royal house of Saxe-Coburg, as well as the authoress Miss Jane Austen, whose elder brother inherited the estate in 1794.'

The crowd nearest the entrance murmured slightly as a striking woman in her thirties came through the mirrored doors and glanced discreetly about the room. She was able to find a seat near the front when several gentlemen, recognising her, jumped up to offer theirs.

Sotheby's assistant director of estate sales, Yardley Sinclair, was watching from the sidelines next to the podium. He was inwardly congratulating himself for arranging the late arrival of the woman, so that the entire room would notice her and the excitement of the day would increase even more. She had visited the auction house several times over the years to inspect various Austen memorabilia, even recently acquiring a rare first edition of *Emma* for a record-setting price. Yardley had made sure she was among the first to learn of the sale of the Godmersham estate. He knew that the Hollywood studios would have her schedule locked down for months in advance, and he wanted her to have every opportunity to fly over in time.

He watched as she leaned forward and caught the eye of a man across the aisle from her. There was some silent signalling between them, and Yardley's heart started to beat faster at the seriousness of the couple's expressions. The gentleman in particular looked thoroughly determined to win at something big today.

Yardley himself was torn about the sale. Godmersham had been one of those historic houses that seemed to survive the First World War, only to lose its final footing with the struggles of the Second. Sotheby's had had its eyes on the Austen-related contents of the estate for several decades, the author's reputation only increasing year after year, especially abroad. Wealthy Americans were aggressively driving up the prices for various editions and letters, and Yardley could foresee the day when certain items would outstrip the average collector's reach. His whole team was hoping today would usher in that new era. For now, items including fragments of Austen's own handwriting were still reasonably priced, and Yardley was holding on to his own first edition of the collected works from 1833, personally acquired from an antiquarian dealer in Charing Cross when Yardley was still in college.

'Lot number ten,' intoned the director of Sotheby's, 'is this exquisite necklace of a cross. In topaz. Acquired by Charles Austen, brother to Jane Austen, from reward money received for capturing an enemy ship whilst in the Royal Navy. Accompanied by a similar but not identical cross, also in topaz. Both on solid-gold chains and described through a series of Austen–Knight family letters as belonging to each of Jane Austen and her sister, Cassandra. Affidavit copies of those letters are included in the catalogue before you.'

Yardley knew that the famous film star now sitting in the third row was most interested in three items from the catalogue: a simple gold ring with a turquoise stone that had verifiably belonged to Austen, the two topaz necklaces and a small portable mahogany writing desk that had passed down through the Austen family over the years. Although Sotheby's could not confirm that Jane Austen herself had written at the desk while at home or travelling, this was one of only two desks known to have belonged to her immediate family. The other one was lost somewhere in private hands.

'Lot number ten,' the director repeated. 'Bidding begins at one hundred pounds, with a presale estimate of one thousand. One hundred pounds – do I hear one hundred?'

The actress gave the slightest nod of her head.

'We have one hundred pounds. Do I hear one fifty? One hundred and fifty pounds?'

Another nod, this time from a few rows back. The actress looked back over her left shoulder, then glanced quickly at the gentleman across the aisle.

Bidding proceeded like this for several minutes. When one of the bids went from one thousand pounds to fifteen hundred, the auction-house director looked over at one of his other colleagues standing along the mirrored wall to the right of the podium. The two men exchanged nods. 'Two thousand pounds,' the director announced sharply. 'Do I hear two thousand?'

Yardley had started watching the gentleman in silent conversation with the actress. He was as handsome as a film star himself and well over six feet tall, his hatless head towering above those of the people seated around him. He was wearing a tailored suit in dark grey, with dark-chocolate-brown brogues. He was not checking anything – not his Cartier watch, not the catalogue, not the faces of anyone else in the room except hers. He showed no apprehension or anxiety of any kind. As the bidding accelerated, the price now far exceeding previous estimates, most of the crowd started to lean forward in their chairs, whispering excitedly to their neighbours. But the man just kept calmly, almost casually, lifting his right index finger, over and over, as if bored with the proceedings.

'Five thousand pounds!' the director was exclaiming, as the audience started to murmur its approval even more loudly. All the faces in the room were now swivelled to watch the famous Hollywood actress and the man across the aisle from her.

'Going once . . . going twice . . . sold! Two topaz crosses belonging to Jane Austen and her sister – sold for five thousand pounds to the gentleman in row three.'

The actress jumped up from her chair and rushed over to the man, and he smiled in his seat while she hugged him. He looked up at her, at that remarkable face, and it was clear to Yardley that everything the man was doing – everything he was bidding on today – was in service to that face. Everyone else got to see it storeys high on a screen – but right now, it belonged to him, as much as those two topaz crosses did.

The ring was sold as lot number fourteen, this time for a record-setting seven thousand pounds, and again to the actress and her partner. The writing desk was sold for almost twice as much, its lack of official verification only slightly dampening the price, and an American collector of no known affiliation outbid the British Museum. Yardley had winced at the sale – he believed that all of these objects should remain in England, or at least be kept together as much as possible.

At the end of the auction, with record amounts raised, Yardley and the director of Sotheby's invited the actress and her fellow buyer to celebrate with the team over champagne. As they raised their crystal flutes in a toast to the day's success, Yardley asked the actress what her plans were for the jewellery.

'My plans?' she repeated. 'I don't know – I guess to wear them.'

The idea of something so invaluable – and so culturally significant – being tossed onto a dressing table or, worse still, lost in the back seat of a cab, started the beginnings of a migraine for Yardley.

'But their worth . . . ,' he began to say.

'Their worth is for Miss Harrison to decide,' the gentleman interjected. 'That is why I bought them for her.'

Yardley noticed for the first time something less than pure exhilaration on the actress's face as the other man said these words. Yardley wondered at the degree of their intimacy – wondered if the purchase was part of a larger transaction of some kind. He had heard the usual rumours about actresses from the stage or screen, yet he would have liked to have given this one the benefit of the doubt.

'Actually I was being a little glib just now,' she said apologetically. 'I seem to be doing that more and more of late. I guess the excitement of the day must be getting to me. I will of course make sure that these most prized possessions are given the care they deserve.'

She looked over at Yardley as if in appeasement, and he

noticed yet again her wonderfully adaptable manner. So very
American, he suspected: she would put a foot wrong, then just
as quickly — and as charmingly as possible — put everything
right as if it cost her nothing.

'Were you pleased, at the sale?' she was now asking him.

Yardley sipped his champagne thoughtfully before putting
the flute down. 'I was pleased at the success, yes — I've been
trying to land the Godmersham estate for years. It's so rare,
as you know, to find any substantive collection of Austen
artefacts. All that's left now is the Knight estate down in
Hampshire — but apparently the current Mr Knight's impossible to deal with, and the sole heir, a Miss Frances Knight, is
an agoraphobic spinster, of all things.'

'Agoraphobic?' the woman's companion asked, finally looking up from the paperwork before him.

Yardley, noticing the woman give the man a curious look,
continued, 'Yes, phobic of the outdoors — doesn't leave the
house.'

'That's such a shame,' the woman said. 'And so very Gothic.'

Yardley smiled. He could tell that she, like himself, lived
with one foot stuck in the past.

'I just hope she cares enough about Austen,' he added. 'You
and I both know how much I would love for as many of her
possessions as possible to stay in England.'

She gave an irrepressible smile and looked over at her companion before speaking further. 'Well, Yardley, I have some
great news for you then — they will. At least mine will. I am
moving to England.'

'Well,' Yardley exclaimed, 'this *is* good news. I had no idea.
Ah, it is all making sense now. Where will you be living?'

'We' — she looked again at the gentleman as she said the
words — 'we will be living in Hampshire. Of all places! What
do you think of that?'

'I think that quite perfect, under the circumstances.' Yardley looked down at the bare engagement finger on her left hand. 'So, the ring?' he asked with a smile.

'Yes, the ring.' She smiled back, and in that smile was an entreaty he was powerless to resist.

The paperwork was being completed for the transactions, with the wiring of the American funds still sitting in the New York bank. Yardley looked at the director of Sotheby's, and with a few discreet nods, they agreed to retrieve the contents of box number fourteen. As the director walked out of the room, Yardley marvelled at how much of his job – the most important parts of his job – seemed to be conducted with absolutely no words whatsoever. Like an actor himself, he was constantly attuned to the needs and demands of others, adapting to them as much as he could, and as much as was necessary to acquire or hold on to some essential power for himself.

The director came back into the room a few minutes later and whispered to Yardley that, following some questions from the Manhattan bank, the lawyers for the buyer had authorised withdrawal from a European account in his name instead. This was greatly speeding up matters, and they now had the final release from the Zurich account confirmed by telegram. Yardley nodded his approval, then walked over and presented the small numbered box to the gentleman.

'I believe this is yours.' Yardley held the marked box out to the man, whose name they now knew to be Jack Leonard, a successful businessman and fledgling Hollywood producer.

The woman stood up quickly, and the high heel of her shoe – the highest set of heels Yardley had ever seen – caught just slightly on the edge of the antique Indian rug that carpeted the floor.

'Oh my goodness,' she exclaimed, her fingers outstretched

towards the small box as she righted herself, her hand shaking perceptibly.

Jack stood up and took the box from Yardley's hand, then playfully held it up high, far out of her reach. Only because Yardley knew the woman to be as big a fan of Austen as himself did he see in the man's behaviour something more than playfulness. Something between teasing and a little cruel.

'Good things come to those who wait,' Jack said to the woman, as she finally gave in and lowered her arms in mock defeat.

But Yardley was not sure he fully trusted the Hollywood mogul with the looks of a matinée idol. And he was left to wonder, as the Americans said their goodbyes and were accompanied by security into the early-September twilight, who the real actor was between them.

Mimi Harrison had met Jack Leonard six months earlier, by the backyard pool of the producer of her latest film. *Home & Glory* was the story of a widow whose two sons are fighting in different battles in the war, strategically kept apart by the British navy to minimise the potential for grievous loss to the family. But the boys desperately want to fight together, and this leads to inevitable and tragic consequences for all. Mimi had heard a real-life story similar to this years ago, on a trip to England, and agreed to the role without even reading the script.

It was a 'weepie' – a woman's picture – the very kind that had made Mimi Harrison a Hollywood star. She had meant to become a great stage actress and, after graduating with a degree in history and drama from Smith, had started out on Broadway in several strong supporting roles in the mid-1930s, reluctantly changing her name along the way from the more sombre Mary Anne. But her dark, exotic features were caught one night by a studio casting director sitting in the front row, and she completed a quick make-up-free screen test in New York, before being sent out West by train to Los Angeles. There she had another screen test, this time in full make-up, followed by facial bleaching to reduce her freckles, and a minor surgical procedure that would have mortified her mother.

'One procedure is a record for around here, honey,' the wardrobe assistant had remarked when Mimi pointed out the scar. Mimi was a slave to the truth and felt that, if her body was no longer 100 per cent a Harrison's, the least she could do would be to not hide the fact.

Mimi's first day at the studio had been an eventful one. The leading actor in a string of successful Depression-era comedies hit on her immediately, and after several days' persistence, she gave in and agreed to dinner at Chasen's. But that was all she agreed to — a fact he had trouble accepting at the end of the night. She would have been more unnerved by all of this if she did not already have a list of successful stage credits behind her. Arriving in Hollywood a little older than most, she believed that none of this would be happening if she did not possess something of value. And if she gave away any of it out of fear, she would be in a race to the bottom. Her father, a notable judge in the Third Circuit Court of Appeals, had taught her this, along with a love of horseback riding, Renaissance art and Jane Austen.

Her first few months were marked by many men's attempts to seduce her for one night — and sometimes even less, if they had an afterparty they hoped to get to — and her meeting them right there on the start line, not budging one bit. She knew she had only one person she needed to keep happy, the head of the studio, Monte Cartwright — and she had carefully and wisely cultivated fatherly feelings in him from the start, until he was patting himself on the back for being such a mensch, at least where Mimi Harrison was concerned.

The past decade in Hollywood, career-wise, had been remarkably successful. She had contractually retained the right to one outside-studio film a year, and she was averaging four in-house movies on top of that, keeping her too busy for much of a social or romantic life. With a per-film take of forty thousand dollars, she was considered one of the highest-paid actresses in the world.

It would be only a matter of time before she met Jack Leonard, who made even more money than that.

He had been watching her box-office ascension from a rival up-and-coming studio with a degree of patience for which he was not usually known. His own success had been less linear and much more questionable. With generations of family money from the garment industry behind him, he had counter-bet the Depression, picking up any stock that looked as if its final days had come, then buying up any surviving competitors. As FDR's antitrust teams moved in, Jack started moving abroad, cultivating alliances with steel and weapons producers in Europe, and becoming both financially and diplomatically indispensable to them as various countries started assembling munitions factories for the increasing military demand. He had an uncanny knack for knowing exactly where things were heading, and for isolating the most critical weaknesses of his opponents, who were many. For Jack Leonard, life was a constant battle.

He possessed not one ounce of introspection and instead directed his total energy at summing up the people around him. Understanding himself was not important because there was nothing there to understand. He knew that, and he knew that no one else would ever believe it. After all, he walked and talked and acted like a normal person, yet he won, again and again, in a way that few others consistently could. If everyone else had had the capacity to imagine how much he was focused on beating *them,* they might have stood a chance. But even then, they would not have been able to live with the terms of success. So Jack Leonard continued to win, and destroy others, and make money, and he convinced himself (because when one is devoid of a soul, it takes little work to convince the self of anything) that his success was due to his own superiority in having figured all of this out.

The more he made money, the more he needed to make – it was a compulsion that he made no qualms about. If you weren't moving forward, you weren't winning – and if you weren't making money while you were at it, you were losing even more. So when a few business associates from New York decided to invest in a new studio venture out West, he hopped on – what better way to meet beautiful young women with little expense or effort. Plus, there was no better time to enter the movie business, with so many prominent producers, actors and directors off fighting the Nazis.

Now, in the spring of 1945, with America fully in the war, and his steel and weapons contracts worth millions, and his studio putting out a film a week, Jack Leonard stood towering down over Mimi Harrison as she lay on a lounge chair in her purple one-piece swimsuit.

Mimi opened one eye against the sun, now partially obscured by Jack standing there, and said simply, 'You're blocking my sun.'

'*Your* sun?' he asked with one eyebrow raised.

She sat up a bit, peering at him from underneath her sunglasses, then placed them back down on her still slightly freckled nose. 'Well, I have it on loan from our host today.'

'Loans. I can give out those. Jack' – he held out his hand to her – 'Jack Leonard.'

No glimpse of recognition passed over her face, and he could feel the back of his neck start to tighten in irritation.

'Mimi Harrison,' she replied, shaking his hand.

He noticed that she had a strong, assured grip for a woman. He also noticed her hands were bare of any jewellery and slightly calloused.

She looked down at her hand still resting in his and added, 'I ride.'

'And you act.'

'When I'm not riding.'

'Or reading.' He casually picked up the book on the unoccupied lounge chair next to her and flipped it over to see the cover.

'*Northanger Abbey,*' he read aloud, then looked at her inquiringly.

It was a test, in a way — at least in L.A. They so rarely knew the books, the studio men — they were numbers guys. The actors — they were the outdoorsy types, always in motion, always too bored to have sat still in school. She had lost count of the number of two-seat airplane, motorcycle and sailboat rides she had been taken on over the years; the golf courses, the canyon hikes, the one-room fishing cabins.

'Jane Austen,' she said with a nonchalant shrug. 'You're not familiar with her?'

He put the book back down and sat on the edge of the lounge chair facing her. 'For a role?'

'I wish. No, just relaxation.'

'Relaxing's overrated.'

He was the most confident man she had ever met. She knew he must know who she was, although she genuinely had no idea about him.

'What rates with you then?' she asked, reaching for a glass

of iced tea from the tray now being held out to her by one of the household staff.

'Winning.'

'At all costs?'

'Nothing costs more – or is worth more – than winning. Look at the war.'

She sighed, and the sudden look of boredom on her face made the irritation start creeping down his spine and right back up to his temples. 'Why do you men have to make everything about the war?'

'Why not? We're all in this together.'

'Oh, I'm sorry, are you shipping out soon?'

Now it was a full-on migraine. Jack stood back up. 'Look, I'm not going anywhere. Not my style. I don't think it's yours, either. I think – well, anyway, it was nice to meet you.' He paused, and something almost yearning appeared in his hazel eyes. 'I always hoped we'd meet.'

It was the first sign of anything approaching vulnerability she had seen in him. She could tell he was supremely used to getting everything he wanted. She could tell he wanted her. The distance between his confident bravura and his interest in her was something only she could bridge. As Elizabeth Bennet would say, it was most gratifying.

She looked at him in his perfectly pressed white shirt and beige khakis that were the exact same shade as his close-cropped sandy-brown hair, and she saw the glint of the Cartier watch around his tanned left wrist, and the slightly faded spot at the base of his ring finger. There would be plenty more to find out about him, of that much she was sure.

Chapter Four

Chawton, Hampshire
August 1945

$\mathcal{D}$r Gray had finished up his rounds for the day and decided to take a walk to clear his head. He headed down the main Winchester road past the Austen cottage, then walked briskly along old Gosport Road until he reached the long gravel drive that led to the Knight estate and the adjoining parish church of St Nicholas.

A little farther down the lane, he could see the Berwick hay wagon, now emptied of its bales of straw and done for the day, sitting next to the kissing gate. But this afternoon he was not looking to stretch his legs with a long walk through the summer fields to Upper and Lower Farringdon.

Instead he walked up the drive to the church. It was only a little past three, and he knew that Reverend Powell would be out on his daily rounds, visiting various ailing villagers either right before or right after him. Their two jobs were probably much more alike than either would want to admit. But where the reverend was being asked to change reality through prayer, Dr Gray was being asked to prescribe hope in the face of reality. Two sides of the same fateful coin. Which side the coin would flip on – which corner of the stairs, which X-ray film, would rear its ugly head – was the darkness that it was his job to somehow manage and disperse, even as he himself so often wanted to surrender to it.

He had always loved the small stone church of St Nicholas, set back from the road on its little walled incline. To him, the church was the perfect size: small enough to always feel intimate, but just big enough to always seem full. Although he was never sure how much visitors were aware of it, the connection to the Austen family was at its most poignant here. The church was on the estate of Chawton Park, which Edward, Jane's older brother, had inherited from the wealthy childless couple who had adopted him, to avoid dying without an heir. The estate also included the little steward's cottage where the Gosport and Winchester roads intersected, and where Jane Austen had finally found a home for her writing after years of dependency on several other male relatives. Here in this church, nearly a century and a half later, the Knights still held sway. The Knight family heraldry stained the panes of glass, the altar stood above the family crypt, and the pews were made from oak that had been felled on the Knight estate.

As Dr Gray entered, he removed his hat and, after crossing himself, looked up to see Adeline Grover alone in the front pew, her long straight brown hair brushing against her full pink cheeks as she kept her head lowered in prayer. She was wearing a simple floral-patterned housedress that had been let out at the waist, with a white girlish collar and cuffs on its short sleeves.

Her husband, Samuel Grover, had ended up perishing last March in a dive-bombing attack off the coast of Croatia, unknowingly leaving her just one month pregnant. The baby was now all that she had, her husband's body lying below one

simple plain white cross on the rocky island of Vis. Dr Gray
had been surprised at the young woman's composure throughout the ordeal. With all her brashness, he would have thought
Adeline would become quite bitter, quite fast, if life dealt her
an unfair hand. But instead she radiated a strange positivity,
almost a desperate determination that somehow everything
would turn out all right. He would have chalked it all up to
her youth, but he knew from patients such as Adam Berwick
that being young when tragedy strikes can make it even harder
to endure.

From across the aisle, he had watched her stand in church
every Sunday for the past six months, both hands on her expanding belly, listening peacefully to the words of Reverend
Powell. Perhaps expecting a child could do that – he would
never know himself. But he wondered if the pregnancy was
keeping her from fully experiencing her grief. He was the last
person on earth to judge anyone for that; he sometimes wondered what good grief did at all.

Adeline looked up at the sound of his heavy step on the old
stone floor but did not turn around. He watched silently as she
crossed herself, then stood to move up the centre aisle towards
him.

He remembered her and Samuel's wedding day here last
February, during the young officer's final leave. Adeline had
been radiant – but then again, she always looked bright-eyed
and game for anything. Yet as wonderful and spirited as Adeline was, she had ended up too interesting and progressive a
teacher for their slumbering Hampshire village. She had quit
halfway through the last spring term, on the heels of her wedding, and dedicated herself to setting up house for Samuel once
he permanently returned from the war. Even now, in the late-
summer heat, with only a trimester left in her pregnancy, Dr
Gray would occasionally wander by the little Grover house to

find Adeline knee-deep in the dirt of her garden patch, pulling up the courgettes and wax beans and beets to be pickled and preserved for the winter ahead.

He smiled at her approach, hoping she would not pass by without stopping to talk.

'Adeline, how are you feeling?'

'Better than last week. Which is unusual, I understand, as all the old women keep telling me it only gets worse.'

'Best not to listen to them,' Dr Gray advised with a laugh. 'They have their line, and they will stick to it. They can be counted on for at least that.'

She made as if to keep on her way, and he fell in step next to her.

'Am I keeping you?' she asked.

'Not at all – I worried I'd done the same to you.'

She shook her head quickly. 'No, I was finished. Said all I needed to. And then some.'

'I'm sure He was listening. You are hard to ignore.'

'Dr Gray!' she exclaimed in mock offense.

He was one of the few people in Chawton who did not recoil whenever they ran into her, as if suddenly flinching from the memory of her loss – which, of course, only made her feel even worse, the opposite of what the other villagers surely intended. She had also always loved Dr Gray's dry sense of humour, and the way he acted so admonishing, even when she suspected that he might be a much softer person inside. During the few times Samuel had been on leave, they would often go to the pictures in Alton – always her pick – and she was sometimes surprised to catch a glimpse of Dr Gray watching a Mimi Harrison 'weepie' all alone in the back, half-hidden by the whirls of cigarette smoke, surrounded by couples at what were highly wrought romantic films designed to make the audience cry.

Maybe the film-going was some kind of weird catharsis for him. Certainly, she marvelled at how he stood it all, the terrible random diagnoses he carried around inside him, knowing that sharing any of it was only going to make someone's pain even worse – knowing that just a few words from him could destroy a life. Even as colleagues fighting over her teaching methods at the school, she had always looked up to Dr Gray as one of the kinder souls in the village, quick with a comforting and attentive smile. Since his wife's tragic death, she wondered if he had found anyone else to confide in. She knew his nurse, Harriet Peckham, was up to something about him, for all the gossip she liked to spread in town about his comings and goings.

They emerged together into the sunshine. Two female tourists could be seen loitering in the lane, gazing up the gravel path and past the church in its tree-sheltered hollow, to the large Elizabethan house standing on rising ground behind.

'They're back,' Adeline said. 'That didn't take long. I guess only a world war could keep them away.'

'Do you ever stop and think how lucky we are, the way we get to live here every day, like Jane Austen did? I know I do. I sometimes think it was one of the reasons I moved back.'

Adeline turned to look at him with interest. 'Actually, yes, I do. I always have. It made this place magical for me when I was young. That someone could spin such stories from *this:* this walk, this lane, this little church. Those gorgeous sunlit fields, that kissing gate, all of it. So very English. They come to see it because it exists. Here, at least, it exists. Here, at least, it is real.'

He nodded in agreement. 'I should tell you I am reading *Emma* again. Every time, I find a new clue, something I missed before. It's like she's still writing these stories, still giving them life.'

Adeline always loved discussing books with Dr Gray. When

she had been essentially fired from the local village school – although she had quit before the town could have its way with her, shrewdly using her wedding as a way out – there had been increasing concern over her class discussions. Certain subjects and authors continued to be deemed inappropriate; Adeline, on the other hand, did not think it was for a village to decide which of the classics counted. That job, presumably, had already been done, by people much more learned and wise than any of them. Of everyone in the village, only with Dr Gray could she speak with total freedom about the books she loved.

'I don't know about Emma, Dr Gray. I mean, I am all for high spirits myself, as you so often point out, but I sometimes fail to see where the selfishness ends and the spirits begin.'

'Emma is not selfish, per se. She is self-*interested*, in a way that most people can't afford to be.'

Adeline was not so sure of this. She would never want the amount of attention that Emma gladly soaked up. Even though Adeline was now an object of anxious concern among the villagers, she could never endure it for long without wanting to rotate the intense beam of attention elsewhere. She wondered what it said about Emma that she was always so content to keep the beam shining directly on herself.

The two women tourists were still standing at the bottom of the drive, and Dr Gray, for all his manners, was not quite in the mood for an encounter. He looked back up at the Great House, then over at Adeline, noticing for the first time the faint shadows of fatigue beneath her eyes.

'Shall we stop and see into the back kitchens and get you some tea?'

Adeline nodded quickly. 'Yes, let's do.'

The Knights had long been known throughout the area for their generous hospitality. The back kitchens were kept open for those in the know, and even the occasional tourist who was brazen enough to walk all the way up to the front door and knock was never turned away. The kitchen at the back of the house was entered from a beautiful open courtyard, surrounded by four high walls of red brick, green ivy and stained glass containing more Knight heraldry. There they could sit with their tea and a sugar bun hot from the ovens and, for a little while longer, capture the peace and calm of the church nearby.

Josephine, the cook, was an arthritic, hunched-over old woman who had been with the family for as long as anyone could remember. Always eager to see visitors, she motioned Dr Gray and Adeline into the kitchen the minute their boots hit the threshold. Soon, they were back outside on a bench in the courtyard with their arms full, balancing plates of hot buns on their knees as their hands cradled warming mugs of milky black tea.

'So what little secrets are you gleaning from *Emma* this time around?' Adeline asked, curious to hear his reply, wondering if she could possibly be one step ahead of him for once.

'Ah, yes, it was this tiny set of words, thrown into the middle of a rumination by Mr Knightley on Emma's lack of discipline. Remember in *Pride and Prejudice* when Darcy is listening, enrapt, to Elizabeth playing the piano, and she is mocking his lack of ease with strangers, saying he should practise more – saying she should herself practise the piano more to be better?'

Adeline loved that scene. 'Yes, of course! And he so gallantly replies – because he is wooing her – except she has no idea he is wooing her, and neither even does he – that she has employed her time much better than with practise, because "no one admitted to the privilege of hearing you could think anything wanting." I used to muddle over that phrasing when I was younger – was he saying she is only exactly as good as her limited amount of practising can achieve? "Wanting" in the sense of something missing, like in an equation, or a puzzle? But eventually I realised he means that she is so smart not to practise very often because no one hearing her would be anything but pleased, and so she is efficiently mastering her time. Darcy is so in over his head at this point.'

'Now, I know *Pride and Prejudice* is your favourite' – Dr Gray smiled indulgently – 'but back to Emma. So last night I am reading this scene, where Mr Knightley is thinking the opposite of Darcy – he's thinking that Emma never reaches her potential, never even thinks about how best to spend her time. And he mentions this list she once composed of great books to read, remember?'

'Yes, and she never finishes any of them! She has the attention span of an eight-year-old boy – and I should know, seeing as I used to teach them. Always distracted by something new. That's one reason I disagree with you on her heroine status – she's all about pleasing herself, never about improving.'

Dr Gray shook his head. 'Yet she gets there all the same. She is, after all, only twenty-one when the book begins.'

'That's not so young. I am only a few years older than that and look at what I've endured.'

'Very true, Adeline,' he answered thoughtfully, then paused for so long that she ended up egging him on.

'Anyway, and the little clue is . . . the little secret . . . ?'

'Well, right in the middle of this rumination, Mr Knightley mentions Emma's handmade list of books, and then almost as an afterthought he very briefly adds that he once held on to a copy of her list for a period of time. And I was brought up short by that. Because this is well before even the most astute reader can see that Knightley is in love with Emma. Perhaps Austen thought her readers were even less intelligent than I fear. I know I myself never picked up on that so many times . . .'

'Oh, I am sure she did!' Adeline was laughing with delight,

so happy to disappear into this conversation about unreal people with very real flaws. 'I know I never noticed that line before either. My goodness, no – wait – it's like Harriet and her little collection of "most precious treasures" from Mr Elton – the bandage he gave her, the pencil she stole, all the stuff that ends up in the fire at the end! Mr Knightley has acted just like Harriet, holding on to something so trivial to everyone else, and so subconsciously important to him – and yet Jane Austen takes such pains in the book to put Mr Knightley above everyone else and Harriet so far below them, at least intellectually.'

Dr Gray put his mug down on top of his now-empty plate. 'There. See? I hadn't even made *that* connection yet. Imagine, giving Mr Knightley something in common with Harriet.'

'We are all fools in love, as they say.'

'My Jennie would have loved this.'

'My poor Samuel would have had no patience for it,' Adeline answered with a melancholy smile. 'He never got my love for the books. Something about her voice left him cold. He needed characters to be straightforward, the plot like the engine of a runaway train. You were lucky you and your wife could share this.'

'We shared a lot of things.'

'Samuel and I shared our childhood together. We didn't get the chance for much more than that.'

'There is something to be said for growing up with someone.'

'Yet that's what Knightley and Emma fight against the entire book. How funny.'

Sitting there on the bench together, with no one else to confide in, Dr Gray and Adeline felt a strange connection through these books.

During the Great War, shell-shocked soldiers had been encouraged to read Jane Austen in particular – Kipling had coped with the loss of his soldier son by reading her books aloud to his family each night – Winston Churchill had recently used them to get through the Second World War. Adeline and Dr Gray had always loved Jane Austen's writing and could talk together for hours about her characters, but her books now eased their own grief, too.

Part of the comfort they derived from rereading was the satisfaction of knowing there would be closure – of feeling, each time, an inexplicable anxiety over whether the main characters would find love and happiness, while all the while knowing, on some different parallel interior track, that it was all going to work out in the end. Of being both one step ahead of the characters and one step behind Austen on every single reading.

But part of it was the heroism of Austen herself, in writing through illness and despair, and facing her own early death. If she could do it, Dr Gray and Adeline each thought, then certainly, in homage if nothing else, they could, too.

Chapter Five

Chawton, Hampshire
At that same moment

*F*rances Knight could see the two of them on the bench in the courtyard below, having tea outside in the late-summer air. She had a little window seat in the second-floor gallery where she could sit beneath the Elizabethan stained-glass panelling, each window decorated by a different coat of arms for every successive freeholder of the estate, as well as their dates of ascension. She had used this window seat the most as a young girl growing up in the Great House, and again now, when getting out of doors seemed to be growing harder for her to do.

She recognised Adeline Grover from church and had at one time been somewhat friendly with Beatrix Lewis, the young woman's mother. Dr Gray, on the other hand, was the most visible person in the entire community – he had birthed dozens of babies in the village, and tended to even more deaths, and had dealt with a whole host of injuries and ailments in between. In recent months, he had been ministering to her own father, although she knew that Dr Gray had not been due at the Great House that day.

She wondered what the two of them were talking about and opened the lead crank of the window next to her in an effort to listen.

It was not at all what she had expected.

'Another little secret moment I just discovered . . . the scene where Mr Knightley calls, and old Mr Woodhouse hesitates to leave him to go out on his planned walk, and both Mr Knightley and Emma are so quick to encourage him to walk alone . . . Here, let me find it for you . . .'

Frances watched from above as Dr Gray pulled a small, slight volume from inside his coat pocket, while Adeline gave a slightly mocking gasp.

'You're carrying Emma around now, Dr Gray, right by your heart?'

He grinned as he flipped through the pages, until he found the line he had been searching for:

'"Mr Knightley called, and sat some time with Mr Woodhouse and Emma, till Mr Woodhouse, who had previously made up his mind to walk out, was persuaded by his daughter not to defer it, and was induced by the entreaties of both, though against the scruples of his own civility, to leave Mr Knightley for that purpose."'

Adeline wrinkled her nose. 'I think you might be reading too much into *that* one.'

'Hmm, well, yes and no, perhaps. Certainly, this part of the scene – which goes on for several lines, with Mr Woodhouse continuing to demur, and Mr Knightley continuing to not budge a bit – comically reduces the two men to their intractable natures, one all fussiness to his detriment and one all abrupt and overly decided to his. But if you think about it, this is the absolute *most* that Austen would be willing to show at this point, about the hidden currents of attraction between Emma and Knightley that they are way too bogged down by history and situation to acknowledge. This helps us to first mistake Knightley's dislike of Frank Churchill as that of an elder overprotective family member – since she has her father wrapped around her little finger, *someone* in the book has to be up to the task – rather than the raging jealousy he is starting to be consumed by.'

'Mr Knightley is another one who is so clueless – do none of these men know they are in love? Why are so many of her characters so lacking in self-awareness, do you think?' asked Adeline. 'Is that the essence of our folly, our fate as humans: to not understand why we do things, or whom we love? Is that why so much of it ends up rubbish – and if it doesn't, it's just dumb luck?'

'It does seem to me that when her characters truly know and understand themselves from the start, they are less successful to the reader. Fanny Price comes to mind.'

Adeline knew how much Dr Gray disliked Fanny Price.

'I think the reader on some level resents that purity of intent and action,' he continued. 'It's like, "Come on now, mess it up – do what other people would do. Fall for the Henry Crawfords." We love Jane Austen because her characters, as sparkling as they are, are no better and no worse than us. They're so eminently, so completely, human. I, for one, find it greatly consoling that she had us all figured out.'

Frances slowly shut the window, then leaned back against the side of the nook and closed her eyes. It had been a long time since she had chatted with a friend about anything meaningful. The more she stayed indoors, the less people visited. She understood the logic to that – for all that friendship was not supposed to be logical.

It was now only her, her father – the ailing patriarch in his second-floor suite – and Josephine who resided in the Great House, along with the two young house girls, Charlotte Dewar and Evie Stone, who took care of the laundry and cleaning. For day employ, there was Tom, the stable boy, who also looked after the walled garden, caring for her beloved roses and apples and squash, and Adam Berwick, that sad, silent man, who tilled the fields for her.

But she was the last in line of the Knight family, now that her father was dying. The very thing her ancestors had fought so hard against, in adopting Edward Knight, had come to pass after all, and on her watch. She felt such pain over that, a pain far out of proportion to the simple sad fact that she had never been lucky enough to marry and bear a child. That she would feel obliged, from the weight of family history, to mourn for even more than that – for the crumbling Elizabethan bricks around her, for the break in a chain that included the world's greatest writer – was something a good friend would have tried to talk her out of.

She also berated herself for failing at friendship itself. She had once been one of the most prominent members of the community, sharing the privilege of her beautiful estate, opening it up for autumn fêtes and spring fairs and winter tobogganing down the back hill. And she had always had a natural compassion and concern for other people. The energy that she got from learning about others, hearing their stories and thinking of ways to help them had been a real gift. She resented greatly that, for some unfathomable reason, she no longer had the energy for the very things that had always sustained her. If ever there was a recipe for decline, that surely would be it.

She did not mean to feel so sorry for herself – and she was fully aware of the great losses many others in her village had survived. Look at the Berwick family, losing both the father and two of the sons so soon after each other – the two boys in the exact same battle even. And poor Dr Gray, whose beautiful wife could not have children, and then one day took just one little misstep and died – and now Dr Gray had to spend all of his days listening to other people's stories of woe, with the same engagement and care he always had. She couldn't even begin to imagine doing that.

She also knew that if life was indeed a process of loss, then she had been gifted at the beginning with simply much more to lose: a precious family heritage, and the tremendous comforts of wealth. She might not be fully to blame for losing it all, but unfortunately she was the only one left to blame, and she felt the weight and gravity of that as much as anyone would.

Small raindrops were starting to hit against the windowpanes, and she rang the bell next to her on the plush red velvet seat. After a few minutes, Josephine appeared at the top of the stairs that led to the second-floor gallery.

'Josephine, thank you – I do dislike having to use this bell so much.'

Josephine nodded. 'I know, ma'am. You were never one to begrudge a trip to the kitchens.'

'Has the solicitor arrived yet, for Father?'

'Yes, ma'am, right on the half-hour. He is a right prompt one, Mr Forrester.'

'I suppose they are discussing the estate, for such a long visit.' Frances squinted out the window again and saw Dr Gray starting to shelter Adeline from the stray drops with the coat he had taken off. 'Josephine, I think Tom and Adam should be finishing up in the barn by now – they were tending earlier to one of the mothering sheep. Why don't you suggest that Adeline get a ride home in the automobile with Tom, to keep her out of the rain in her condition?'

Josephine went back down the old oak staircase and out into the courtyard with both an umbrella and Miss Knight's unexpected invitation.

Adeline and Dr Gray looked at each other quickly as Josephine made the offer on her employer's behalf, and then

Dr Gray started to stand, Adeline still holding up one side of his coat as shelter with her right hand. With her left, she pulled on his sleeve, a movement so intimate and pleading that he stopped to look down at her again.

'I'm fine, really – the rain is nothing. But I would love to see the new lambing in the barn if I can. We can wait out the worst of the rain there.'

Dr Gray hesitated a bit, then nodded to Josephine. 'Please thank Miss Knight for her thoughtfulness, as always. But we shall do as the young lady suggests.'

Adeline now stood up, too, a little more slowly in her state.

Josephine passed the umbrella over to her, muttering, 'That coat's not much up to the job.'

Adeline nodded her thanks and passed Dr Gray's coat back to him, all under the protective gaze of the old woman.

'What was that about?' Adeline asked Dr Gray as they hurried together under the umbrella and along the red-brick path that led from the courtyard down to the medieval stable block. 'Did we offend her?'

'I don't think Josephine Barrow is sensitive to offence.'

'Maybe it's all that rattling about in such a huge, empty house, just those two old women and that crusty, spiteful old man. I was even a little intimidated by Miss Knight when I was little – although not in a bad way. Just, growing up, she always seemed so calm and elegant, so unflappable. One hardly sees her now.'

'I have long admired Frances. I had hoped she would not end up alone like this. Perhaps it wears on one.'

'Why do you think she never married?'

'Her parents were quite particular, you know, and so her choices were fairly limited from the start. Rather ironic as her own early ancestors were yeomen, not even gentlemen farmers. And goodness knows it's hard enough to find the right person without strictures or limits of any kind.'

'Did she ever come close? What about you – you're the same age, aren't you? Grew up together?'

'The exact same age, actually – we were both born right before the turn of the century, in 1898. Went to school together our entire lives.'

'Long enough for romance to bud,' Adeline suggested.

'And still never good enough for the Knights,' he replied light-heartedly. 'A lowly country doctor and all.'

'Nonsense,' scolded Adeline with a teasing smile. 'I bet you were quite the catch as a bachelor.'

Dr Gray never enjoyed it when people pressed him about his love life before meeting his late wife, and he quickly changed the subject. 'Well, anyway, even then Frances Knight kept pretty much to herself. I do know several of our classmates were after her, but nothing ever came of it. I suppose she eventually gave up on ever finding the right one, stuck as she was in this small village.'

'It's strange, don't you think, that I found my right person in this very town where I grew up? But I bet it happens more than one would think.'

Dr Gray nodded somewhat distractedly as he focused on pulling the umbrella down to shake it off.

They were now standing in front of the open door to the stable and peered inside. In the middle stall, under a single dangling lantern, Tom Edgewaite and Adam Berwick were tending to the mother sheep and her newborn lamb. Both men jumped up from what they were doing when Dr Gray and Mrs Grover unexpectedly walked in.

Adam pulled off his cap, even though he was only two years younger than Dr Gray, but he barely looked at Adeline to say hello. He had known the Lewis family his entire life and yet had never really spoken to their only daughter. Adam saw her as one of the village's bright young things, highly energetic and friendly to everyone, but her direct manner always brought out his shyness. Even in the relaxed environment of the barn, he could only give her a quick nod.

Tom was much more outgoing and a bit of a scamp, and couldn't help commenting on how well Mrs Grover looked given her condition.

Dr Gray gave him a curt look. 'Let's leave the medical pronouncements to me, Tom, shall we?'

Adeline took her time sitting down in the hay next to the mother sheep and the baby lamb suckling at its side. Tears suddenly started in her eyes. One minute she and Dr Gray had been laughing in the rain together, and now here was life, new life, no father to be seen, her own husband gone, her own baby about to arrive, and the overwhelming reality of everything was hitting her all at once. She reached out to pet the baby lamb to distract herself, and Adam moved forward quickly.

'I'm sorry, miss, but they're plenty protective, these ones. Don't want the baby touched as of yet. Not like people that way.'

With a noticeable struggle, Adeline started to get back up. 'Maybe not so different from people after all,' she offered, then smiled obligingly as Dr Gray came forward faster than the other two men to help her up. 'Thank you for letting us see. Your mother is well, Mr Berwick?'

He nodded.

'And how is young Evie Stone? Is she well, too?'

He nodded again.

'She was my star pupil, you know, before she had to leave school and come to work at the House. I hope you are all taking good care of her.'

'Tom's looking to that, ma'am, as always.'

Adeline looked at Adam curiously. Perhaps there was more to the quiet farmer than she had always thought.

'Well' – she smiled at all three men – 'the rain looks to have eased up. We should get going.'

The two other men watched as Dr Gray led Adeline out of the stable and across the fields leading back to the main road.

'He knows what side his bread's buttered on, don't he,' remarked Tom.

Adam frowned as he watched the two figures beneath the umbrella head back to town. 'He's a good man, Dr Gray.'

'I'm not saying he's not,' laughed Tom. 'But he puts us two bachelors to shame.'

Adam scoffed, 'You're full of nonsense, Tom Edgewaite.'

'I'm just saying,' Tom persisted, as he turned back to the nursing lamb. 'I knows what I see – I see it all day long.'

Adam left the stable without a word and headed home himself. It was getting close to his supper, and after that he would do some reading. He didn't care to hang around for Tom's constant gossip and innuendo – he would read some Jane Austen instead.

⌣

Adam had not ended up adoring Emma Woodhouse as he had once been promised by the young American woman.

He loved Elizabeth Bennet instead – loved her in a way he had not thought possible with a fictional character. Loved the way she always spoke her mind but with such humanity and humour. He wished he could be her – wished he always had the perfect, tart remark at the end of his tongue, the ability to draw people to him, and the strength to assert himself with his mother. He saw Elizabeth as the lynchpin to the entire Bennet family, the one whose boldness and emotional intelligence was keeping her own family from the brink. But she never flaunted herself as a saviour – she just loved so thoroughly, and so wisely, that the saving of others was the inevitable result.

Adam felt as if he could hardly save himself, let alone anyone else. Yet, on his loneliest of days, he sometimes felt as if he was being saved by Jane Austen. He could only imagine what the villagers would say about him if they suspected any of that. Still, he often wished there were someone with whom he could discuss Austen and her books. The only person he had met so far lived on the other side of the world.

Of course, he had recognised the young woman in blue the very first time he had seen her face at the cinema. He had since become a devoted fan of Mimi Harrison and had watched all of her films, including *Home & Glory* three times. He thought of her out in Hollywood, reading the books again and again. It bemused him to have something in common like this with a movie star. He knew it said a lot more about Austen than it did about him, but it also made him feel a little less odd, a little less damaged, all the same.

On his walk home from the stables, Adam stopped to rest at the junction where Winchester Road split in two. If he turned a sharp left instead of proceeding on his way, he would end up at the old farmhouse where he had been born, now home to the substantial Stone clan. If he went on past that, he would eventually end up in the city of Winchester, a good sixteen miles away.

Adam had never been as far away as that, but he knew that Jane Austen, in her final days, had moved to rented rooms there, vainly hoping to find a cure for the mysterious illness that would soon claim her at only age forty-one. One month later, Cassandra would watch from the upper-room windows as Jane's coffin was transported by carriage to the famous Winchester Cathedral. Her beloved sister's words of record – '. . . it turned from my sight . . . I had lost her forever' – never failed to bring tears to Adam's eyes. His own two brothers were buried hundreds of miles away beneath the Aegean Sea, nothing left of them at all but unmarked graves that he would surely never see.

The unnatural loss of youth not only hits us harder, it seems to insist on invading our days, as if the memory of the person lost too soon has a hidden, persistent source of energy. Cassandra had spent her final decades in Chawton heeding this force and safeguarding her sister's legacy, whereas Adam feared he had failed the legacy of his brothers in not making more of his own life. Yet, despite his depressed spirits, he was still always searching for something, for some way to make meaning from his life. He simply had no idea how to begin.

Heading now in the direction of home, the rain having stopped and the sun out again, Adam opened the low wooden gate next to the old steward's cottage and walked over to the bench in the farthest corner of the yard. He often sat and rested here at the end of his day, preparing himself for his mother's relentless questions the minute he got home. She was keeping close tabs on the state of the now-dying Mr Knight, as well as tracking the social deterioration of Miss Frances Knight, one of the gentlest souls among them and an easy target for someone as aggressive as his mother.

Sitting on the bench, Adam could only imagine Jane Austen walking about the gardens, or resting on this very spot, as there was little physical sign of the house's famous former resident. Instead he watched the new litter of tabby kittens dozing in the courtyard under the late-afternoon sun, heard the sound of the village junkman's hand-pulled cart approaching and caught sight of Dr Gray and Adeline only now passing by the outside brick wall after him. They must have taken a longer route home through the fields.

Adam got up and walked back towards the gate. Turning to his left, he spied the pile of rubbish in front of the cottage, lying in wait for the junkman's rounds. Protruding from the mound were the remaining three legs under the flat square seat of an antique chair. As a self-taught carpenter, Adam recognised the column shape of the chair legs and the straight lines of the seat as harking from the Regency period. His pulse quickened at the thought that perhaps this chair had once been used by the Austen family, maybe even by Jane herself.

He reached the pile of rubbish just as the junkman did.

'Having a little poke around as usual, are you, Mr Berwick?'

Adam nodded and pulled at the chair, only to discover that most of its dark mahogany back was missing. In its present state the chair was useless, and he doubted he could carry it home without raising alarm at his own damaged state. As he released the chair, he spied something else, a small wooden toy of some sort, not immediately recognisable to him. Known in the village for his own handiwork, the gifts of small rattles and wooden ring-toss sets that he worked on when he wasn't tending to the fields or reading, Adam wondered how old this forgotten object might be. Maybe it meant something more, a connection of some kind to the Austen family – maybe it meant nothing at all. But no one else in the village seemed to care about finding out any of that.

'You can keep that there, haven't much use for something so slight.'

Adam gave a quick murmur of thanks and, tucking the object into his front jacket pocket, continued on his way. He was convinced that the other villagers viewed him as a subdued, broken man, not good for much, not creating any kind of legacy of his own. But at times like this, he wondered if he was also the only one paying attention to the shortening of the days, the rubbish left by the side of the road, and the neglected and forgotten past.

Chapter Six

Los Angeles, California
August 1945

At first, Jack Leonard had found it mystifying, the obsession with Jane Austen.

The shelves of Mimi Harrison's living room in the small bungalow perched high in the canyon were full of old leather-bound books (the one called *Emma* looked particularly beat-up) and the collected works of writers he had never even heard of: Burney, Richardson, and some poet called Cowper. He did recognise the name of Walter Scott, but only because the movie *Ivanhoe* had recently made another studio a ton of money.

The most common denominator with all of these writers appeared to be their connection to Austen, about whom he had been smart enough to ask around following that first encounter by the pool and the sight of the well-thumbed copy of *Northanger Abbey* in Mimi's suntanned hands. Eventually she had mentioned her dad reading her the books as a girl, and the trip to some small town in England to walk in Austen's footsteps (at that point he had wondered if she was both red-hot *and* insane), and the dream of one day making a film of *Sense and Sensibility*.

He had listened, patiently for him, to all of this, all the while wondering if Jane Austen was somehow the key to getting Mimi Harrison into bed. But between dinners out and cocktail receptions and red-carpet walks, Jack Leonard was starting to feel that migraine coming on again, as he walked Mimi to her front door night after night. For one thing, she was no spring chicken any more, as her latest box-office receipts were finally starting to reflect, so all the games made less sense to him and – worse still – would have less of a physical pay-off. For another, he could tell she was interested in him, too.

That Mimi might have been fighting against a strong physical attraction to him, in deference to her usual better judgement, would never have crossed his mind.

One thing he had learned in Hollywood was that there was no better way to sleep with a leading lady than to make her one. He hadn't paid much attention to the recent Laurence Olivier–Greer Garson adaptation of *Pride and Prejudice*, but now that that was out of the running, he turned to Mimi's own interest in *Sense and Sensibility*. He liked the idea of three young sisters under twenty (casting was already going on in his head on that one) and had a genuine appreciation for Willoughby's willingness to seduce young women out of wedlock. He thought there was a backstory in there that could be alluded to in defiance of the Code. The more he learned about Austen from Mimi, the more he was impressed by how she mostly wrote about bad behaviour. As far as Jack could tell, there weren't too many pure heroes in the books. Everyone was making mistakes, and falling for cads, and giving the wrong people the benefit of the doubt. He loved it.

Of course, he wasn't reading any of it – but he had one of the screenwriters, a famous debauched novelist living in bungalow seventeen on the back lot, working on a treatment of it. So far, Jack liked what he saw.

Mimi, on the other hand, was not so thrilled.

'The scene in the script, where Willoughby shows up, because he's heard Marianne is near death – I never bought that. Of all of Jane Austen, that is the one scene that rang hollow for me. Willoughby doesn't care about anyone but himself – if he's visiting Marianne, it's totally out of guilt. But he doesn't care about guilt either. Why on earth would he ride there all night and demand that Elinor see things from his point of view? Why on earth would he care?'

They were sitting in two facing armchairs in Jack's spacious office, which was in bungalow number five, at the perimeter of the main studio lot. Outside the front bay window were huge pink hydrangea bushes and a white picket fence leading to the Main Street façade that featured in every 'Let's put on a show' musical that the studio was currently cranking out. As Mimi continued speaking at length about Willoughby, Jack was getting the feeling that she was projecting that character onto him, and it bothered him greatly that she could underestimate him in this way. He didn't mind being a cad, but he was the hero of his own life, and he would always get the girl in the end.

The scene as she described it was bothering him, too, but for different reasons. From what he understood from both Mimi and the script, Willoughby was acting here like a loser, yet had gotten everything that he'd wanted in the end. He'd impregnated an underage girl, seduced one of the heroines into visiting an empty house unchaperoned and married an heiress.

If Jack Leonard could get even half as far with Mimi Harrison, he would be a happy man.

'Isn't the point of the scene to show that Marianne was not wrong for thinking Willoughby loved her, just wrong in thinking he would do anything about it? Isn't it really about redeeming *her*?' Jack was parroting the words of the scriptwriter, who had explained exactly this in a recent meeting, after one of the co-producers had voiced the same concern as Mimi.

Mimi shook her head. 'The reader knows all that already. I really think Austen slipped up here – I think she actually responded to Willoughby. I think she liked Henry Crawford, too.' Jack stared at her blankly. 'Henry Crawford, from *Mansfield Park,* remember? Anyway, I think part of her *wanted* us to forgive them, or at least feel sorry for them. I think this is where her religious sincerity sometimes got in the way – goodness knows, Fanny Price was the poster girl for *that*. But if Willoughby is genuinely seeking expiation for his sins—'

'Seeking what?'

Mimi stared back at Jack just as blankly. He had claimed to have gone to an Ivy League business school, but this was one of those times when she wondered if he really had.

'*Expiation*. Seeking atonement; forgiveness.'

Jack downed the Scotch he had been cradling in his hands. 'Yeah, yeah, I know. So,' he said in a relaxed tone, 'I've been thinking. Angela Cummings. For Marianne. Monte tells me you two make quite a team.'

Mimi was not surprised to hear the name of her latest co-star, who was taking Hollywood by storm following a brief modelling career out East. But it was hard to begrudge Angela anything. For one thing, she was a most supportive castmate, having stood up for Mimi many times to Terry Tremont, the director on the Western they had just filmed in the Nevada desert in the scorching heat of summer. Mimi was secretly impressed with the way the girl went after anything and everything that she wanted, the bigger the better. Mimi was also one of the only people in Hollywood who knew that Angela was juggling a torrid affair with Terry alongside a new relationship with her married co-star on an upcoming film. Next to the twenty-year-old and her lovers, Mimi's relationship with the equally notorious Jack Leonard seemed positively chaste.

'Well, she's certainly young enough,' Mimi finally replied. 'And I like her – she's easy to work with. Doesn't take any of this too seriously.'

Jack was watching her with a look of surprised relief. 'Listen. I have a five o'clock with Harold at the Beverly Hills to discuss Eleanor and her "liquid diet". Why don't we meet for dinner after that and keep this talk going?'

'What is it with all the hotel meetings all the time? Monte wants to meet at the Chateau Marmont tonight to discuss the grinding promo tour for *I'll Never Sing Again*.'

'You be careful with him. Can't keep his dick in his pants. Waves it about like the goddamned flag.'

'Jack, honestly, the swearing.'

'Oh, trust me, honey, swearing will be the least of your problems with that guy.'

'I can handle myself.'

'I know you can,' Jack replied, although he wished this weren't true. Wished there were some crack in the façade, some little chink in the armour, that would finally let him in. That was the problem with well-bred college girls like her – they seemed to always be holding out for something, putting a guy through his paces, making sure there was something of value at the end of it all – otherwise they didn't budge an inch.

Jack may not have been book-smart, but he was shrewd enough to know that what he had to offer Mimi (the money, the power – but mainly the money) wasn't anything she couldn't get on her own. He was not used to feeling this redundant – it was one reason he had leapt at the chance to make a Jane Austen movie of all things. He was feeling checkmated completely off the board right now. Mimi hadn't even let him kiss her yet, at least not a proper full-throated kiss. Her powers of restraint were proving to be unexpectedly formidable.

'Listen, Mimi, let's make this movie. Together. We'll be a great team, you'll see. You don't put up with any of my crap, and you keep me honest. And you'll get your beloved Jane Austen out of it.'

He came over and sat down on the arm of her chair with his glass of Scotch in hand, and he heard her give the softest sound, almost a sigh. Almost, he thought, his ears pricking up, the sound of resignation.

Mimi was becoming resigned, but not to him: to herself. She had a weakness for handsome men, be they farmers or actors or university professors. Jack Leonard was definitely handsome – movie-star handsome – and a constant frisson of energy came from his striking looks meeting hers every step of the way. She was not used to that, even in Hollywood. Jack also had an over-the-top extravagance that made everything he touched jump to life. For the first and only time, she identified with Mary Crawford in *Mansfield Park,* repining over the otherwise ill-suited Edmund Bertram: 'he gets into my head more than is good for me.'

Mimi Harrison was also becoming resigned to the fact that she wanted Jack Leonard: wanted to be kissed by him, and held by him, and have him say things she knew a woman would only ever hear from him in bed. There was power in that, to be sure, but it wasn't just about feeling emboldened. Jack had a little-boy quality that she still couldn't quite put her finger on. The degree to which a certain look from her could hurt him – the degree to which she thought she could get him to open up his heart – seemed to be behind her crumbling resistance. Maybe this was all part of his routine with women, but if it was, he was the best damn actor she'd ever worked against.

'Jack, honestly, you don't need to buy me – you don't need to buy me a movie.'

He smiled, a very slow, mischievous smile. 'Oh, I don't want to buy you, Mimi. I want you for free. I want you to give yourself to me, all of you, every last inch, because you can't stand it one more second either.'

He dipped his finger in his glass of Scotch and started to trace it along her collarbone and just below her long neck, then moved his hand down farther still. As he leaned in more, he brushed his long sleeve across her right breast (she had noticed that he never wore short-sleeved shirts except on the tennis court, no matter the heat), and she felt her skin grow warm and flushed under his touch. He tilted her chin up towards him with his other hand, and then their lips met, and everything up until that point finally made some weird kind of sense. It was as if her physical attraction to him was so deep, it had bypassed her mind, and now her mind was finally catching up to her body.

Mimi could no longer judge Marianne for preferring Willoughby over the older and more muted Colonel Brandon, only to wind up close to feverish death; she just hoped and prayed that she wouldn't end up a sobbing, reclusive mess by the end of it all, too.

⌐

'Mimi, how lovely you look. Let me get you some champagne.'

Monte Cartwright was an older, portly man well into his fifties. The head of the studio that had made Mimi a star, he had a preternatural knack for sizing up a young actor's marquee value from the first screen test, then locking them into a long-term contract so punitive that they would spend at least the next decade ruing the day they had ever met him.

Mimi's ten-year contract had three years left on it, and every time she saw Monte, she mentally checked off another square on the calendar of her servitude. The out-of-house projects she was allowed to do, such as the burgeoning *Sense and Sensibility* adaptation with Jack, had been hard-earned over time, through contract negotiations aided by her business-lawyer brother back home in Philadelphia. At age thirty-five, Mimi shrewdly understood that her only leverage with the studio came from her box-office receipts, so she continued to take on as many promising projects as she could. Some of her fellow ageing actresses were already raising families or otherwise taking 'breaks' that quickly became permanent in an industry where perception and momentum were everything. But Mimi kept working at building up career capital, before the tiny lines about her eyes deepened and the first grey hair showed up.

Monte was now sitting on the matching sofa facing hers in his hotel room, staring at the hair about her brow, that famous raven-black mane, wondering when that first grey hair would show up. Mimi was finally starting to look just the tiniest bit different from before – he knew the signs well, as he was constantly on the lookout for them, as if circling his prey for any indications of injury or fatigue.

'You're looking a little tired, Mimi, although as lovely as ever. Is Terry running you ragged on the Western shoot? Those early-morning calls out in Nevada for his goddamned sunrises – what are you now, two hours in the make-up chair?'

Mimi shifted about in her seat, losing count of the number of references to her age he could make in one single ramble.

'It's all good, we're all wrapped up now. Angela's going to be a revelation in it.'

He looked at her in surprise, unable to figure out her end-game in singling out her much-younger co-star for his attention.

'Yeah, that kid's a real find. What is she, twenty? Twenty-one at most? You'd never know it – smokes like a teamster and swears like one, too. Hell, she even *sounds* like one sometimes – we've been working on that. There's husky, and then there's just goddamned menacing.'

On some level, Mimi always enjoyed her infrequent meetings with Monte, as his love of hearing himself talk and his need to put others in their place kept him so fully occupied, she could usually just sit back and think about something else. Lately, that something else had been Jack Leonard, to her complete surprise and consternation. He was indeed getting into her head – and, worse still, she worried that he knew it. If he didn't before, that kiss a few hours earlier had probably done the trick.

Meanwhile, Monte was talking about some poor 'dimwit' actress, and her recent shotgun marriage, and a conflict of laws with the Dominican Republic over the equally recent divorce (Mimi had to hand it to Monte, he did know the law, at least well enough to get around it). She was half listening, sipping the second glass of Piper-Heidsieck that he had poured her, when Monte finished his Scotch, got up and sat down, uninvited, next to her.

Patting her knee, he asked most solicitously, 'Did he tell you, yet?'

'Did who tell me what, Monte?'

'Terry. Did he tell you about Angela?'

'Tell me what about Angela, Monte?'

'Her billing.'

'What about her billing?'

Monte smiled at her. 'Well, I guess we could play this little game all day. About Angela's billing going right next to yours, above the titles.'

Mimi forced herself to breathe. 'But that's preposterous. It's only her second feature.'

'Yeah, but you're both vying for Cooper and he's the lead, so it makes sense, optically at least – or at least that's what Terry thinks. Look, Mimi, I'm all for saying something to him – but I need to know how much you care.'

'Monte, what do you think? We both know I've been one of the top money-makers around here for years, and there is no way some novice should get equal billing. It's not a question of anything but fairness – I'm sure Angela's time will come, she is very talented, but her time can't come at the expense of mine. That's ridiculous.'

Monte sighed. 'I know. It's tough. But my hands are pretty tied. Terry had the right of approval over the credits baked into his contract on this one, given the Crawford-Gable-Davis debacle a few years back.' He shifted a little closer to her on the sofa. 'Look, Mimi, we both knew this time in your career would eventually come. I'll step up if you want me to, but I'd be a chump not to get something in return.'

His hand now rested on her thigh, and he was so close, she could smell the mix of nicotine and Scotch on his breath.

'Monte,' she said with a stern look, moving his hand away with hers.

'Mimi, there's no one else in the stable that can touch you for a clear two years. We still have to teach Betty Winters how to sing, and Janice Starling how to act. You're still hanging on at the top and you know it. And I can help keep you there. You know how much I believe in you. You're the face of the studio.'

'If I'm the face of the studio, then I should have top billing.'

'Mimi, look, I'm no one to talk when it comes to the looks department – thank God they ain't paying me around here for that. But we're getting test-screening feedback on the Nevada outtakes, and they're all over Angela.'

'And?'

He sighed again. 'And they think you're looking old. Look, it's been a harsh location shoot and in-studio will always fare better for you now. You're on the *Scheherazade* shoot next, right?'

Mimi put her champagne flute down on the small table next to the sofa. 'Monte, I'm not giving up my billing, there's just no way. I've worked too hard for it. I'd personally rather never have to think about billing at all, but it totally matters in this business, and I am not stupid enough to give up something I don't have to.'

'But that's just it' – he moved his hand back up her thigh again – 'you might have to, and yet you don't have to. I'm always on your side, you know that.'

'Monte . . .'

'Look, Mimi, I just want to help you, I always have.'

She stood up and he got up, too, and grabbed her and pushed her against the arm of the sofa.

'Monte Cartwright, you get your goddamned hands off of me this instant.'

He was a hundred pounds heavier than her and a good foot taller except for her heels. 'Mimi, come on, stop it.' He started trying to kiss her, and at first she was in shock, as his sheer size and power overwhelmed her. His smell was what she would always remember later, the Scotch and the cigar smoke and the too-strong cologne full of spice and patchouli and sweat. She tried with all her might to push him off, but already he was rubbing himself hard against her, and the idea that he might ejaculate any minute finally helped her find her voice.

'Monte, get the fuck off of me . . . Monte . . . Monte, I swear I will scream!'

He was now panting so hard that she was finally able to push herself free, and he fell back and finished off on the sofa while she stared at him, shaking in horror and disgust.

'I am going to sue the pants off of you, you animal.'

'No, you won't,' he replied with eerie calm, taking a crisp linen handkerchief out of his front jacket pocket to wipe his hands. 'You're on your way down, Mimi, and you know it. Say a word and I'll put your name below Angela's. Say a word and see if anyone gives a fuck.'

She left him there, splayed back onto the sofa, cleaning himself like an animal, clearly not caring one little bit for his degradation, while – she feared – revelling in hers.

When Jack arrived at the bungalow a few hours later to take Mimi to dinner, he found her sitting curled up in an armchair with her housecoat wrapped tight about her, and her long black hair hanging loose and wet about her neck.

'I scrubbed and scrubbed in the shower until my skin was raw, trying to get rid of the smell of him,' she told Jack after recounting what had happened.

Jack said nothing – a myriad of conflicting emotions and thoughts were running through him, the predominant of which was rage – and instead stormed out of the bungalow, re-appearing an hour later with a cut above one eye and his right hand swollen and bruised.

Mimi cleaned the cut with some disinfectant and put some ice on the hand, then knelt on the carpet before Jack, who was sitting there with a gratified ego, a distressed heart and a splitting headache.

'I wish you hadn't,' Mimi finally said, after they had stared at each other for several seconds. 'I told you I handled it as best I could. He won't get away with it.'

'As best you could is way too good for someone like him,' Jack practically growled.

'So you left him bruised and battered – now what? He'll probably come down even harder on me. And charge you with assault. And I'll end up unemployed, just watch, and *you'll* end up in jail.'

Jack pulled her onto his lap in the single most tender motion he had ever made in his life. 'So here's the deal, okay? You're not going to charge him with rape, he knows that – and he isn't going to charge me with assault. He knows I know that, too. And you're out of your contract, if you want. He said he'll release you.'

'Because I'm old.'

'You're not old.'

'I'm not *young*. Or at least, not as young as Angela Cummings or Janice Starling.'

'Screw him, Mimi. The writing's on the wall over there. Go free agent and name your price and work when you want. I can take care of you the rest of the time.'

'I can take care of myself. God knows I have enough money.'

'There's no such thing,' he corrected her, taking both her hands in his.

Mimi looked at him in surprise. 'What are you saying, Jack?'

'We'll get married. And you can retire.'

'I don't want to retire.'

'Well, then, semi-retire. Like what's-her-name. Make the occasional prestige picture, get that summer place in England you're always going on about, and read Jane Austen the rest of the time for all I care.'

'I don't trust Monte, Jack, if I don't stay busy – he's just the sort of person who would start spreading lies. Before you know it, my name will be mud in this town.'

'Screw him, Mimi. Look at what you've pulled off so far with your career. He can't touch that.'

'What about babies?' she suddenly asked, almost holding her breath.

'What *about* babies?'

'I dunno, Jack. Do you *eat* them? What do you *think* I mean?'

He smiled. 'Well, if you're already thinking about making babies with me . . .'

From the open bungalow window, she could smell the dahlias and the roses that her gardener took such care of, hear the far-off cries of the coyotes that stalked the canyon, and see every star in the August night through the skylight above their heads.

'My head hurts.' She sighed. 'I shouldn't be making any decisions right now.'

'Don't then. Just think about it.' He smiled. 'But not too long. Time is money after all.'

Chapter Seven

Chawton, Hampshire
September 1945

*F*rances Knight sat in the main-floor library of the Great
House, staring at the floor-to-ceiling bookshelves made
of oak and walnut from the woodland on the estate. Two
thousand books, Evie the house girl had recently informed
her. Two thousand books dating as far back as the 1700s, and
many of them bound in leather especially for the family, the
front covers imprinted with the Knight family seal. The Austen family would have read these books: Jane and her brother
Edward and his daughter Fanny Knight Knatchbull, Jane's beloved niece, along with Cassandra and many other aunts and
uncles and cousins too numerous to mention.

Two thousand books. And all now just for her.

Even more ironically, she had only read a few of them.
Mainly the Brontës, the Georges Eliot and Gissing, and
Thomas Hardy and Trollope. Over and over again.

This had started in her thirties, after the death of her mother
from pneumonia and her older brother in a shooting accident
just two years later. Not at all close to her one remaining

relative, her distant and judgemental father, Frances had retreated into these familiar worlds of literature. Something about her favourite books gave her tremendous comfort, and even a strange feeling of control, although she could not quite put her finger on why. She just knew that she did not want to invest her time trying to figure out a new world, whom to like and whom to trust in it, and how to bear the author's choices for tragedy and closure – or lack thereof.

When she was younger, before the Great War, she had read widely and profusely, eschewing the outdoor activities so beloved by her rambunctious and rebellious brother – the riding, the hunting, the daredevil activities that young boys always seem to devise – and choosing instead to remain indoors, sitting in one of her favourite windows, with a stack of books by her side. Reading, she now understood, had been her own choice of rebellion. A most private activity, it was the perfect alibi for a young woman in a demanding household like theirs. She could maintain a healthy distance from both her parents and their dwindling expectations and increasing disappointment in her. She could simply never do right by them, and they all knew it.

She had also been the only true reader in the family, her mother having been extremely social and her father preoccupied with the failing income of the estate. The history behind all these ancient family books, and the legacy of Jane Austen in which the Knights had a share, was of little interest to them. Even today her father bemoaned the presence of random gawkers at the gate, especially the American ones, searching for any trace of their beloved author.

She heard someone stop in the threshold of the open doorway, followed by the slight rustling of paperwork, and she turned to see Andrew Forrester, her father's solicitor, standing there.

'Miss Knight,' he said with an abrupt bow of his head. He was a very tall, ramrod-straight man of her exact age – forty-seven – with a long face, high Roman cheekbones and a severe boyish side part to his dark brown hair.

Frances gave a slight nod back. She always had such a wistful, faraway look in her pale grey eyes, a look he did not enjoy seeing, and he hesitated before venturing farther into the room.

'I hope I am not disturbing you.' He looked about a little awkwardly.

'Not at all. How did you find my father?'

Andrew took a few steps closer, then stopped to fold the set of papers he was holding and discreetly slipped them into his brown leather lawyer's bag. 'The same, I'm afraid. Has Dr Gray been round yet this week?'

Frances nodded. 'Yes, he still comes every Tuesday and Thursday morning. Early, when Father is at his most lucid.'

'And his least intimidating,' Andrew replied, then quickly stopped himself. 'Oh, I'm terribly sorry, Frances – I mean Miss Knight. That was extremely impolite of me.'

'It's fine, really. And anyway, it's true.' She turned to the tray of tea still warm before her. 'Would you like a cup of tea before you head back into Alton? The sugar buns are straight out of Josephine's oven this past hour.'

Andrew hesitated briefly, then went over to the wingback chair across from hers. Sitting down, he reached for the cup she held out to him, noticing she had remembered to add the squeeze of lemon he always preferred.

'You must have a great deal of business to talk over with Father. I know our investments are scattered at best.'

Andrew took a long sip of his tea before answering. 'How much has your father involved you in any of that?'

She shook her head. 'Not at all. Apparently I do not have a head for business.'

Andrew stared up at the ceiling as if remembering something. 'That surprises me. After all, back in our schooldays, you used to trump both Benjamin Gray and me in mathematics.'

She shrugged. 'I used to be able to do a lot of things. Not so much any more. And you – how is business?'

Andrew was listening carefully to her words, and she noticed for the first time the frown lines of anxiety between his eyes.

'Business is good, just fine. Always is. Although I'd rather not be busy with the estates work.'

'It must be difficult for you. And for Benjamin, too, I suppose. Tending to the hard times in the lives of the people with whom you have grown up.'

'Well, we none of us moved away for a reason, I suppose. Nothing is perfect – certainly being able to stay in Alton has had its share of recompense.'

She found that an interesting statement given that Andrew, despite everything, had never married nor had children. She wondered what else could have been so gratifying about staying so close to home – she certainly knew it fell plenty short for her at times.

'And helping people – especially people one knows – is rather a privilege, I think,' he added.

'They say it is the key to happiness.'

Now it was his turn to wonder at her words, knowing how rarely she left the Great House, knowing how little she now interacted with the world outside it.

'I guess that statement speaks for itself,' she added quickly, catching the look on his face.

He took another long sip of tea, then placed the cup down on the tray between them and cleared his throat.

'About the estate – I know you say your father has not

involved you much – and I know this must be an extremely difficult time. But decisions, sadly, will always have to be made, both in good times and in bad. The books for the estate are not in the best of shape, and I have been trying – so far as I am able – to work through as much of it with your father as I can. I do think the two of you should talk though. I mean, generally speaking, it is always wise. Times will be hard enough without too much being, um, thrown at you when the inevitable time comes.'

She was looking down now, as if at an invisible book on her lap. 'My father and I are ill-suited to conversation at the best of times.'

'Yes. I know.'

It was the first allusion he had ever made to their shared past, and she looked up quickly at his concerned face as if to double-check his words.

'And anyway, it won't make a difference. My father does as he wants.'

'Yes, I know that, too.'

She sighed. 'I just want us all to get through the year in one piece, now that this awful war is finally over.'

Immediately she wondered what had come over her to say something as emotional as that. She took a final sip of her own tea, then placed the empty cup down with the tiniest chink of the china against the silver tray.

Andrew felt as if this was his cue to leave and stood up. 'Well, I best get back to the office.'

'Did you walk, by the way?'

'Yes. It's my favourite walk. Always has been.'

With those words, he nodded goodbye and left.

Frances sat quite still. She usually found herself lingering behind in empty rooms to mull over difficult conversations like this. For one thing, her mind worked slower now, probably due to lack of engagement more than anything else. Certainly, everyone in her family who had lived to old age had remained sharp as a tack. That was why, as much as the accounting ledgers might look to be in a state, she knew that her father was still completely on top of everything. So she was a little curious as to why Andrew had been checking in on all of that with her.

But before she could think about his words any further, Josephine appeared in the other doorway, the one leading from the library to the back gallery and the warren-like complex of kitchens and cellars beyond.

'Miss Frances, telephone call for you. A Mr Yardley Sinclair, from Sotheby's.'

Frances made a small face. 'I don't know anyone by that name.'

'Should we tell him you're indisposed, ma'am?'

Frances stood up. 'No, it's fine, I'll take it in the hall. Thank you, Josephine.'

She headed into the hallway just as Evie Stone passed by, duster in hand, on her way to the library. Frances smiled at the young girl's diligence when it came to dusting the thousands of books. Goodness knows the many volumes had sat neglected on those shelves for far too long.

Frances picked up the phone that rested on a small desk at the far end of the hallway, below the substantial hanging Jacobean staircase that led to the upstairs rooms.

'Frances Knight,' she said uncertainly, making it sound more like a question than a statement.

She heard a man clear his throat on the other end, as if he had been waiting quite some time to speak with her.

'Miss Knight, hello — my name is Yardley Sinclair. I work with Sotheby's, the auction house, here in London.'

'Yes.' She waited.

'Yes, I see, thank you – thank you for taking my call. I am telephoning because I just supervised the sale of the Godmersham estate a few weeks past.'

This estate had once also belonged to the Knights but had been sold decades earlier to pay off significant tax and other debt owed by the family.

'Oh, yes, so I'd heard.' She and her father had learned about the sale of the estate and all its contents from Andrew Forrester, who had obtained a copy of the Sotheby's catalogue through a colleague in the City for their perusal.

'I'm terribly sorry, I hope you don't mind my calling like this – I would much rather visit in person. You see, I am the biggest fan of your famous ancestor. The biggest.'

'How would one measure that?' Frances asked, and she heard a panicked pause, followed by a strange attempt at a laugh.

'Oh, I see, how funny – yes – I suppose you hear that all the time.'

'Yes,' she replied again, and waited.

'Yes, well, you see, with the Godmersham sale, we saw a few of Miss Austen's possessions go off to America, to different buyers, and one of them has asked me to reach out to you.'

'Mr Sinclair, is it? Look, I'm terribly sorry, but this is not a good time. My father, James Knight, is not well.'

'Oh, I see. I am so sorry.'

'Thank you. I am sure you understand.'

'Oh, yes, of course, it's just, this particular buyer – well, he is very persistent – he's in love, you see, and extremely well-off – and apparently the sky's the limit when it comes to his fiancée. And she, too, is quite obsessed with Miss Austen.'

'That's all fine, but of no concern to me. Not at present.'

There was a long pause.

'Oh, I see. Yes. Well, I shall carry that message back to him.'

'Please do.'

Frances hung up and looked about herself at the empty hallway that led to equally empty rooms. She was the care-taker now, and the gatekeeper, of this once-great estate and its connection to one of the world's greatest writers. She would have to learn to step into her father's place and protect, as much as possible, what was left of the legacy of their family.

So she hoped Mr Sinclair did not call again. She had always felt herself far too liable to persuasion.

~

Evie Stone sat alone on a little stool in the far corner of the library. It was well past midnight.

Unbeknownst to Frances and the other staff, Evie had been doing more than just diligently dusting the volumes in the Knight family library; for the past year and a half, she had also been doing a secret sort of cataloguing under the pretence of her daily tasks.

She was far more interested in Jane Austen than she had let on when first hired as house girl to the estate. She had read all of Austen's six novels at the age of fourteen, giving her a signif-icant chunk of her teens to reread them, then to fall inevitably into the same hole as so many others before her, in wanting to know more, to understand more, to figure out exactly how Jane Austen did it.

If Evie had anyone else but herself to blame for this pre-occupation, it would have been that one great teacher the village had managed to provide, the year before Evie's own premature exit from school. Adeline Lewis had come into the classroom with both a sense of urgency and a sense of humour. She seemed to intuitively know how long she could keep the attention of the most inattentive student and to work back-wards from there. Suddenly the children were being read to from diverse works ranging over the centuries, from *The Rime of the Ancient Mariner* and *Evelina,* to *Orlando* and *All Quiet on the Western Front.* Miss Lewis always took the time to explain various characters' behaviour and motivations, connecting a wealthy landowner in Georgian England, or an army general in one of Shakespeare's plays, to real-life figures of the day, the war providing ample examples of people both born and made for greatness.

The children had listened, rapt, as the war raged on outside their little village school, and the newsreels during the Saturday matinee films showed the bombs dropping on London and Europe, and the telegrams started arriving more and more often to their own families' doors. It seemed as if every other week another grief-stricken child would show up in class, their face white and tear-stained as they went about their lessons. The adults in the village appeared intent on instructing the children that it could be a long road ahead, and breaking down along the way wouldn't help any of them. It was a lesson in stoicism and persistence that Evie would never forget.

It was now nearly one A.M., and Evie's work that night had been proceeding unimpeded, until she came upon one of the earliest editions of *Pride and Prejudice* on the library shelves. Slowly opening the leather-bound book, she was delighted to find an inscription by Austen herself to one of her brother Edward Knight's many children. Evie sat there running her fingers over Austen's handwriting, as sacred as anything she had ever touched. This was Evie's absolute favourite of all of Austen's books, and of all the books she had read so far in her young life. For this, too, she had Adeline Lewis to thank.

Right from the start, Miss Lewis had noticed what she called Evie's 'intellectual precociousness', and the very first book she had pressed into the girl's hands was her own well-worn copy of *Pride and Prejudice.* As Adeline suspected, Evie had quickly picked up on the subtle and ironic humour in the text. The young girl had particularly loved moments such as Mr Bennet's asking Mrs Bennet – after her one-sided litany on which of their five daughters the wealthy new neighbour, Mr Bingley, might marry – if she supposed that to be Bingley's 'design' in moving there. Mrs Bennet rudely scoffs, 'Design? Nonsense, how can you talk so! But it is very likely that he *may* fall in love with one of them. . . .' To the delight of Evie, everything about Mrs Bennet's obtuseness and desperate one-track mind could be thoroughly and efficiently summed up in that one throwaway line.

But no sooner had Miss Lewis started at the school than the visits from a myriad of different, sheepish, male school board trustees had begun. Evie had watched with fascination as Miss Lewis held her ground with each of them, reinforced the value of her lesson plans and practically dared the men to do something about it. One by one, the men would leave the classroom visibly disturbed by their exchanges with her – even Dr Gray seemed unable to manage Adeline Lewis, despite his usual calm but insistent bedside manner. When the students learned of Miss Lewis's engagement to her childhood sweetheart, they suspected that she would not stay their teacher for long. Evie herself left school for good in the spring of 1944 – a year later she learned that Miss Lewis had resigned from teaching, only to lose her new husband in battle, leaving her pregnant, unemployed and alone.

Meanwhile, Evie, confident in her high impression of Miss Lewis's flawless literary judgement and her own untested gifts, had spent the past year and a half ploughing through the list of classics that Adeline had given her on her last day at school – a very different list from the one she had given Evie's father during his long convalescence from that terrible tractor accident. Even without a clear sense of where further study could lead her, Evie was keeping up her reading in the hope that one day a grand opportunity would present itself. She was convinced that she only had to work hard in the meantime and be ready for it when it came.

Then one day Evie read a piece on Virginia Woolf in a copy of *The Times Literary Supplement* left by the fire for kindling, and it quoted Woolf as saying that Jane Austen was the hardest of all great writers to catch in the act of greatness. For Evie, working for the Knight family, although on the decline, was bringing her one step closer to that greatness. Miss Lewis had said as much to her one day in the village, when she learned where the young girl would be working. Evie continued to console herself over the early departure from school by thinking about her unique proximity to the very environment that had helped inform some of the greatest novels ever written.

This was when the idea of trying to get even closer to the Austen legacy had first popped into Evie's head.

As she had learned from Miss Lewis in school, Austen's father had enjoyed a library of hundreds of books in their parsonage home in the village of Steventon, and young Jane had been encouraged to read anything and everything she found on its shelves. Miss Lewis similarly believed that there was no such thing as a 'bad' book in terms of content: her mantra to both the class and the trustees was that if something had ever happened before in real life, then it was completely fair game to put it down in print. In fact, it was demanded of it. Miss Lewis was convinced that young Jane's being allowed to run rampant among fairly 'adult' material had informed her gift for irony at an ideal age, giving her years of juvenile writing to perfect it.

Evie knew that the Knight family library, as it stood today, must also contain books that Austen would have borrowed, and the more time that Evie spent both overtly dusting and covertly examining the volumes in the library, analysing their bookplates and marginalia and degree of wear, the more it occurred to her that a cataloguing of sorts could help compose a picture of Jane's reading tastes from that last critical decade of her life.

So Evie secretly kept a small scrapbook hidden in one of the shelves, and in it she wrote down anything of note as she worked her way through the thousands of volumes, one by one. She had been at this for nearly a year and a half, most often late at night when everyone else had gone to bed, having herself been allocated a small bedroom in the third-floor attic. This was generous of Miss Knight to provide, as it saved Evie a long walk home at the end of the day. But she had not yet confided in anyone, not even Miss Knight, about what she was doing, sitting here on the little stool, night after night. Young and unschooled though she was, Evie was convinced that this library held valuable insights into Jane Austen – and possibly a few books of immeasurable worth – and she was canny enough to know to keep this pursuit to herself, at least for now. Earlier that same day, she had heard Miss Knight on the phone with someone from Sotheby's and learned just enough to confirm that, with the war now over, interest in Jane Austen's possessions, letters and handwriting was starting to significantly heat up.

So far, Evie had catalogued fifteen hundred of the over two thousand books on the shelves, averaging a handful of volumes a night. She had estimated from the start that it would take close to two years to get through each and every book to the extent that she intended. She knew that the entire exercise would end up meaningless unless she went through every single page of every single book. The risk of missing a small set of initials, a scratch of handwriting – or, God forbid, a marking by Jane Austen herself – was simply too great.

The most onerous and time-consuming work involved copying down all the title and copyright page information, as well as any lengthy marginalia, into her little notebook. Some nights, only a few volumes could be summarised as a result. She did give herself weekend nights off, primarily because she usually went home to help her mother on the farm and to visit with her father. She knew herself well enough to know that – just as with Miss Adeline's list of books – she would otherwise compulsively proceed apace, day after day, with no nightly break from the challenge she had set herself.

Now, on this quiet, moonlit September night, with only a low-placed kerosene lamp to guide her, Evie was turning the pages of a volume – one of ten in a set – of an ancient Germanic-language text. Each volume was several hundred pages long, making the entire collection thousands of pages of work for her. The odds of finding any margin notations at all in a work on the German language and its origins struck even her, for all her investigative spirit, as virtually non-existent.

At moments such as this, Evie always felt the most tempted to cut a few corners and race ahead. But her ability to forge on and heed that other voice in her head – the one that told her she was special, no matter what the outside world reflected back at her – was one of the things that she knew made her unique. So she always listened to this insistent inner voice, no matter how apathetic or tired she felt, and right now this voice was telling her not to give up.

It was now nearing two A.M., Evie's usual finishing time. Through trial and exercise, she was learning to live on four hours of sleep a night. She was confident she could keep to this routine for at least several more months. Besides, lack of sleep was no deterrence – her days at the house were busy yet so mundane, so bereft of intellectual challenge, that she found herself living for these quiet nights to herself.

As Evie turned the pages of the large, dense volume still in her hands — pages so thick that it took actual effort sometimes to pry their edges open — she could feel a slight bulging in the section coming up. She skipped eagerly ahead to it, and as she flipped over the final page, a letter fell out.

The handwriting was familiar to her from some of the earlier annotations, inscriptions and margin markings she had found. No postmark was on the outside folded cover, the letter apparently having never been mailed.

She could not believe her eyes as she read it — at first too quickly, as if convinced the paper might disappear as mysteriously as it had been found, and then three more times, each time more slowly than before. It was the very thing she would have been looking for, if only she could have guessed what that could possibly be.

Immediately she set out to copy the complete letter into her little notebook as faithfully as she could, making sure her own lines began and ended with the exact same words as those in the letter, and inserting every grammatical or spelling error, and every well-known dash.

She had had moments before in the library, late at night, that had approached a small degree of the euphoria she now felt as she scribbled away, but nothing else had ever come close to this. She finally understood why she had spent so many futile nights sitting here, on her little stool, alone. This was why she had never given up. And this was why Miss Adeline had been right all along.

She had, with this discovery, brought the world closer than it had ever been before to the greatness.

She had, as Miss Woolf herself once described it, caught Jane Austen in the act.

Chapter Eight

*H*arriet Peckham knocked on Dr Gray's half-open office door late one Friday afternoon, and he looked up to see a new expression on her face. Lately he had taken to mentally cataloguing Miss Peckham's various expressions, which he did not think boded well for any longevity in their working relationship. He would have preferred a nurse who was always pleasant of face and no-nonsense in manner – none of the hinting and insinuations that Harriet liked to throw about, as if trying to see what would stick.

'I'm sorry, Dr Gray, to interrupt, but Mrs Lewis is on the phone.' Harriet leaned forward a bit and added, almost in a hush, 'Adeline Grover's mother.'

'I know who she is, Miss Peckham,' Dr Gray replied quickly. 'I will take the call in here.'

'Very well, Doctor.' Harriet whirled about in the doorway and left.

Dr Gray picked up the phone, then waited for the telltale click from the hallway line before saying a single word.

'Mrs Lewis, what is it? Is it Adeline?'

'Yes, Doctor, we're sorry to bother you so close to the dinner hour.'

'It's no bother at all. Is she starting her labour?' He looked over at the calendar on the wall. 'Although I should think it's a bit early for that – she has, what, one more month to go?'

'We're not sure, Dr Gray – she's just not right. And she's very worried, more than I have ever seen her.'

'Well, that's saying something.' He got up and started packing his medical bag from the desk. 'You were right to call. I am leaving now – tell Adeline I'll be there in five minutes.' That would give him just enough time to get to the other side of the village.

He walked as fast as possible along the main road with his black medical bag in hand. When he reached the little thatched Grover cottage set back from the road, he slowed himself down, as his breathing was becoming a little laboured and he didn't want to worry Mrs Lewis any more than necessary. Already he could see her standing in the open cottage doorway waiting for him.

'You made remarkable time. Adeline will be so grateful,' she said, and he followed her straight up the narrow staircase without removing his coat.

Adeline looked a little less than grateful when he entered her bedroom. 'Mother, honestly, I told you, I am sure it is nothing serious.'

Dr Gray came over and sat down next to her on the edge of the bed, ignoring her words, and took her wrist in his hand to feel for her pulse. With his stethoscope already about his neck, he listened to her heart and lungs, then felt her forehead with the back of his hand.

'Well, did I pass?' Adeline said, with only the hint of her usual teasing smile.

'Tell me your symptoms.'

She looked over at her mother in the doorway. 'Mum, can you please go and make Dr Gray a nice stiff gin and tonic? He's going to need one by the time we're both done with him.'

Her mother reluctantly headed back down the stairs, leaving the door open.

'I am sorry that you had to go to all this bother.' Adeline pulled herself up against the pillows he was now propping for her. 'It's just some cramping.'

'Where?'

'Quite low in my stomach.'

'Any pain in your lower back as well?'

'Not really – just the tiniest bit, and it comes and goes.'

'Any bleeding?'

She shook her head. 'No, not today. There was a little spotting last night, but that seems to have gone away. That's a good sign, right?' she asked him eagerly.

He was listening to her belly with the stethoscope now. 'The heartbeat is strong enough, but I'd still like to keep you monitored.'

'Oh, no worries there – my mother has me under lock and key.'

'Well, it's her first grandchild, after all.' He put the stethoscope away in his bag and was starting to stand up, when Adeline put her hand out to stop him.

'Might you stay, for a bit? I mean, it's already after hours, thanks to me.'

'I should get going. You need to rest.'

'Well, make sure you get that drink on your way out.'

She looked very tired to him, sitting up in bed against the white pillows in her white lace nightgown, her face so pale that he hesitated to leave.

'Adeline, do you promise to have your mother call me if

anything changes, anything at all? I don't care how insignificant it might seem.'

'You sound worried.'

He picked up his medical bag. 'No, not worried. I just know how stoic you can be, and I don't want anything to get missed.'

'Stoic? Me? But I was such a rabble-rouser with the school board, remember? Couldn't keep my mouth shut, if I recall correctly.'

He smiled. 'You are not remotely stoical about others, yes, that is correct.'

'Well, I promise then, but you have to promise to not come flying over here every time my mother telephones. You looked quite unlike yourself when you came through that door.'

He headed down the stairs, testing part of the old oak banister as he did so, then looked back up when he reached Mrs Lewis waiting at the bottom with his gin and tonic in hand.

'Make sure she uses that banister, especially in this last month. Her balance will be off. She is quite large already.'

Mrs Lewis passed him the drink and showed him into the front drawing room. 'I hope you didn't tell her that – Adeline can be surprisingly vain.'

'Oh, I know that,' he said between sips. 'She is missed at the school, you know.'

Mrs Lewis sat down on a nearby sofa. 'Adeline is doing exactly what she wants to do.'

'I know that, too. But the board was foolish to come down on her so hard.' He sat back against the sofa facing hers. 'Will she return to teaching one day, do you think? It would be quite a waste of her talents otherwise.'

'I have no idea. Right now the baby is all she thinks about, as it should be.'

'Quite right.' He felt strangely self-conscious under Mrs

Lewis's gaze, as if he were being told off for something he hadn't even done yet. Looking about the room for a distraction, he spotted a framed photo from Adeline's wedding to Samuel the previous winter. 'Does she talk about Samuel much?'

'Why do you ask?' Mrs Lewis replied curtly.

'No reason. I just, well, I know how it feels. Although I can't imagine how it feels when one is expecting.'

'No, Dr Gray, you can't. And you were fortunate – we both were – to have had so much time with our late spouses, to at least give us memories to spare.' He shifted uncomfortably in his seat as she kept on talking. 'Although, sadly, I don't think being briefly married is any kind of insurance against the loss. It's the hole someone leaves behind that matters most. Adeline and Sam knew each other from the time they were babies – she was his entire world. He spoke about marrying her from the time he could talk. And then they had – what? – all of one week together before he had to return to that god-awful war. One week of marriage. And now a baby to raise all on her own.'

'She might marry again.'

'Will you?'

He smiled and downed the rest of his drink in one go. 'No, I am getting old now. Nobody would want me.'

'Oh, come now, Dr Gray,' Mrs Lewis said archly. 'You sell yourself short. There's Miss Peckham, for one.'

He stood up. He could see where Adeline got both her nerve and her sharp tongue.

'Promise me you'll call, Mrs Lewis, no matter the hour, if anything changes. Anything at all. Especially any new bleeding. All right?'

He was in deepest sleep – a second gin and tonic back at home had done the trick, and thinking he had the night to himself, he had collapsed early into bed. So when the phone rang at midnight, it took him a few seconds to pull himself awake and process what was going on.

When he entered the bedroom behind her stricken mother, he saw the bedsheets covered in blood, and a bucket and towels scattered about the floor, and in the centre of it all lay Adeline, her white lace nightgown shredded and stained as she writhed and screamed in pain, gripping the headboard posts, one in each ash-white hand.

Dr Gray felt her abdomen as gingerly yet as thoroughly as possible, watching Adeline flinch at every negligible pressure of his hands. He took out his stethoscope and listened carefully to both her and the baby's hearts, then turned back to Mrs Lewis, standing trembling behind him.

'The baby's heart rate is irregular – and her pain – the bleeding – it's happening way too fast. Get the hospital on the phone and make bloody sure the ambulance I requested is on its way.'

Stunned by his tone, Mrs Lewis rushed out of the room in a panic.

The minute she was gone, Adeline grabbed wildly at Dr Gray's arm. 'Is the baby okay?'

'We need to get you to the hospital right away. You're not in labour yet, but you're bleeding profusely, and the baby is feeling the stress.'

She grabbed his arm even harder. 'Am I going to lose this baby? Tell me the truth, Dr Gray, please, I'm begging you.'

'We're going to get you into surgery for a Caesarean section – the baby is too distressed to wait for a natural labour. But I have no reason to believe that he or she can't be delivered safely that way. Time, however, is of the essence, so I will get you downstairs now, all right?'

Dr Gray wrapped Adeline in her housecoat and carried her down the narrow staircase as carefully and as quickly as he dared. By the time they reached the bottom landing, the ambulance was pulling up at the end of the garden path. The ambulance driver and the attendant jumped down from the vehicle and rushed up to meet them with the stretcher.

As the ambulance raced in the night to Alton, Dr Gray stayed by her side, holding a damp towel to her forehead with one hand while holding her ice-cold hand in his other. He could do nothing else for her.

Dr Howard Westlake, the surgeon and a longtime colleague of Dr Gray's, was not hopeful and called for additional blood supplies to be rushed over from the Winchester hospital's new blood depot eighteen miles away, in case transfusion became necessary. Both he and Dr Gray had learned the hard way over the years to plan ahead whenever local villagers ran into serious trouble, given the distance from the better-prepared urban Hampshire hospital. Dr Gray asked for a quick second of private consultation as Adeline was prepped for surgery.

'I think it's placenta abruption,' Dr Gray said in a half whisper. 'All the signs are there. The bleeding, the uterine tenderness, the foetal heart rate.'

Dr Westlake was watching him carefully. 'Did you think of trying to deliver the baby right then and there?'

Dr Gray shook his head. 'The foetus is in too much distress. And besides, they are both in danger, as you know. They needed to be here in the hospital, just in case.'

He paused to look through the long narrow window to the operating theatre and could just make out Adeline's long brown hair fanned out behind her head, now obscured by the anaesthesia mask.

'Howard, you agree with me, that she should be the primary patient, right? All the literature says that—'

'Benjamin, we've talked about this plenty before – you know how I feel. You know you have nothing to worry about there.'

Dr Gray nodded but looked so stricken, the surgeon wasn't sure his words were sinking in.

'Go home and get some rest, Ben, all right? It's going to be a long night, and no matter what happens, Mrs Grover is going to need you on the morrow. We'll call when it's over.'

But Dr Gray stayed all night at the hospital, unable to sleep. He knew he could make sleep come soon enough, when he wanted it to. Right now he wanted to stand sentinel at the gates of hell and keep Adeline from falling through. She was so young, with so many years ahead of her. This did not have to be the end, for her, no matter what happened – he would do his absolute best to see to that. And with that notion, something inarticulate and grasping stirred inside him, the very essence of life.

Chapter Nine

Chawton, Hampshire
November 1945

*I*t had been over a month since the loss of Adeline's daughter, and Dr Gray had been summoned to her bedside yet again.

He knew that the degree of her loss was incalculable. It was measured both in reality and in the extinguishing of all the motherly hopes and dreams that had carried her through the earlier waves of grief over Samuel's death. By holding on to the idea of the baby in order to survive that pain, she had invested all she had left, only to now be left with nothing. From all his years of practise, Dr Gray knew only one thing for sure: that some of us are given too much to bear, and this burden is made worse by the hidden nature of that toll, a toll that others cannot even begin to guess at.

She had grabbed at his arm that very day, pulling hard on the sleeve of the suit jacket he always wore, as if to keep her back from some invisible brink.

'I just want the pain to end. You have to help me.'

'I know, Adeline, I know. But it will ease, somewhat, with time, I promise you.'

'Don't lie to me – you of all people know it won't.' She turned her face away from him and let his arm drop hard, almost hostilely. 'How can it, when I've lost everything – everyone – that I've ever loved? What would that say about me, if I could just go on?'

He stared down at the back of her head. 'No one will ever judge you for trying to be happy again.'

'I don't care what others think,' she said harshly. 'I gave everything I had to Samuel and then to our baby, every last bit of me. I did it knowing how much I could get hurt – I took my chance and I was wrong.' She gave a strange, bitter laugh.

'You speak as if you could have held back somehow, from life.'

She turned back to look at him.

'Can't I? Don't you? You certainly act like you do.'

He shifted his weight a bit under her gaze. 'We're not talking about me, Adeline.'

'Maybe we should be.'

'Adeline, you have every right to be angry and upset. But I don't think it's appropriate to direct it at me, as your doctor and, I hope, your friend – do you?'

She turned her head away from him again. 'Appropriate. Fine. I'm sorry. Just give me something, please, anything to help me sleep. Please, just for a bit. Just this once.'

He reached into his black bag and took out the tiny vial he had filled back in his office, knowing she would ask for it again, knowing he would not be able to say no. He prayed she wouldn't ask him for anything more.

He placed the vial down on the bedside table without a word, then left the darkened bedroom just as silently.

Emerging into the purple dusk of early winter, Dr Gray walked the half-mile home weighed down by both Adeline's loss and his own futility in the face of it. He had been so panicked and distraught that terrible night at the hospital, and weeks later he continued to feel a pervasive helplessness where Adeline was concerned.

Worst of all, he had just left medicine with Adeline that — like him — was doing nothing to help. All that the morphine was doing was helping her *not* to live — to avoid what she must endure — to deafen the voices inside. That was all he could do for her now: keep her alive by letting her kill the very essence inside her. He could not stop the pain, he could not give her a reason to live — he could not heal the trauma in her brain. As he thought back on all of this, he struggled to think of what recompense a good doctor got for having to face such life-destroying failure. He struggled at the best of times to figure that out; tonight he couldn't even try.

His nurse had gone home for the day — as usual, he entered a quiet and lonely house. Throwing down his coat and bag on the old deacon's bench in the front vestibule, he walked slowly into the examination room and back through to his office, shutting the door behind him.

The rest of the bottle still sat on his desk. He had not locked it away earlier, as he was supposed to; he just made sure to leave only enough for one dose. Then he had shut his office door unlatched behind him, as if hoping someone would steal the bottle while he was away.

He sat down at his desk, staring at the clear, slow-moving liquid. He always tried so hard, always came up with a thousand reasons not to. And then always, always, came up with one or two really good ones why. He could hear all the voices in his own head, not yet deafened — those of his late wife, his medical colleagues like Dr Westlake, Reverend Powell to whom he had confessed. But the thing that no one warns you about, when the pain is too great – when the pain is so great that you'd rather die than face another day of it – is that the pain becomes bigger, and more real, than anything else. It's like that circle of grief which is not supposed to shrink, even with time, but also not to grow – it's as if it is still expanding with the pain, feeding on it, infecting everything else around you. A calculating, inextinguishable darkness that covers everything, even the few things that you were promised would remain outside the grief, by all those well-meaning people who simply had not yet experienced a grief as bad as yours.

You feel so trapped, with no way out, and you stop caring about the best way to be. About the proper way to live, the smart way. For if merely living becomes the sole endgame, then what does it matter what you do to sustain it?

The bottle sat before him, promising something that no one – that nothing else – could give him. He defied his Lord to judge him – he was past caring what would happen if he got caught. If he did end up caught one day, at least it would mean he had survived longer than he had thought possible.

He reached out for the bottle, and just like poor Adeline, all alone in her own bedroom, curtains pulled against the light of day, he took his first sip and let deliverance – however temporary, however illusory – wash over him, too.

⌣

Adam Berwick was home early from work, now that the harvest season had ended and the days were becoming increasingly short. By the middle of the afternoon, he could feel night waiting impatiently to descend in the sudden silence of the songbirds and the long shadows of the sun. With his ploughing almost done for the year and the stable chores limited to feeding the livestock, he looked forward to the upcoming seasonal respite.

For one thing, it would give him plenty of time to read. Adam needed that because he now spent every winter rereading the collected works of Jane Austen; sometimes he even read *Pride and Prejudice* twice.

He was sitting at the kitchen table with a strong cup of coffee and his well-worn copy of *Pride and Prejudice* before him, enjoying the first botched proposal scene with Mr Darcy, astonished every time at the man's insensitivity. Adam was nothing if not sensitive – perhaps too much so. Reading as Mr Darcy unknowingly dug a bigger and bigger hole for himself – 'Could you expect me to rejoice in the inferiority of your connections? To congratulate myself on the hope of relations, whose condition in life is so decidedly beneath my own?' – Adam always found himself practically yelling out loud to Fitzwilliam Darcy to stop and save himself from further humiliation at his own hands.

Adam loved being in this world, transported, where people were honest with each other, but also sincerely cared for each other, no matter their rank. Where the Miss Bateses of the world would always have a family to dine with, and the Harvilles would take in the grief-stricken Captain Benwick following the loss of his fiancée, and even the imperious and insensitive Bertrams would give Fanny Price a roof above her head. And the letters people sent – long, regular missives designed to keep people as close to one's heart and thoughts as possible, whatever insurmountable distance might be between them at present. He wondered at the solicitude in that, the deep and unwavering caring, and what he could do – at as little risk socially as possible – to experience any of that in his own, stymied life.

'Queues were awful again today – one orange per customer, and only the bitter ones at that. Then I run into Harriet Peckham at the post office – no mail for us as usual, by the way – and she tells me Adeline Grover's not doing so well,' his mother announced almost triumphantly as she walked straight past him into the kitchen and threw her ration book, small string bag of groceries, and a rolled-up newspaper onto the counter. She went over to put the kettle on, still not having looked over at Adam. 'Just as I'd feared, of course.'

Adam knew best to shut his book.

'Tells me the poor girl can't get out of bed. That Dr Gray is beside himself with worry, for all he apparently botched that delivery – has taken to checking in on her so regularly, you'd think she was his only patient.'

'Maybe right now she's his most important one.'

His mother turned about at the stove to stare pointedly at him. 'Now there's a pretty young thing. Why didn't you ever have your eye on her?'

Adam pushed the book a little farther away from him.

'Adam, my boy, one has to be on the lookout for these things. You need to find someone to take care of you. I won't be around forever, you know.'

He did know – she reminded him regularly. He hated when she talked like this. To him, it felt the opposite of caring. It wasn't helping him find the key to those happier worlds he read about in books; it only made him feel trapped and desperate and even more alone.

'Adeline Grover's never going to be interested in the likes of me, Mother. And now's surely not the time to discuss it.'

'Suit yourself. Just know the village is always speculating about you, whether you want to discuss it or not,' she said with a shrug, then went and cut herself some bread and butter on the counter. Sitting down across from him with her tea, she glanced at the book before him. 'Didn't you just read that?'

'Last winter.'

'You read too much. You read *her* too much. You should be out, go to Alton more.'

'I go to Alton.'

'You go to the *pictures*. You sit alone in the cinema, watching some romantic silliness. Or reading it,' she added, with an insolent nod at his book. 'Your nose always in a book, just like your father.'

He took another sip of his coffee, then stood up.

'Where are you off to?' she asked, unrolling the afternoon newspaper that she had brought in with her.

'I just remembered I did promise Mrs Lewis to help with the mulching in the garden before there's a hard frost. Sun will be down in an hour or so.'

'There's a boy.' His mother smiled approvingly at him as she picked up her newspaper.

Adeline Grover sat in the window seat she had improvised for herself at the front of the drawing room. She had taken half of an old swinging door she had found in the garden shed and laid it over both the deep windowsill and the level top of the adjoining radiator. She had covered it all with a thick quilted counterpane and a variety of cushions, and there she could often be found, sitting with a stack of books, but mostly staring out the window, watching the rest of the village move on with their lives.

She was in trouble and she knew it. She was very aware that she had not allowed herself to fully feel the loss of Sam, often pushing the thought of him out of her mind, as if he were simply off somewhere, still fighting the war. Losing Sam had been difficult and complicated enough, let alone the death of their baby. She was not coping with either of these losses, not in the way one had to in order to move on. She had surprised herself with this shortcoming – she was very proud and very smart, and it had never occurred to her that she would get something so significant, and unavoidable, so wrong. But she was at least smart enough to be able to trick everyone else into thinking she was doing well enough. It had become almost a game to her. And while playing the game of appearing well enough, she felt so completely detached – even liberated – from her real self, the person she had been before everything went wrong, that she marvelled at this ability to be so objective and cut off from one's own feelings. As if this were the real achievement.

She was starting to get a bit of a window into the male mind as a result. She could only wonder at what a lifetime of both emotional avoidance and overactivity yielded as a result. She thought about Sam's impenetrable optimism even in the face of an opposite reality – his determination that they would be married, his forgiving of her every slip, his bright and happy surface. She had loved that about him and how he helped keep her so moored to daily life: how every day was a new day, and yesterday didn't matter, and there was no point in ever worrying about the future.

She pictured him in his bomber plane, the gauges rattling before him, and the sea and the rocks below, and both the intensity and the detachment that he would have brought to this one terrifying moment. He would have given his all, even though the effort didn't matter – you were just a speck on someone else's gauge, a tightrope walk across an abyss, an entire human life balanced on the point of a needle.

Now she was on the point of the needle, too. There were only two ways that this could go. If she kept this up and fell off and into the abyss, she might pull herself out one day – but she also might not. So she had to find a way to stop what she was doing, this medicating away of her unavoidable pain and taking advantage of poor Dr Gray. For she was certainly taking advantage of him – of his guilt, and his compassion, and the confusing little soft spot he seemed to have for her, and of all the things that made him an especially caring man, outside of being a doctor.

She looked out the window at the setting sun, and at Adam Berwick in the garden with her mother, cutting back the dead growth and covering up the more delicate perennials ahead of the winter frost. When the two of them spied her in the window seat, her mother must have said something to Adam, because he put down the shovel and picked up a basket at his side as they headed into the house together.

'Adeline, darling, look what Mr Berwick has brought you.'

Adeline looked down from her perch and peered into the basket to see a little kitten fast asleep.

She started to cry.

Mrs Lewis was used to all this emotion, but the poor man could only stand there frozen in place, having no idea what to do or say, gripping the basket in his white-knuckled hands.

Mrs Lewis put out her hand to touch his forearm gently. 'Don't mind her, it's so sweet of you. She's just still quite worn down. Look, I'll go and get us all some tea, shall I?'

As Mrs Lewis left the drawing room, Adam put the basket down next to the stack of books in the window seat and noticed *Persuasion* at the very top.

Adeline was wiping her eyes with the edge of her housecoat. 'I'm sorry, Mr Berwick.'

'It's Adam,' he said simply, then gently reached down into the basket and put the kitten in her arms. 'Came from the old tabby at the steward's cottage. It's a few months along now.'

She stroked the tiny animal's brown-and-ginger coat. 'It was so thoughtful of you. I really am very sorry.' She had interacted so rarely with Adam Berwick in the past, such a shy and silent man, that she was now feeling terrible for having frightened him with this display.

He gave a little cough and looked about for a place to sit.
She was sitting up there in the window, looking as if she could
stay there for hours, with her books and her little pot of tea on
a small wicker tray. Suddenly a mental image from years ago
flashed through his head – lying up on the edge of a stone wall,
surrounded by death in the little church graveyard, feeling like
an effigy himself.

'Oh, I'm sorry, please, have a seat – bring that chair over,
the rocking chair. It's my favourite. Keeps me in motion.' She
smiled wearily.

He brought the chair over from beside the fireplace and sat
it down next to her. 'You're reading *Persuasion*.'

'You know it?'

He nodded. 'A hard book, that.'

'Hard to read?'

'Hard to feel.'

'Oh, dear, yes, I don't know what I was thinking when I
picked it up – although it always makes me so happy in the
end. You like Jane Austen, too, then?'

He nodded again while simultaneously looking everywhere about the room except directly at her.

'Of course I have to ask then, which of the books is your
favourite?'

He looked down at his lap and gave her a small, self-conscious
smile. 'All of them. But Elizabeth Bennet is my favourite character.'

'Oh, me, too. There's no one like her in all of literature.
Dr Gray goes on and on about his Emma, but I'll take Lizzie
over Emma any day.'

Adam was staring directly at her now, at the way she was
speaking about the characters as if they were real people. They
had always seemed so alive to him – it had never occurred to
him that anyone else might feel that way, too.

'You talk to Dr Gray about the books?' he asked, leaning over to give the kitten a little pat.

'Yes, he is a singular fan of hers, let me tell you. But it makes sense – he is such an odd mixture himself of – how did Austen describe Mr Bennet? So "odd a mixture of quick parts, sarcastic humour, reserve, and caprice"?'

'Dr Gray is a good man,' Adam replied simply.

'Yes, he is – which is remarkable, given how clearly he sees everyone and everything.'

'Like Austen herself.'

'Yes.' Adeline sat up even straighter in agreement. 'Exactly. The humanity – the love for people – mixed with seeing them for who they really are. Loving them enough to do that. Loving them in *spite* of that.'

Adam nodded. He had never loved anyone enough to do that. Had not been given the chance. Had not given himself the chance. Like Adeline right now, he had been sitting in a window seat, watching everyone else go by, not putting himself out there. And getting nothing in return.

That night, he returned to his copy of *Pride and Prejudice* yet again. He thought back to his talk with Adeline, and of how they both loved Elizabeth Bennet, and he wondered how much of Jane Austen might be in that wonderful character after all. He would often stare at the small sketch of the baby-cheeked woman with tight brown curls and strong nose on the frontispiece of some of the books, and he wished he knew more. Wished the letters to her sister had been preserved – wished that the one sketch Cassandra Austen had done out of doors had revealed more than loose bonnet strings and an outward-seeking gaze.

It mystified him that he could have grown up in the same

village where Austen had once lived — where she had written the final three books from scratch — yet see so little of her around him. Yes, there was the Great House still owned by the Knights, and the graves of the mother and the sister, and the old steward's cottage in the heart of the village. But aside from one small memorial plaque placed on the cottage in 1917 on the centenary of Austen's death — the kind that the country gave out to hundreds of distinguished Englishmen — there were no other traces of her life.

Adam found the courage to say as much to Dr Gray a few days later at his annual check-up, now that Adam knew he was not the only man in Chawton to be so interested in the great writer. Harriet Peckham led him brusquely into the office, then remained in the front examining room tidying about as the two men spoke.

Dr Gray put down Adam's medical file and looked at him curiously. 'I must admit, Adam, I wasn't expecting something like this from you. I mean, honouring Miss Austen's legacy has always struck me as more of a—'

'—Woman's job?'

'No, not exactly — more of a historian's. Or an educator of some kind.'

Adam shook his head. 'It's been over a hundred years, and no one else has jumped into the breach.'

'But what are you thinking about, then? A museum of some kind?'

'Yes, of some kind. I was thinking, if the cottage could be repurposed again, as a single residence, and we were able to retrieve some of her things, then we could assemble it all together and people would actually have something to see, and touch, when they came. Look here.' Adam fumbled about in the pocket of the overcoat he was still wearing and pulled out a misshapen wooden object. 'It's a small child's toy — Georgian

I think, I looked it up in the library – and it was in a heap of rubbish I found in front of the house. They've been digging up the garden a bit of late. What if? What if this toy belonged to Jane's family? And now it's got no home, and it's just lying there, trash, in the street.'

It was the most Dr Gray had ever heard the man speak, and the doctor nodded thoughtfully in response. 'A home of sorts, then, to honour Austen. That seems right to me. You know, I always did feel that this village retained an old-world feel to it, as if one had stepped back in time.'

'Then it might not take much.'

'Well, it will take a house, for one thing. The cottage as it is won't suffice, you are right – there'd have to be renovations, and town approvals for all that, and the Russell place up the road just sold for one thousand pounds. I think, with this lot size and the costs to repair, we'd be looking at a few thousand pounds at least, if not more.'

Adam ruminated quietly. 'The cottage still belongs to the Knights?'

Dr Gray nodded. 'As far as I know. In better times, they might have sold for less than market value – but now I am not so sure. Adam, forgive me, because I am actually quite impressed by your initiative, but will you really have time to think about any of this come spring?'

No sooner had the words left his mouth than Dr Gray realised that time was the one thing so many in their sleepy little village seemed to have. Jane Austen had used her time here for housework and visits and composing works of genius. That the population of Chawton had barely varied since then made Dr Gray suddenly see each of the villagers as almost pure one-to-one substitutes for those of the past. If they weren't up to the task of preserving Austen's legacy, who on earth ever would be?

Adam shifted his weight about in the uncomfortable

wooden chair facing Dr Gray behind his desk. 'If I have time to read her over and over, I've time for this.'

It was the most declarative statement Dr Gray had ever heard come from the man.

'Okay, Adam, let me think about this – and possibly we can approach Frances Knight together, at the house. Best to start with her – old Mr Knight only ever complains about all the Austen tourists we attract.' He suddenly stopped talking, having heard a noise just outside his office, and went over to slowly and discreetly close the door before returning to his desk. 'In the meantime, let's both think about others who might be interested in helping with our little project. Your mother perhaps?'

Adam shook his head. 'Not Mum – doesn't care for all the tourists and whatnot that Austen brings around either.'

Dr Gray looked at Adam curiously. Having been school-mates with all three Berwick boys, he had always had a partic-ular concern for the farmer and his obviously depressed mental state. As part of his medical internship decades earlier, Dr Gray had been on duty at Alton Hospital when Mr Berwick had tragically died from the Spanish flu. And Dr Gray was well aware of the mother's domineering personality, which seemed to have grown only more difficult and self-pitying over the years. He had assumed Adam had been introduced to Austen by a woman – and the only woman anyone knew about when it came to the bachelor farmer was the old widow Berwick. Perhaps a teacher then, years ago, when Adam was studying for his placement and won the scholarship. A teacher such as Adeline Grover had been.

And with that, Dr Gray's head shot up. 'I think I know someone else who can help.'

Chapter Ten

Alton, Hampshire
15 November, 1945

Andrew Forrester sat alone in his office, the door firmly shut. Before him on the desk blotter was the last will and testament of James Edward Knight.

Andrew felt sick to his stomach. Frances Knight, the woman he had loved and lost decades ago due to this same man and his meddling, was about to lose everything she had.

That very morning, James Edward Knight had summoned Andrew Forrester to his sickbed, confined to a room he would never leave again. In all the years that Andrew had provided legal advice to Mr Knight, Frances's name had rarely come up. They had all functioned best by never mentioning the past.

But on this occasion, Mr Knight finally mentioned his daughter:

'Frances has no head for business.'

Andrew appeared to listen patiently, but doubted that was true. Frances might be a little shy and yielding, but she had a firm grasp of the value of the estate and its contents. He also knew that she had done her best with household decisions to conserve expenses as much as possible, often to her own detriment, in order to attend to the costs of running the estate.

'Sir, your daughter cares greatly both for you and for this estate,' Andrew countered, suspecting that the conversation was about to take a very difficult turn.

James Knight shook his head. 'Who knows what that girl cares about. I surely don't. Certainly, she never bothered to marry or bear children to carry on the family name, her one female duty.'

Andrew could feel an old familiar anger rising within him, and he practically had to bite his lip, given what he knew of James Knight's involvement in Frances's few chances at love. Andrew wasn't sure he had ever met a greater hypocrite than this man now dying before him.

James Knight sat up in bed and Andrew went to adjust the pillows behind him, then sat back down on the chair left by the bedside for the infrequent visitors.

'Pass me some paper,' the old man ordered, 'and go and get Dr Gray's nurse. She should be downstairs by now, to give me my bath. Oh, and that writing desk over in the corner – I'll take that, too.'

Andrew hesitated but did what he was told, then gritted his teeth and walked one floor down to find Harriet Peckham standing in the front entrance, inspecting the visitors' log on the small side table.

He had never liked Harriet, whom he suspected of being a busybody. But trained nurses were hard to entice out to Chawton – a village with all of one hundred homes and practically no commercial business to speak of. At least Harriet, who had grown up in town, was a familiar sight to the villagers and could be relied upon to show up in any emergency.

When Andrew and the nurse entered the bedroom together, James Knight held up a sheet of the paper that Andrew had given him. 'I need you both to witness my signature on this. I don't want any questions about it, no bloody argument about my state of mind. I am completely satisfied as to its contents, and there's not to be another word about it, do you hear?'

He then placed the document back down on the mahogany writing desk and signed it with a flourish. Andrew went slowly over to the side of the bed and added his signature, then motioned for Harriet to come over and do the same.

'That's done then. As it should be. Maybe this estate — including the cottage — will now stand a chance. The last thing I want when I'm gone is a bunch of American tourists hanging over the fencing, trying to sneak a peek inside, and I don't trust that daughter of mine to keep any such thing from happening.' James Knight glanced quickly at Miss Peckham, then over to Andrew, where he saw increasing anger darting across his long-time lawyer's face. 'You're going to take this and lock it away, and that is the end of it, understood? And, as my lawyer, you are, of course, required to keep its contents completely confidential.'

Andrew sighed. He knew when he was beat. He had been here before.

Back in the privacy of his office, Andrew now read the new will before him.

Inside his locked cabinet was another will, one that had been executed nearly half a century ago, in 1896, soon after the passing of the new death-taxation laws. This earlier document had left the entire estate to the eldest surviving child of James Knight. At the time of execution, this would have been Frances's brother, Cecil, who had been born that same year and ended up dying in his thirties in a hunting accident. The estate would then pass to the next eldest child, being Frances, born two years after her brother in 1898. This was similar to the pattern of inheritance that the Knight family had prescribed for generations. To keep the property in the Knight family, the estate had often been inherited by women laterally over the centuries, rather than being passed down to some distant male relative.

This 1896 will was the only one that the various Knight relatives would have been aware of over the years. Now everything was about to be upended by this most bitter, disapproving man.

So this was the daughter's reward, an inheritance of exactly nothing. Her recompense for all the years of loneliness, the caregiving, the apparently unforgivable sin of not providing an heir.

Andrew stood up. He dreaded one day having to give the news to Frances. But they had been here, before, too.

They were nothing if not familiar, the two of them, with sharing crushing disappointment.

Chapter Eleven

Chawton, Hampshire
14 December, 1945

$\mathcal{D}$r Gray had not visited Adeline Grover for several weeks.
He did not think it appropriate – her care was now entirely up to her and needed to be. He also did not want to be
put in an uncomfortable position again or asked to do something he shouldn't. The longer he went without seeing her, the
greater the chance she would move through some of her anger
(which so often of late seemed, disturbingly, to be directed at
him) towards the start, at least, of resignation.

He was sitting at his desk one dark, wintry Friday morning, when his nurse came in with a small envelope. He
opened the holiday card in front of her, read it quickly, then
stood up. Stuffing the card into the front left pocket of his suit
jacket, he tried to simultaneously retrieve a small parcel from
his desk drawer as nonchalantly as possible under Harriet's eager gaze.

'I'm going to go out on my rounds a little early this morning, Miss Peckham.'

She stared at him curiously. He had never cared for her,

even though she was a thorough and diligent enough nurse. But at moments such as this he could see the small eyes of the town upon him. He suspected she was a big source of the gossiping behind his back.

So he did not tell her where he was going and hoped she had not recognised the handwriting on the envelope – he couldn't imagine how.

He picked up his coat and hat from the hallway stand and was gone before Harriet Peckham could say – or intimate – another word.

A light sprinkling of snow covered the rooftops and the surrounding fields as he headed out, just enough whiteness to make it finally feel like Christmas – the first one since the war had ended. Dr Gray knew that for many in the village, with the constant loss of life and increasing rationing, recent holidays had been much more muted than was good for the soul. At least they still had Christmas Eve service in the little parish church of St Nicholas, which would be beautifully decorated with boughs of fir and ivy from the estate's woodland, and he hoped that Frances Knight would once again invite everyone to the Great House afterwards for roasted chestnuts and mulled wine. This had been a Chawton village tradition for generations. For a second he wondered if it was how Jane Austen had celebrated Christmas with the Knight family, too, and he realised that Adam Berwick's surprising plan must be getting to him.

He opened the small wooden gate to the Grover garden and, noticing the top hinge was loose, made a mental note to arrange to have that fixed. As he walked up the frosted pathway, he saw the empty stakes from the tomato plants and the delphiniums, and the willow cloches for the sweet pea – everything looking just a little desolate and forgotten. He gave the red-painted door a firm knock or two, then waited as a light turned on in the centre hall against the dark December morning, and the door opened.

'Dr Gray,' Beatrix Lewis stated, then kept standing there as if waiting for him to say something. She had been staying with Adeline in her little cottage for months now, given her daughter's low spirits and the lack of a man about the house to help her out.

'Mrs Lewis, hello, I came to pay a call on Adeline. Is she — is she up?' Something about the woman's hard stare was making him uncomfortable.

'Yes, but I wasn't aware that she had called for you.'

He unconsciously felt for the Christmas card now packed against his left chest, inside his jacket pocket. 'Not precisely, but she had written, and with the holidays so soon upon us, I thought I would quickly check in on her, if that is all right.'

Given that he had once carried her daughter's near-lifeless body out of this same doorway and into an arriving ambulance, she was acting in a fairly cool way towards him. 'Yes, well, your nurse telephoned just now to let us know you might be coming by today, so it's not a total surprise.'

'Look, if this isn't a good time, I can really—'

He heard Adeline's footsteps coming down the stairs — such a rickety, narrow staircase it was — and the strangest feeling shot through him, a pang of inexplicable anxiety such as he had never before known.

'Dr Gray, hello. Mother, I'll see Dr Gray into the drawing room.'

He followed her thin figure into the room on the right, then waited to sit down while she shut the double doors.

'Please, have a seat.' She motioned to the larger settee a few feet in front of the bay window, behind which he noticed a makeshift window seat over an old water radiator. Several needlepoint cushions were piled high across the deep window ledge, along with an impressive stack of books and a little kitten curled up asleep. He gave it a tender pat, then looked back at Adeline inquisitively.

'A present. From Adam Berwick.'

He stopped petting the kitten and looked about himself. 'I see you are all set up here,' he remarked as he fluffed up some of the cushions and started turning over some of the books.

'Looking for clues?' She smiled wanly. 'My little perch. Where I watch the world go by.'

'Adeline,' he started to admonish her, then tried to soften his tone, 'please don't talk like – please don't be so hard on yourself. This is an awful time – I know.'

'I know you know.' She stared at him, not coldly like her mother, but resignedly. Finally she motioned again for him to sit down, while she sat primly in a carved wooden rocking chair across from the fireplace, facing him at an angle.

'Thank you for your card,' he offered after a few seconds of silence.

'You came over just to tell me that?'

'Adeline,' he sighed, 'please, let's not do this.'

'It's just easier this way,' she sighed in return.

'What – being rude to everybody – to your mother – to me?'

'I just don't have the energy like I used to.'

'You were indeed quite energetic – almost too much so,' he said, attempting to coax a smile onto her pale, tightly drawn face.

She couldn't help but smile back. Sometimes she forgot how much he knew about her – forgot how long he had known the real her, the person she now only remembered herself to be.

'Well, you're welcome. For the card, I mean.'

'Ah, that reminds me.' He reached into the pocket of his coat, which he had thrown over the back of the settee. 'I brought you something. 'Tis the season and all that.'

He pulled out the small rectangular package and stood up to hand it to her. She gave a slight, self-conscious frown as she said, 'I didn't get you anything.'

'Your card was enough.' He sat back down on the settee. 'And anyway, as they say, it's the thought that counts.'

'I can only think of myself, it seems, of late. How to get through today, this hour. How to distract myself. How to forget.'

'Have you thought about going back to teaching? I'm sorry, maybe I shouldn't ask – I know it's still early days.'

She shook her head as she continued to hold the wrapped package in her hands. 'No, I haven't thought about it, not one little bit.' She raised the package up to her right ear and gently shook it. 'Dickens? Too light . . . Eliot? No, too thin . . . Hmm . . . what could it be . . . ?'

She came over and sat down next to him on the small settee. He realised that they hadn't sat like this since the time last summer when they had taken tea together in the courtyard of the Great House. So much had happened since then, in a year when she had already had to endure more than her fair share. He looked forward to 1945 coming to an end for both of them – there was always something to be said for a new year.

She unwrapped the package slowly – she had enjoyed watching him try to act patient while she had teased him – and realised it was the same edition of Austen's *Pride and Prejudice* as the one of *Emma* that he had read to her while sitting in the courtyard together.

'My favourite.' She smiled. 'Thank you.'

He smiled back. 'It wasn't hard to guess. You must have other editions – but this one you can carry around if you like. Look, Adeline, you need to start getting out again. You need to start walking, long walks, need to get the fresh, brisk air into your lungs and your head, need to just get out. I am always much better for getting out on my rounds. Always much better for talking to, and helping, others. It's no magic prescription, but it's a start. Reading is wonderful, but it does keep us in our heads. It's why I can't read certain authors when I am in low spirits.'

'But one can always read Austen.'

'And that's exactly what Austen gives us. A world so a part of our own, yet so separate, that entering it is like some kind of tonic. Even with so many flawed and even silly characters, it all makes sense in the end. It may be the most sense we'll ever get to make out of our own messed-up world. That's why she lasts, like Shakespeare. It's all in there, all of life, all the stuff that counts, and keeps counting, all the way to here, to you.'

He watched as Adeline kept her head bowed slightly as he talked, not looking at him, just gazing down at the small book in her hands.

'It's amazing, though, how she tricks you with the surface of things,' Adeline finally answered, looking up at him. 'When you think about Anne Elliot, for example, and this totally disastrous decision she makes at, what – eighteen, nineteen? – not to marry Wentworth, it has to be partly because her mother has died only a few years earlier. I can't imagine feeling any different a year or two from now than I do today.'

Dr Gray didn't even try to persuade her otherwise this time, but just let her talk, hoping it would help her get out of herself, if only for a moment.

'Austen must have picked her to be fifteen when it happened for a reason,' Adeline continued. 'In the book, the ages of everyone when the mother dies are set out fully, right from the start, when we know Austen was no stickler for details like that – but that is her way of cluing us in, that Anne is still in full mourning when she first meets Wentworth, and very vulnerable both to him but also to the ties and pressures of family, still so impressionable. So grief is in there, deep-seated in those books, even when it doesn't look like it.'

'We all live with grief eventually, every last one of us. Austen knew that. I also think she knew she was dying when she wrote parts of this book, knew that nothing could help her, and so tried not to worry her family when there was nothing to be done.'

'She's a better woman than me. I've got the whole village on edge.'

It was the first joke he had heard Adeline make in months, and again he felt the essence of life break through. Just a crack – but it was there.

'Listen, Adeline, when you are ready, I have a little project for you. Something else that I think might help. Ironically, it has to do with Jane Austen. Adam Berwick suggested it, of all people. Can we entice you out to hear more?'

'Not out, no, but we could meet here.'

The Adeline of old would not have let him pique her interest like this without demanding to know more. But it was a start, nonetheless.

'That's fine. We understand.' He paused. 'Everyone is very worried about you, you are right about that. But I know you. I know what you are made of.'

It was the most honest and personal thing she had ever heard him say, and she was sure her mouth was still open as he turned and left the room.

From the front window seat, she watched him leave down the garden path. She let the kitten curl up in her lap, then waited until Dr Gray was no longer in sight, before turning to his little present and opening it to page one.

'Right, well now, what is it you two wanted to talk to me about?'

Adam gave a little cough and looked as if he were going to bolt.

'Adam . . .' Adeline started, feeling more familiar with him ever since he had come by with the kitten.

The farmer shuffled a bit in his seat by the fireplace in the Grover front parlour. 'We've been thinking, Dr Gray and I, about trying to make a place in honour of Jane Austen. In Chawton. Maybe the old steward's cottage.'

Adeline looked over at Dr Gray, who was sitting on the small settee in front of the bay window. 'The two of you cooked this up? Two men?'

'Yes, I'm afraid.' Dr Gray grinned at her almost sheepishly. 'It would be a big project – we'd need to incorporate as a charity or a trust of some kind, then find the money to acquire the property and any artefacts we can get our hands on, including a lot of what's kicking about the old Knight estate, I suspect.'

'Have you talked to Miss Frances yet about any of this?'

The two men shook their heads.

'The Knights still own the cottage as far as I know,' Adeline said with her typical directness. 'So you're going to have to start there – and with old Mr Knight so ill, it may not be the best time to raise any of this.'

'Well, what do you think?' Dr Gray asked gently. 'Would you be interested in helping?'

She narrowed her eyes at him. 'Am I a project then, too?'

'No, not at all – I mean, I – we – wouldn't ask if we didn't think you'd normally want to help.'

'If I was still normal, you mean.'

Dr Gray sighed and could feel both their eyes now upon him, making him unusually flustered. 'No, again, not at all

– we just wouldn't want you to feel obligated to help if you weren't up to it, right, Adam? We just wanted to invite you to join. Just in case.'

Adeline stopped rocking in her chair next to Adam on the sofa by the fire. 'Okay, fine, count me in – I surely have nothing better to do. So, it's the three of us to start, and hopefully, of course, Miss Knight, if she's up to it herself. We'll need to get a solicitor on board, too – Samuel was training with one over in Alton when he got called up . . .'

'Andrew Forrester.'

She looked over at Dr Gray, surprised as always by his razor-sharp memory. 'You know him, then?'

'We went to school together.'

'You're the same age?' she said in surprise again. 'Really? He just seems so . . . old. Or at least old-fashioned. And quite a stickler for detail, as I understand. He might not want to get involved with something as amateur as this.'

'Why don't I ask him about first steps at least?' Dr Gray said to them both.

Adam concurred, then he and Dr Gray both waited for Adeline, with her natural air of authority, to resume talking. She looked at their expectant faces and asked, 'And what will we call ourselves then? The Society for . . .'

'. . . the Preservation of . . . ?' Dr Gray suggested.

'How about simply the Jane Austen Society?' Adam spoke up without missing a beat, and the other two both turned to him in surprise.

'Perfect,' agreed Adeline, a wide smile breaking across her face for the first time in weeks. 'Absolutely perfect.'

Chapter Twelve

A few mornings later, Dr Gray ran into Andrew Forrester as he was leaving Mr Knight's sickbed. Eager to speak with Andrew on behalf of the newly formed society, Dr Gray asked if they could take a walk outdoors to talk in private.

They exited from the southside door of the Great House and walked along the lower bricked terrace surrounded by towering conical yew hedges. They then proceeded along a gravel path adjoined on one side by deep forest until they reached the upper terrace, a low-walled site topped with lattice brickwork, fanciful balusters and a view of the entire estate below.

'All right, we seem to be far enough out of earshot now,' announced a bemused Andrew. He looked down at the beautiful Elizabethan house and the sloping expanse of snow-covered lawn before them, recalling the hours of tobogganing they had done there as boys. 'You said you had a proposal to make me.'

As Dr Gray now described the 'little project', as he liked to call it, Andrew at first was not sure that he needed to hear more. After all, he had read a few of the Austen books over the years and enjoyed them well enough, but the idea of devoting hours each month to preserving her physical history in the small farming village of Chawton seemed – as fastidious as he was – a bit exacting for his moderate level of interest.

But as his old friend spoke, Andrew realised that the very thing the society wanted to do might soon be out of reach. He was the only one of them who knew just what was at stake, for Frances most of all. If Mr Knight had his way, the entire estate could end up one day in the hands of some unknown distant male relative, and then who knew what would happen to any of it. Worse still, the new will included a particularly punitive clause, one that provided Frances with nothing more than a small annual allowance and a right to reside in the steward's cottage only for so long as the property belonged to the Knights. The minute any male heir sold off the cottage, Frances would essentially be homeless, in what appeared to be a back-door attempt to keep the cottage from being turned into some kind of Austen amusement park. It was as if Mr Knight had already been clued into the society's plans.

But if the society could somehow get their hands on the cottage, Andrew told himself, either now from Mr Knight or in the future, then they were the one group that could ensure Frances always had a place to live – the cottage was already subdivided enough to preserve sufficient rooms for her upstairs.

'I'm afraid we are only three members, at present,' Dr Gray continued. 'Myself, Adeline Grover and Adam Berwick. We will need more than that to form a decent quorum for voting. Over time, of course, we hope to invite Miss Frances herself.'

'Miss Frances, too?' Andrew asked with surprise. 'Really?'

Benjamin Gray watched the other man carefully as they approached the back walled garden, his favourite spot on the entire estate. Andrew seemed to have a deep and unresolved interest in Frances Knight, which confused Dr Gray. His two childhood friends practically managed the Knight estate together, both still single and unmarried, and he knew Andrew had been besotted with Frances when they were young. Dr Gray could not imagine the man still caring for the woman and not ever having done anything about it, for all his fastidiousness.

'All the same, I'm afraid I would be conflicted out of most decisions, as solicitor for the estate,' Andrew was saying, the intricacy of his situation continuing to dawn on him. He could never tell any of them what he knew about the contents of the will. He wondered, though, if, by being involved at all, even just as a fly on the wall, he could at least observe their decisions as a group and subtly steer them in a way that helped protect Frances's interests, while not violating the duty he owed Mr Knight as his solicitor. In his lengthy career, Andrew had never before allowed himself to even contemplate such a morally grey area, and it was making him feel more than a little queasy.

'Perhaps, when it comes to voting,' Dr Gray responded. 'But your general legal knowledge – not to mention your peerless knowledge of Chawton itself and its history – would be invaluable to the other members.'

Andrew took a seat on a carved-oak bench just outside the entrance to the walled garden, and Benjamin joined him.

'Have you contemplated yet a legal structure to carry out the charitable goals of this society? To protect yourself from liability, raise money and minimise taxes and the like?'

Dr Gray was gratified to see the wheels already turning in Andrew's lawyer brain. 'We were thinking of a separate charitable trust to administer the actual property and any assets we acquire.'

'Very good, very good. Whose idea was all this to begin with, anyway?'

'Adam Berwick, believe it or not. Seems he has been reading and rereading Jane Austen every winter for many years now.'

'I would never have guessed that in a thousand years.' The lawyer shook his head in amused disbelief.

'They say that certain books can really help patients with trauma, and for some reason Jane Austen is one of the ones they recommend. I know she has helped me.'

'Is this medicine then for poor Adeline Grover as well?'

'Yes, I suppose.'

Andrew stared pensively at the Great House and the grounds stretching out before him. 'I still feel uncomfortable about my position as the Knight solicitor of record. My duty is to protect the interests of my clients, financial and legal and otherwise. Inevitably things will come up – conversations will happen – in which I will need to abstain or absent myself altogether.'

'Andy, of course – I took a professional oath, too, you know. Look, it's a charity – we're certainly none of us going to be making any money for all our efforts. I would like to think we can manage any conflicts that arise without too much fuss.'

'All right,' Andrew finally agreed with a sigh. 'I will help out, too. But I think we should meet soon, before the holidays occupy us.'

'Andrew, honestly, are we any of us four so busy right now?'

The two men sat on the bench and looked about at the scene of so many earlier festivities from their shared youth. Maybe, just maybe, they were both silently thinking, the society could help them recapture even a small degree of that.

Chapter Thirteen

Chawton, Hampshire
December 22, 1945
The First Meeting of the Jane Austen Society

In which the Jane Austen Memorial Trust is established, with the charitable objects of the advancement of education and, in particular, the study of English Literature, especially the works of Jane Austen.

The first order of business was to establish a trust as a legal means to carry out any dealings supported by the society, and to nominate three trustees, including the chairman, treasurer and secretary.

Adeline Grover agreed to act as secretary for the meeting being held in her front parlour again, given her speed at note-taking, and by the end of the meeting was permanently acclaimed in that role. Dr Gray agreed to be the first chairman of the trust for a term of two years, given his prior experience on the local school board. Andrew agreed to be the first treasurer, given his solicitor's training and knowledge of trust accounts and separate banking practises. This was all to the palpable relief of Adam Berwick, whose financial situation was understood to require his full commitment to his regular employment.

The trust deed, as drawn up in advance by Andrew Forrester, provided for funds raised through both subscription and donation, and thirty pounds was quickly pledged by the three trustees to create an account from which any incidental expenses could be withdrawn going forward.

Each of the three trustees also pledged to uphold various duties, primary of which was the duty to carry out the charitable purposes of the trust and to avoid any conflicts or perceptions thereof. With Andrew Forrester's role as executor of the Knight estate, the situation felt ripe for conflict, and he agreed to abstain from any voting on the use of funds to purchase the property.

'It's all still a little dodgy – don't write that down, Adeline – but it is a charity after all, and we're none of us doing this for profit, so I am comfortable with the provision for abstention as it stands. We'll just have to stay very mindful of these issues going forward.'

'What are the rules for voting, with such a small group?' Dr Gray asked.

'Historically, one abides by the rules of parliamentary procedure, which require a majority of the full board, including any who abstain. So, right now, if I abstain from a vote, you and Adeline must both agree for anything to move forward.'

'Ha!' Adeline laughed outright, causing all three men to turn to her.

'Right, well,' Andrew quickly replied, 'that in and of itself is reason to invite at least two more members to join us. Five trustees in total should do it.'

'And money?' Adam asked. 'To buy the cottage?'

'According to local sales of late,' Andrew replied, 'we're

looking at several thousand pounds to buy the cottage no matter what. I move that we try to raise sufficient funds through public subscription as soon as possible. Then we can go to Miss Frances with a pure business proposition and hope that she can prevail upon her father to agree in time.'

Dr Gray caught these last two words and gave Andrew a curious look.

'You think we should hurry then? Before he passes?'

Andrew shuffled the papers before him on his lap. 'It is my understanding from Adam here that there is outside interest in the Knight estate. Similar to the recent sale of the contents of the Godmersham estate, that also once belonged to Austen's brother. I brought the catalogue with me – it's of public record, so I don't feel it improper to share it with you.'

The other three members of the society passed the catalogue around.

'A reserve price of five thousand pounds for a writing desk?' Dr Gray exclaimed.

'Apparently it went for almost three times that amount. Adam, tell them what else you know.'

'Apparently someone from Sotheby's keeps calling Miss Frances.'

Adeline looked at him in surprise. 'How do you know that?'

'Evie. She told me as much.'

'Evie Stone?' asked Dr Gray. 'Whatever is the child up to?'

'Whatever it is,' replied Adeline, 'I bet it's more than sweeping out the hearths. She was far too young to have to leave school when she did. She's whip-smart – smarter than any of us.'

'I am sure that's an exaggeration.' Dr Gray smiled.

'Speak for yourself,' Adeline replied in all seriousness.

'All right, back to my motion,' Andrew interjected. 'I move that early in the New Year we post a small advertisement in *The Times* and the local Hampshire papers, notifying the public of the incorporation of a trust to accept monies supporting the initiatives of the society.'

'Should we mention trying to acquire the cottage?' asked Adam.

'I think it best,' Dr Gray answered. 'We need to give the public a tangible goal of some kind. Something more impressive than acquiring writing desks and topaz crosses.'

'Again, speak for yourself,' Adeline said pointedly to him. 'I wouldn't mind getting my hands on Austen's jewellery.'

Dr Gray felt strangely gratified – the old Adeline, so sharp-tongued and direct, was slowly, but surely, starting to come back.

Chapter Fourteen

Chawton, Hampshire
Christmas Week, 1945

'Do you think we'll get the old girl to church this Christmas Eve?' asked Tom. He and Evie Stone were picking ivy and holly in the woods to drape about the main entrance hall and drawing room of the Great House, in preparation for the upcoming annual village reception, following Christmas Eve service at St Nicholas.

'It's always a toss-up,' replied Evie. She was only sixteen to Tom's twenty, and as she foraged in the snow for the trimmings, her cheeks had that pure ruddy blush that one only ever saw on the very young and unblemished. 'Did you read that book yet, that I found you from the library?'

Despite her continued and extensive reading, Evie's favourite book remained *Pride and Prejudice*. Almost as a type of test, she had pressed it on her limited social circle at the Great House – Josephine the cook, Charlotte the other house girl and Tom the stable hand and gardener – with as much enthusiasm as she ever did anything. If they failed to enjoy or – even worse – finish the book, she wrote them off just as dismissively.

'Um, no, not quite.' Tom coughed. He had meant to start the book, mostly because he was in a race against time and two other young men in the village, when it came to romancing Evie Stone. But even that potential reward could not overcome a notable fidgetiness and lack of discipline on his part.

'Well, you should, Tom, you really should. It's so good. It's so funny.' Evie stood up straight with her hands full of greenery and smiled at him. 'I can't carry any more, can you?'

He looked through the lime grove and out onto the west-facing fields, separated from the woods and the house by a little ha-ha – the deceptive fencing sunk down into a ditch so as not to impinge on the sightline of the view while keeping the sheep out of the gardens.

'Sun's setting fast enough, must be close to tea. Say, listen, can I hold on to that book a little longer?'

'Miss Knight says she's thrilled if we're any of us reading, so I'm sure she won't miss it yet.'

Evie headed down the lime grove back towards the house, letting Tom straggle along behind her. She suspected that he had not even bothered to pick up the book and wondered whether this reflected either a limit to his interest in her or just an antipathy to sitting still. Either way, she was not overly impressed – nor did she think Jane Austen would have been.

Evie entered the Great House and placed her pile of greenery on a side table to the inside left of the huge wooden front door. Tom did the same, then headed off down the centre hallway to the kitchen to grab tea from Josephine. Evie took the longer, more circuitous way, through the drawing room that the family called the Great Hall, which opened up onto the main-floor library, and then along a small gallery until reaching Evie's other favourite room, the dining room.

In the centre of that room sat the immensely long mahogany

table at which Jane and Cassandra and their brother, his eleven children, and an evolving assortment of other guests, would all have dined. Part of a three-storey extension that protruded from the western face of the house, the dining room contained two huge window seats with thick brocaded curtain covers, which one could pull closed along a high brass rod for total privacy. Sitting in the southern window, you could also watch, unobserved, the approach up the long drive of any of the infrequent visitors to the house.

There, as Evie had suspected, sat Miss Knight.

'Excuse me, miss,' she started, and Miss Knight turned to look at her.

Evie was concerned about her employer. Miss Knight had a pervasive greyness about her, a lack of life in her face and posture, that made it seem as if she had one foot in this world and one foot somewhere else. She was a woman essentially alone and increasingly without friends, as she began to spend all her time indoors. Although still young, Evie already understood that true friendship was not earned without hard work and vigilance. Having left school and the easy camaraderie of classmates, Evie could see how working inside a big, empty house with minimal staff was keeping her from more typical social pursuits. Going to the cinema in Alton with girlfriends was her only outside form of recreation – reading and cataloguing the books late into the night took up the rest of her leisure time.

'Tom and I were wondering, miss, if you'll be attending the service this Christmas Eve. Many of the villagers have been asking on my rounds.'

Frances shook her head. She was already not up to seeing too many people, and now half the village was about to descend on her very home.

'No, but you and Charlotte and Tom should all go. Josephine is going to stay back to get things ready and keep me

company. And, of course, I should spend some time visiting
with my father.'

Evie walked farther into the room. Above the fireplace was
a beautiful, almost life-size portrait of Edward Austen Knight,
Jane's brother, shortly after his grand tour of Europe as a
young man. He had inherited several well-known estates from
the Knights, and two of Jane's other brothers had been successful naval commanders, sailing to places as far away as the
Caribbean and the China seas. Evie thought about the Austen
women being circumscribed by the four corners of England
instead, venturing perhaps as far north as the Peak District and
as far south as Southampton, but in the main staying in villages
such as Chawton. Evie wondered if she, too, would be stuck
here forever. Wondered what on earth would ever be her ticket
out.

'Miss Knight, I hope you know how much everyone looks
forward to this to-do. It's awful kind of you and your father to
welcome everyone into your home like this.'

'Thank you, Evie. It's a family tradition after all – and family tradition is important. Will your own parents be able to
come?'

'Dad is still having trouble walking with the canes, but
Adam Berwick is going to pick him up at the house and pull
his wagon right up to the church to let him off.'

'Oh, Evie, how wonderful for you. Two years is a very long
time to be confined to bed.'

As soon as the words left her mouth, Frances realised that
she had, in her own way, been voluntarily doing much the
same thing. In that moment, something dawned on her, the
sense of spiting the little good fortune she'd been left with, and
she was religious – and superstitious – enough to pay attention.

'Evie' – Frances stood up from the window seat – 'I think I
will go to the service this year after all. I should like to add my

prayers to your father's. He is a very strong man. But I'm sure you know that.'

At rare moments such as this, when Miss Knight seemed up for conversation, Evie was dying to say something to her about the late-night cataloguing. She truly cared about Miss Knight and wanted her to be less depressed and fretful, and part of Evie's hope with the secret project was to uncover enough indisputable treasures to help keep the Knight family legacy alive and thriving. But her instincts told her that the longer she could go unimpeded by anybody else's concerns or priorities, the greater the chance she might trip over something of import. The idea that she could ask her own questions and decide where to look for answers was intoxicating to her.

Evie was a born academic; she just didn't know it yet.

So instead the girl nodded and headed off to the kitchen for her tea, and Frances looked up at the oversized oil painting of her ancestor above the mantel. She accepted, for the first time, that she was doing, in her own small way, the best that she could. She wasn't sure that Jane and Cassandra Austen would have expected anything more than that.

Chapter Fifteen

The villagers streamed into the parish church, full of the excitement of the season. Parents let their smallest children run about the gravestones in the twilight, and the men and women were all wearing their finest outdoor hats and coats against the frosty air.

The Stones descended from the Berwicks' wagon, the four children having walked alongside during the trip from the farming fields at the perimeter of town. Adam helped his mother and Mrs Stone get down from the wagon, then attended to Mr Stone, who was unable to bend his legs due to his injuries but could finally shuffle a bit with a cane in each hand.

Dr Gray was already inside the church, looking about, wondering if this year Miss Knight would make an appearance. His nurse, Harriet, was in the same row as him, along with her older unmarried sister, but he was avoiding too much social interaction. He was still smarting from the completely inappropriate and insinuating phone call that Harriet had made to the Grover cottage in advance of his recent visit.

The Berwick and Stone families entered slowly together to take their seats in the back rows, and then there was quite a bit of commotion as Miss Knight herself entered, accompanied by Evie Stone and the stable boy Tom. As her physician and long-time friend, Dr Gray knew how much effort this must be for Frances, and he gave her an encouraging smile as she walked down the aisle to take her traditional place in the front row to the right of the altar.

Everyone settled down again and Reverend Powell approached from the back of the chancery to commence the service. As he asked everyone to rise for the opening hymn, the door to the church opened to let in Adeline Grover and her mother, along with one final blast of winter wind. They snuck in as quietly as possible, then walked down the centre aisle until they, too, had reached their regular seats.

Dr Gray did not look over at the two women as they entered the row directly across the aisle from his. He could feel Harriet's and her sister's eyes upon him, but right now his mind was focused on composing the letter of termination that he would be delivering to Miss Peckham in the New Year, no matter how hard it was to find a nurse willing to come out to Chawton every day. Being the subject of gossip and speculation by one's own staff was ludicrous enough – being such when there was absolutely nothing amiss going on was altogether unacceptable.

The service on Christmas Eve was always short, Reverend Powell being as fond of celebrating the season as anyone else. After singing the last carol of the night, 'O Come, All Ye Faithful', the villagers waited for Miss Knight to depart from the front-row pew and exit the church, then all followed in their turn.

The tombstones outside were dusted with snow, and as he passed them, Dr Gray thought about the newest grave, laid in the farthest corner of the churchyard, just below the stone wall that looked down over the fields from a slight incline. He wondered if this was the first time the grieving young mother had been to visit. Following his wife's death, it had taken him several months before he had been able to do the same. Instead he had continued to wake up each morning and reach over for her in bed, and to call upstairs when the kettle had boiled, and even thought – in his most desperate moments – that he had just caught the quickest glimpse of her housedress out of the corner of his eye, as if she had simply left the room and would be back any second.

Dr Gray let the other villagers pass him, until he was the last one left in the graveyard. He waited for the sound of the lychgate latching shut, then walked over to where the newest small tombstone lay, illuminated in the silvery moonlight. Just a few yards away was a larger gravestone, set flat into the cold, hard winter ground.

> *Jennie Clarissa Thomson Gray,*
> *Born 23 May, 1900—Died 15 August, 1939.*
> *Beloved wife of Dr Benjamin Michael Gray.*
> *May she rest in peace.*

Dr Gray looked down at the carved slab of stone and prayed. He did not pray often – he was not convinced it did anything much but pacify a completely reasonable anger at the world – but tonight he wanted God to hear him. Because he needed help. He needed to figure out how to live with the pain, without hurting himself or anyone else. He was in violation of his oath, and that struck him as one of the greater sins, because he was in a state of knowledge, and with knowledge should come grace. He thought of Mr Stone literally having to drag himself through life, and Frances Knight afraid to leave

her house, and Adam Berwick and his sad inner state, and realised that they were all wounded in some way. Bookended by
the two worst wars the world had ever seen, they were ironically the survivors, yet it was beyond him what they were all
surviving for.

He thought of Adam and his interest in somehow preserving Jane Austen's legacy in the village. The list of books that
Adeline Grover had given Mr Stone and Evie each – a cup of
tea and a sugar bun in a courtyard – the party now starting in
the Great House without him. These were small things in a
way, much smaller than a war, yet they seemed to him more
important to survival than he had previously understood.

He bent down, pressed his right fingers to his lips, and ran
his hand across the lettering on his wife's grave. It had been
nearly seven years, and for the longest time he thought he had
been giving something to her by indulging his grief. But Jennie
had been the most alive person he had ever known, with the
quickest mind and a completely open, unguarded heart. She
had not lived one day – not even one minute – as he was now.
She would have seen absolutely no worth in it. If he was completely honest with himself, he was letting them both down.

He straightened himself and headed through the tiny back
gate, the one that hung askew from its hinges, and remembered the broken hinge on the garden gate at the Grovers' and
how that needed fixing, too.

The sideboard in the Great Hall was full of tiered silver platters
piled high with sugar plums and rum balls and warm mince
pies. Josephine had brought up bottles of claret and champagne from the ancient brick wine cellar, and in the large stone
fireplace a dangling black iron pot bubbled with mulled wine
steeped with cinnamon sticks, cloves and nutmeg. Old family

crystal goblets and champagne saucers were lined up in rows along a second sideboard, covered in thick white linens, under which sat the two smallest Stone boys playing a game of Jacks on the deal-and-oak floor.

Adam stood shyly along the far wall of the room, near the door to the adjoining library, as if about to make a break for it at any minute. He felt relief when Dr Gray finally entered the room, long after the service had ended.

Dr Gray accepted a glass of champagne from Charlotte the house girl and went over to join Adam, his back firmly against the wall, with its high dark wainscotting reaching nearly to the ceiling.

'Well, Adam, that's certainly a lot of noise and crowd. A tall price to pay, even for Josephine's delicious mince tarts. How are you faring?' asked Dr Gray.

'Fine enough,' Adam replied in as amiable a voice as he could muster.

The two men watched the many villagers in the room happily milling about, making quick and passing conversation with each other, but mainly, and generously, helping themselves to the rare sight of oranges piled high on a platter and the alcoholic treasures from the Knight family's cellar. Frances Knight sat on a chintz sofa in the middle of all the festive activity, her usually sallow cheeks flushed from the heat of the nearby fireplace.

'I guess now's not the time to ask Miss Knight about the steward's cottage and our plans,' said Adam.

'I'm afraid not. I think this evening takes all her energy as it is.'

Adam cocked his head around the open doorway to his right. 'Have you seen all the books in there?'

Dr Gray shook his head. 'Not recently, no. I think there are several libraries in the house – I hear this one is particularly extensive.' He saw the piqued interest on the farmer's face. 'Care to have a quick look, then, Adam? I don't think Miss Knight would mind – she is nothing if not gracious with her home.'

Adam nodded eagerly, and the two men stepped slowly away from the Great Hall and into the library next door.

There, in the farthest corner of the room, they found young Evie Stone. She was perched on a wooden stool by a fireplace, much smaller than the medieval one next door and surrounded by Victorian tile. She looked so childlike sitting there, with her pixie features, cropped hair and small hands gripping at something in her lap.

'Oh,' she said with surprise, slipping a notebook of some kind back onto the nearest shelf as she stood up.

'Please, Evie, don't let us disturb you.' Dr Gray smiled. 'But why aren't you with the crowd next door?'

Evie pressed down the folds in her plain navy knit dress from having been perched on the stool for so long. 'Well, for one thing, my brothers are either betting, or imbibing, or stealing goodness knows what, so I prefer being in here, away from all that.'

'And for the other?' Dr Gray asked with a laugh. Evie's antipathy towards her four younger brothers, ranging in age from five to thirteen, was well-known among the villagers.

'Well, it's just glorious in here, isn't it? I mean, I think I've counted two thousand books in this room alone.' She took one down from a nearby shelf to show them. 'Do you see this? This special binding? It's the Knight family binding – they had their books specially bound from the printers, see, with their family coat of arms imprinted on the leather cover. As if they'd made the book themselves.'

Dr Gray took the book from Evie and opened the cover. It was a first edition of Lord Byron's *Childe Harold's Pilgrimage*, published in London in 1812.

'Evie, have you gone through many of these books?'

She nodded.

'Does Miss Knight know?'

'Oh, definitely – she's always encouraging everyone in the house to use the library.'

'Does she spend much time in here herself?' Dr Gray asked, as both he and Adam silently started to run their hands along the tops of the books on various different shelves.

'I don't think so. At least, I never really catch her in here much. She does read, she has her favourites – but I think she prefers to reread a lot.'

Adam laughed, a sound that surprised the other two for its rarity. 'Oh, sorry, it's just, I'm as guilty of that as anyone.'

Evie looked at the farmer. 'You are? What do you reread?'

Adam turned back to the long shelf. 'Just, you know.'

Dr Gray smiled at Evie, then turned to Adam's back. 'Adam, it's certainly nothing to be ashamed of.'

Evie's eyes widened.

'Austen,' Adam finally declared.

Evie stared at the farmer. 'But Jane Austen is my favourite. I reread her all the time.' She came over to Adam and pulled two matching books out from in front of him.

'Look, Mr Berwick, isn't it amazing? Another first edition.' She placed the two volumes in his hands.

He turned them onto their sides. 'Two volumes of *Emma*. How strange.'

Dr Gray found a comfortable chair in the corner opposite from them and sat down, sensing they were all three going to be in here for quite some time. 'Strange in what way?' he asked Adam.

'Well, *Emma* was three volumes.'

Evie continued to stare at him in disbelief. 'How do *you* know that?'

Adam opened the book. 'All her books were, at least I think so. Oh,' he said suddenly, and held the book out to Evie. 'Look. Says here it was published in Philadelphia. In 1816.'

Evie nodded. 'I know. How did a book, printed in America, get all the way here, do you think?'

Dr Gray crossed his legs, watching the two of them with great amusement. It was the most animated he had ever seen Adam – and the most speechless he had seen Evie Stone yet.

'Perhaps,' Dr Gray interrupted, 'a relative or someone sent a copy here, or to Austen herself. Evie, you said there were two thousand books in this room alone. Have you gone through the other studies?'

'Just the one right on top of us, on the second floor. I have dusting duty on the two bottom floors, Charlotte's the top.'

'How much dusting can you possibly be getting done?' asked Adam in all seriousness.

Evie laughed. She had never spent much time around Adam Berwick, who had always struck her as so quiet and lonely. It would never have occurred to her that they would have something in common like Jane Austen.

'Evie,' Dr Gray spoke up again. He looked over at Adam, eyes raised, and gave him an inquiring nod.

Adam nodded back in silent agreement.

'Evie, Adam and I have been working on something for a little while now. It was Adam's idea, a little project.'

'Oh, I *love* projects,' she said brightly.

Dr Gray and Adam both smiled at her youthful energy. 'We are hoping to make some kind of memorial to Jane Austen, here, in Chawton.'

Evie sat back down on the stool. 'Like a statue, or another plaque of some kind?'

'No, more than that.' Dr Gray looked over at Adam. 'You explain. After all, it was your idea.'

Adam put the two volumes of *Emma* back on the shelf and took a few tentative steps towards Evie. 'What if we could buy the cottage, the little steward's cottage, and restore it? Make it look like Jane Austen's time there, with some of the furniture and paintings and whatnot? Then all the tourists would really have something to see when they came.'

Evie looked from one older man to the other. 'But where would you get the money? And where would all the stuff come from?'

'Those are all good questions, my dear,' answered Dr Gray. 'We decided to form a society that would help raise funds through donations, and then we'd buy the house and source objects for it. I mean, we've all heard the stories over the years, about some of her letters and even the family's furniture showing up in various Chawton homes. Apparently old Mrs Austen gave away quite a bit to the servants and their families over time. Who knows what we might find if we set about trying.'

'Who are the members – you and Adam?'

'For now, plus Andrew Forrester, the Alton solicitor, and Miss Lewis – I mean Grover.' Dr Gray hesitated and looked over at Adam first, before adding, 'And you, if you are interested.'

'Me?' she said in astonishment, her eyes widening again.

'Well, to be honest, at some point soon we will need to broach all this with Miss Knight. It might help having you on our side. I mean, you clearly know this library inside and out.'

'That's because I'm compulsive,' she said in all seriousness, and Dr Gray's head shot up at her self-awareness for such a young person. 'Like my father. He and I both worked through Miss Lewis's reading lists line by line.'

'But it's more than that, isn't it?' asked Dr Gray.

She looked at him curiously. 'Dr Gray, why are *you* doing this? I mean, when I was in school, you were always taking Miss Lewis to task for teaching so much Jane Austen.'

'Yes, Dr Gray, why are you?' said a voice from the doorway, and the three of them looked over to see Adeline standing there herself, dressed head to toe in mourning black, which only emphasised her pale, tired features.

Dr Gray motioned for her to take his chair, but she shook her head and came over to the shelves nearest Adam. She slid out a thick volume that he had just been reshelving when she entered. She looked carefully at the cover, then flipped the book open, before turning back to the three of them.

'I haven't seen this before – the Knight family imprint. Are there a lot of these in here?'

Dr Gray nodded towards Evie. 'Ask Miss Stone, your former pupil. She seems to have inherited your thoroughness when it comes to books.'

'You realise this is a second edition of *Belinda*?' Adeline asked the room. 'By Maria Edgeworth, only the most important female educator in our history? This very edition is priceless – it references an interracial marriage between an African servant and an English farm girl that later got edited out. Quite astonishing.'

Adeline put the book back and went and sat down in the chair that Dr Gray had earlier offered, then looked at each of their faces one by one, before saying, 'Well, did you ask her?'

Dr Gray smiled at her astuteness. 'Yes, of course – she will be a real asset to the society.'

'Has she said yes?' Adeline smiled back, nodding at the still-astonished house girl.

Evie looked at her revered former teacher and her trusted childhood doctor, and she wondered if this was the grand opportunity that she had been hoping and preparing for all along. Being part of something that would normally have been so far out of her reach. Having something to contribute. Knowing something that others did not.

'Yes,' she answered happily.

Chapter Sixteen

London, England
Midnight, 3 January, 1946

Mimi sat by the open French doors to the suite at The Ritz, where she and Jack had been staying on holiday since New Year's Eve. She was unable to get to sleep and was instead examining yet again the small box containing the two topaz crosses. As was his nature, Jack had immediately taken her at her word last autumn when she had expressed interest in acquiring the jewellery from Sotheby's. She had had to explain to him after the auction that she did not necessarily want to wear the necklaces – she wanted, instead, to safeguard them. She thought no one else could do a better job than a privileged fan like herself. Jack Leonard felt himself stumped, yet again, by the kind of worshipful love Mimi Harrison was doling out to everyone, it seemed, but him.

Work on *Sense and Sensibility* continued apace, and for every extra line that he got the screenwriter to give Mimi's character, Elinor, Jack sneaked in a few extra ones for Willoughby, too. Jack was not the most experienced of producers, but he did have a knack for spotting the most interesting character in a script. In the alchemy that was all of Jack Leonard's unique and uniquely questionable qualities mixed together, his understanding of the pulse of the moment struck Mimi as almost uncanny. Sometimes she felt as if he had been sent back in time by about two years, so intuitively correct was that understanding.

If she could have gone back two years in time herself, she would never have believed that she would have ended up engaged to Jack Leonard and wearing Jane Austen's ring. Or moving to Hampshire. Or – dare she admit – even quite in love. Jack's willingness to practically move mountains where she was concerned was extremely seductive and persuasive. It was as if she could see the wheels turning in his mind, could see the ulterior motives, yet the journey getting there was just too damn fun, and the destination too remarkable. She would have hated herself for falling for him, except that she was a big girl and certainly not risking hurting anyone but – in all likelihood – herself.

It was also extremely difficult not to confuse Jack's more extravagant and stubborn actions with a flair for generosity, if not a pure and selfless heart. She knew that his heart was both uncomplicated (the physical rewards of lust being paramount at all times) and highly compartmentalised into little separate chambers. Right now she might have the master suite and the upper hand, and all the privileges that entailed – but she also knew, from the string of conquests in Jack's past, that she could end up just as easily relegated to the little garret at the very top, like Fanny Price at Mansfield Park.

All of this was why, after that first night they had slept together following the auction at Sotheby's, she had tried her best to keep him from taking over too much of her. Jack, she intuited, didn't just want a woman to give herself completely to him for free: he wanted squatter's rights, a leeway, and a right of first refusal. For a man who approached everything at full velocity, proof of love and fit and courtship required, in Jack's eyes, complete abandon and surrender.

She had to admit, as she looked back at his sleeping figure in the king-size bed behind her, physically at least, Jack gave as good as he got. Perhaps the chemical attraction from the start had been the key after all – perhaps that was what everyone out there was getting wrong. She remembered her mother telling her once that you need to be extremely attracted to the person you married because one day that would be all that was keeping you together, as well as the only viable way of making up.

At the time, Mimi, on her way to study history and drama at Smith, had thought her mother full of it. But life with Jack Leonard the past six months had shown her that there was a reason so much of popular culture came down to sex, and the having, or not having, of it, with the people to whom we were most in thrall. In her darker moments, recalling how a professor had once referred to an acting career for women as glorified prostitution, Mimi feared that so much of her on-screen success came from eliciting those same feelings in complete strangers. This had probably been one of the big drivers behind her quest, as she acquired more and more leverage in Hollywood, to take on increasingly complex and less glamorous roles.

She now knew that this was what Jane Austen was onto as well, with all her attending to the bad boys in her fiction. For if Fanny Price could almost capitulate and let Henry Crawford 'make a small hole' in her heart, then there was no hope for the rest of us. Mr Darcy was the perfect example of a man used to being eminently in control, and then within seconds of meeting Elizabeth Bennet, finding himself so at the mercy of his passion for her that he starts doing the very things he condemns and prohibits in everyone else. Terrified by his human vulnerability, Darcy proceeds to do everything to push Lizzie away except accuse her of some unspecified crime and have her carted off. Austen seemed to know the power of physical attraction (see Mary Crawford and the upstanding Edmund Bertram, or Wickham and Lydia, or even the Bennets twenty years before the plot). Mimi sighed at the idea that the big secret behind Jane Austen's fiction could be something as prosaic, and animalistic, as that.

Jack started to stir in bed, and Mimi watched as, half-asleep, his hand patted the empty space next to him where she had earlier been. Eventually his arm started to flail about until he finally opened his eyes and saw her sitting by the balcony.

'Trying to make your escape?' He smiled, rubbing his eyes and jaw as he sat up in bed.

She smiled back, then came over, and he started to tug at the belt of her pink silk robe. 'Not so fast there, mister. You have a call soon – it's four P.M. L.A. time, remember?'

He yawned and sat up, and she affectionately patted down the shock of sandy-brown hair that was several shades lighter than his beard stubble. He had such a healthy Californian colour to him, for an East Coast businessman; next to the City solicitors he had been meeting with in London all week, he practically glowed.

'Fine, but after that we're going back to bed – early start in the morning.'

'Where are you taking me now?' She went and picked up the phone with its base from the desk nearby and carried it over into bed with her, then lay down next to his warm, lean body.

'It's a surprise.'

'Is it far? Will I be blindfolded?'

'Do you want to be?' he teased.

'I don't ever want what you think I want, which is usually what *you* want,' she teased back. 'So, it will never work.'

'That's what they always say, until it does.'

Starting to pull at her robe again, he was kissing her neck when the phone rang.

'Don't go anywhere, just lie here, with me.' He picked up the receiver and held his hand over the mouthpiece. 'I'll sell at a loss, and then we can pick up where we left off.'

'Oh, Jack, don't go getting all noble on *my* account.' She curled up against him and closed her eyes, wondering where he would be taking her next.

Because she had only been here once before, and by train from the opposite direction, she did not at first recognise the surrounding vistas. They approached the village by driving south from outer London and then directly west from Kent, stopping along the way at Hever Castle, where Anne Boleyn had spent a dreamy girlhood full of Tudor splendour and scheming. Mimi thought the Astor addition and gardens beautiful, but the story of the young woman who had seduced King Henry VIII had always left her cold. She had even turned down the role a few years ago, when she was still young enough to play the ingénue. Now in her mid-thirties and free of her contract with the biggest movie studio in the world, she could see only a limited number of good years left in terms of roles. This was one reason why the idea of a summer escape in Hampshire had been so appealing. Perhaps she would even go back on the stage, an idea that Jack found ludicrous.

'I wouldn't be doing it for the money,' she explained, as their rented 1939 Aston Martin hugged the hedgerows whipping past.

'There's no such thing,' he scoffed from behind the wheel. 'There's no such thing as not doing it for the money. It just means it's not worth much to anyone.'

'It'd be worth something to me. You and I both know the roles have been drying up of late. I'm worried Monte is out there blackballing me, what with the few lousy scripts I've been getting.'

'He wouldn't dare – he knows we have too much on him.'

Mimi shook her head. 'I don't think that worries him one little bit.'

Jack reached over with his left hand and patted her thigh. 'Well, *Sense and Sensibility* will change all that, don't you worry.'

'Yeah, but we're still only in pre-production – anything could happen. God help me if any grey hairs start showing up between now and then. At least on the stage I can age gracefully. And besides, I don't know how healthy it is to leave *all* the dreams of one's youth behind.'

He looked over at her quickly. 'What else have you left behind? Certainly not your scruples – I can't get you to do anything you don't want to do.'

'That's not necessarily due to scruples, Jack,' she teased. 'Unless your goal is to corrupt me. Is it?'

'Not at all. In fact' – he yanked the leather-covered steering wheel to the left as they passed an intersection of three long white arrow-shaped signs – 'in fact I think you've corrupted *me*. Look how far I've strayed from my regular course because of you. Producing Regency films, buying overpriced necklaces at auction that you are never going to wear, moving to the rolling hills of merry old England.'

She laughed out loud. 'You do have a point. But knowing you, you must be getting *something* out of it.'

He looked over at her again. For the first time in his life, Jack Leonard was with a beautiful woman and it was her character he most wanted to seduce. He wanted Mimi Harrison to love him despite every voice of reason in her head, just like a character out of her beloved Jane Austen. Mimi mentioned often a Henry Crawford from Austen's books, but of all the volumes on her bookshelves, *Mansfield Park* was the thickest, and even Mimi couldn't sell the plot. A bunch of young people half-related to each other putting on a play so that they can make out with all the people they are not supposed to was the best she could do. Even for Jack, that would not be enough to get him to read an actual book. Which was too bad, because contained within the pages of *Mansfield Park* was the playbook for making a good woman fall for a cad.

'What do I get out of it?' he repeated. 'I get the love of a good woman – a very good woman.'

She stifled a fake yawn. 'How boring. That will never be enough for you.' She suddenly put her right hand out across his chest and half exclaimed, 'Wait, what did that sign say?'

'Yardley told me about this place, said you'd been here years and years ago, said you always dreamed of coming back.' Jack parked the car at the side of the road where it intersected with another and turned off the ignition.

'Oh my God, Jack, I can't believe it.' She got out of the car, smoothing her tweed skirt beneath her winter coat, and held her hands to her cheeks. 'Look at it – chocolate-box perfect. Seriously.'

Jack got out of the car, too. If a village could be asleep, Chawton was it. There weren't even any sidewalks. Just one pub, one tearoom, one little post office that they had passed along the way.

'I think I'm getting the jitters.' He leaned in to grab the car keys out of the ignition. 'Oh, wait, what am I thinking, locking up? Not even the criminal element would bother with this place.'

'No, you're so wrong,' Mimi gushed, and she grabbed his hand and pulled him across the road, until they were standing in front of a fairly substantial, L-shaped two-storey house, with a bricked-up window, red-brick walls and a little white portico over the front door.

He watched in amusement as she looked side to side before taking a step closer to the building.

'No worries, Mimi my dear — I doubt there are any news photographers in a place like this.'

'No, it's not that — I just don't want to be intrusive. We both know how that feels. But see, this window — I read somewhere that this is the parlour where Austen wrote.'

Mimi turned to him, and the look on her face was as priceless as anything could ever be in Jack Leonard's world.

'There was a door to the dining parlour that creaked, and she wouldn't let it be fixed,' Mimi was rambling on, 'so she'd write in the morning — while her mother and Cassandra helped with the household — they let her write, you see, because they knew. Because she was such a goddamn genius, you couldn't help but know. And the creaking door would warn her when someone was entering, and she'd slip the blotter over the papers, and underneath are Captain Wentworth, and Anne, and "you pierce my soul" and "half-agony, half-hope" and, oh, God, how fantastic is this!'

'I thought Henry wanted to do the piercing of the holes' was all Jack could rejoin, and Mimi still had the presence of mind to playfully swat him as he started to step back into the road.

'It's too perfect that *that's* what you remember from five hundred pages of *Mansfield Park*.'

He did not bother correcting her that he hadn't read it yet; he didn't see the point.

'It's just such a "vivid" image,' he teased instead, as he pulled her back from the house. 'Look, this is swell and all, but I actually brought you here to meet someone.'

She stepped back to look at him. 'In Chawton? Whatever for?'

'Yardley set it up. There's that woman here – remember, the one who doesn't go outside? – who has an extremely large estate and some connection to Austen, and to this house, and I've finally managed to convince her to meet with us.'

Mimi just stood there, staring.

'The house, Mimi – this house. I bought it for you. Well, I've made an offer on it. And I haven't had one of those turned down yet.' He gave her a knowing wink.

Mimi turned away from him and felt as if she might throw up.

'I don't understand,' she finally said, leaning back against the red-brick wall that enclosed the cottage garden at a sharp point next to the junction of the two main roads.

'I just told you, I made an offer on the house. Well, to take over a hundred-year lease on it at least – apparently that's how they do things over here. Anyway, Yardley has been working on the deal for me. It's taken quite some time. It turns out the old girl's quite stubborn, reclusive or not.'

'I still don't understand,' she repeated. 'Why?'

'Because I love you, silly. Because I know how much it would mean to you – well, at least, Yardley told me, but it didn't require any imagination, trust me. Why wouldn't this be a dream come true for an Austen fan like you?'

'But I can't *live* there!' she cried as she started to bolt, and he had to pull her back from the road again as they were finally approached by signs of life, a distinguished-looking man in a dark grey coat and hat, carrying a doctor's bag.

'Shh, Mimi, please, it's a *good* thing!' Jack called out, but she had run off. All he could do now was hurriedly nod to the man who had stopped to stare after the retreating

female figure, a confused look on his face. Jack knew that look
well.

'It can't be . . .' Dr Gray was muttering to himself. He
turned to Jack, who simply shrugged nonchalantly. 'Sorry, it's
just, your wife – she looks a lot like—'

'Just doing the tourist thing,' Jack said quickly, cutting him
off.

'She seemed very upset.'

'Don't worry yourself about it, just a bit of carsickness.
These narrow, winding roads, you know. Anyway, what is it
you people say? Cheerio?'

Jack walked quickly after Mimi, who was now kneeling on
the grass in a park across from the lane and next to the village
cricket pitch.

'I really think I'm going to be sick,' she said as he approached.
He put his hand down to help pull her up, and she swatted him
again, this time seriously. 'Jack, no, stop.'

Now he was starting to get a little mad. 'For God's sake,
Mimi, this was supposed to make you happy. Can't you just be
goddamned happy, for once, for me?'

She looked up at him quickly. 'What's that supposed to
mean?'

'Well, my God, you go on and on about Darcy and Pem-
berley and how Elizabeth fell in love with him after seeing his
house—'

'That was irony you goddamned idiot!'

' – and how romantic it all is, and how hot, and here I am,
just trying to make you happy—'

'Or hot.'

'No,' he said firmly, 'just happy, believe it or not.'

'By buying me a practical shrine. What the hell am I supposed to do with a shrine? I can't live there, this can't be our

summer house, that would be insane.' She narrowed her eyes. 'Oh, God, you're not nuts, are you?'

'No, but I'm starting to think you are. Or I am for loving you.' He turned and stormed off.

She stayed kneeling there a few seconds longer, then pulled herself up.

In front of her stood two gigantic oak trees that bordered the eastern edge of the park, the curve of their branches forming a sort of natural proscenium arch. Through this clearing, she could see all the golden-apple sunshine, like something out of a poem by Yeats, streaming through the bare branches of the trees and radiating about the rolling hills in the near distance.

It looked like heaven to her. Jack Leonard was trying to buy her a little piece of heaven.

Eventually she returned to the car and found him standing there, leaning back against it, map in hand. She came up and leaned her head against his chest, nuzzling him hard, and at first he didn't respond. But eventually she could feel him kiss the top of her head and shake her a bit by each shoulder, and she looked up at him and laughed.

He would have loved to stay there against the car, feeling her push up against him like this, but he knew that they needed to get to their meeting with Frances Knight. As they walked down the lane towards the Great House, all the memories for Mimi started to come flooding back.

'You see I got quite lost, and this farmer, this very nice youngish man, showed me the graves of Jane's mother and sister, and I'd had no idea they were there. Actually, you remember when we met, I'd just made *Home & Glory*?'

Jack did remember. He had wanted that script – the movie had gone on to be one of the top ten money-makers of 1944.

'I'd thought about that guy, losing both his brothers in the

Great War. He looked nowhere near over any of it. Shell-shocked himself, in a way. I thought maybe the movie could help people see how much some families were sacrificing. Help them understand.'

'A one-woman USO.'

'Jack, seriously, short of the draft it was the best I could do.'

'No, I know – I'm still just stinging a bit from before.'

They stopped at the base of the gravel drive, and a hundred yards away stood the Great House, practically scowling down from its small incline.

She grabbed his jaw and pulled him in for a soft, open kiss.

'I *am* sorry, Jack – it's not that I don't appreciate it. It's just so much, you know? To take in.'

'Money can buy you anything.' He shrugged as if it was no big deal.

'I don't normally subscribe to that theory, but after this I may be coming round.'

He took her arm and they started up the long drive together.

Chapter Seventeen

Chawton, Hampshire
Three o'clock that same afternoon

*F*rances Knight was sitting in a small room, known as the reading alcove, that jutted out above the main entrance to the Great House as part of its imposing three-storey porch. It was yet another perfect spot to watch out for visitors, both expected and not, and family lore described it as one of Jane Austen's favourite places in the house for that very reason. Even during the war, tourists could occasionally be seen venturing up the drive, not daring to open the low wooden gate a few hundred feet from the front steps, but just standing there, zooming in with their cameras, taking their one shot of the house that Jane Austen had almost lived in, but not quite.

After three months of persistence, and a burgeoning phone relationship with both Josephine and Evie, Yardley Sinclair had finally managed to get Miss Knight to at least entertain an offer on the steward's cottage. She had not told her father yet, as he was in the final stages now, and she wondered if it might not be better just to wait. This was the absolute most calculating and manipulative idea Frances Knight had ever allowed herself to have, and some small strange sense of rebellion reared itself within her as she got a taste of what the future might feel like, once her father was gone.

Over time, Yardley had explained to her, with all the patience of an archaeologist chipping away at an Egyptian ruin, that the rich American was willing to pay well above market value, several thousand pounds above, for the little cottage. That his plan was to immediately restore the cottage into a single-family residence again, ideally using the original layout from Jane Austen's time.

Frances could tell that Mr Sinclair was a huge fan of her ancestor, and during their series of calls, it always took some doing to put off the visits from him that he would often suggest. To sweeten the deal, he kept mentioning that the American and his fiancée had acquired some of the Godmersham estate pieces, and having this cottage might thereby also enable the acquisitions to stay in England, right in their ancestral home.

Frances knew that neither the Knight estate nor the cottage's rental income yielded sufficient funds to keep up the cottage in the way that it deserved. And with her sense of failure over being the end of the Knight family line, a sale seemed a possible chance to redeem herself, if sold to the right person.

Yardley had assured her that the buyer was indeed the right person – more specifically, that the woman affianced to the buyer was such a serious and successful Austen fan that he could vouch for the care and expense that she would put into the place.

Frances now sat alternately watching the front drive and the clock above the fireplace mantel in the larger second-floor room behind her. At three P.M., Mr Jack Leonard and his fiancée were due to arrive, and at exactly on the hour, a man and a woman could indeed be seen turning in from old Gosport Road and approaching the Great House along the gravel drive.

They stopped at one point as the woman gestured towards the graveyard and church sheltered by a grove of beech trees, then the man unlatched the front gate to the house. They were a well-dressed couple who looked to be in their thirties, the man with a map in his hand and the woman nervously twisting at something about her throat. The man looked straight at the house as he approached, but the woman's eyes were everywhere, and even from a distance she looked a little pale and shaken.

Frances made her way down the hanging oak staircase, with its imposing Jacobean balustrade, so that she could be in the Great Hall when they arrived. Afternoon tea had been set out on the sideboard near the row of large mullioned windows, with two different types of cake on display: coffee and walnut, and Victoria sponge filled with preserves made with strawberries from the walled garden and honey from the estate's own apiary.

Placing a tea tray on the ottoman before her, Frances sat down on the faded chintz sofa and looked about the room. She did not sit here often, finding it the largest and coldest room in the house. It was also full of memories from when she was young, the parties and the family gatherings and the welcoming of new neighbours. Now it was reserved mostly for the Christmas Eve gathering, when the villagers joined her after Mass for a warming by the huge fire. She wondered if this past Christmas had been the last of that, as well.

Josephine answered the door, and she led the two strangers into the room as Frances stood to greet them.

'Mr Leonard, welcome.' She smiled as she took a step forward. 'And this must be your lovely fiancée. Mr Sinclair speaks so highly of you,' Frances said to the beautiful woman at his side.

Mimi and Jack were both waiting for the inevitable sinking

in of recognition – the unabashed stare, usually followed by a gasp or even a shriek – but Frances just stood there smiling as if Mimi were merely the future wife of Jack Leonard.

'Mimi,' she said, putting out her hand.

'Mimi? What an unusual name.'

'It's short for Mary Anne.'

Jack looked at Mimi with interest. 'I didn't know that.'

Frances smiled. 'It's best to have some secrets when entering marriage.'

'"It is better to know as little as possible of the defects of the person with whom you are to pass your life,"' quoted Mimi with an endearing and very white smile back.

'So that's what you're doing,' laughed Jack.

Frances motioned for them both to take a seat on the matching chintz sofa across from hers. She immediately poured them each a cup of tea from the tray before her.

'I understand from Mr Sinclair that you are a fan of Jane Austen,' she said to Mimi, while trying hard not to look at Jack. His efficiency and energy unnerved her. She feared that, left alone with him for too long, she might agree to the sale of the antique Indian carpet underfoot, or even a lock of her own hair.

Mimi nodded vigorously. 'I can't tell you how much – I came here once before, you know – on my own, long before the war, before I moved to California – and I saw the little cottage, and the church here, and the graves. I would have given anything back then to be here, in this very room.' She paused. 'I hope – I haven't had much time to process any of this, Jack just told me about the cottage – but I hope you are okay meeting with us. I know this must be an extremely difficult decision. I could never make it myself.'

Jack shot her a recriminating look. Mimi had absolutely no head for business.

'Thank you, it certainly is.' Frances shifted about on the sofa nervously. She was now finding it hard to look straight at Mimi, too. The woman was gorgeous, in an almost alien way, with a strong heart-shaped jawline, a slight dimple in her chin and eyes the most startling colour of violet.

'Let's not look backwards, hmm?' interjected Jack. He knew that in business there was no point – and he believed pretty much the same in life, too. If Frances got to talking too much about giving up any part of the family legacy, he could see himself having to prop up two emotional females, and he'd had enough of that for one day.

'We've got exciting plans as you know,' he continued. 'The cottage would be restored and beautified to do your family proud. No expense would be spared.'

As the words left his mouth, he looked about himself a bit more and saw that everything in the Great House, antique or otherwise, seemed to live under layers of memories thick as dust. There were extremely old photographs along the mantel of relatives in Edwardian dress, and ancient oil paintings of others in the Knight family's past, and not a sign of any modern convenience at all except for the electric lights and a single radiator along the internal wall. Frances, too, looked much older than her years – Jack, with his discerning eye, would have put her well into her fifties, due to the parchment-like skin on her neck and the deeply etched crow's-feet, except that he had been told she was only a decade or so older than himself.

'The way I see it,' he was continuing, 'it's a win-win. Everybody would get something they need. Yardley said you were a very sensible woman, and I like doing business with sensible people.'

'And why do you need the cottage, Mr Leonard?'

'For my lovely fiancée here. She is the world's biggest Austen fan – no, seriously, show her the ring, honey.'

Mimi shook her head in embarrassment, but Jack took her left hand and held it out towards Frances so that she could see the turquoise-and-gold ring on Mimi's finger.

'Oh, my, that looks – that seems – familiar,' the older woman said haltingly as she slowly realised that this was her famous ancestor's ring recently featured in the Sotheby's catalogue, now on the finger of some American stranger whose crass fiancé seemed to only see dollar signs on every object about him.

'It sure is,' replied Jack. 'Mimi's such a fan, we're even making a movie based on one of Jane's books.'

Mimi had been watching Frances closely as Jack tried to keep her onside. Something was a little off about the woman, as if she was going through the motions of life and this small interchange but was not completely present. She looked as if she belonged to another time, with her high-collared white blouse and heavy long skirt and greying blonde hair pulled up high on the back of her head. But as Jack mentioned the movies, the woman's expression finally seemed to relax a bit.

'A movie? Are you a director?'

'Producer,' he corrected.

'Oh.'

Jack cleared his throat. 'Well, actually, more than that, if I say so myself. You see, I heard about *Sense and Sensibility* and I got this writer – you may have heard of him, J. D. Bateman – anyway, I got him to write a script based on the book. What a story.' Jack practically whistled through his teeth.

Frances looked over at Mimi, who was smiling almost apologetically for her fiancé. 'Are you involved with the movie as well?'

Mimi nodded and took a sip of her tea.

'Involved with it?' exclaimed Jack. 'Why, she's the star! She's Elinor!'

Frances looked at the woman with even more interest. 'Are you an actress?'

Mimi nodded again. 'You could call it that.'

'An actress!' exclaimed Jack again. 'Why, she's a movie star – she's Mimi Harrison! Of *Home & Glory*?'

Frances shook her head politely. 'I'm terribly sorry. I don't get out to the pictures very often. I am sure you are most successful,' she added to Mimi with an apologetic look.

Jack was starting to look a little flushed with annoyance under the crisp ironed collar of his starched white Savile Row shirt. Although not wanting to be recognised everywhere he and Mimi went, Jack did want to be recognised when it could work in his favour. But he was also intuiting that the sale of the cottage might be purely financially driven on Miss Knight's part, and he wondered just how much of a predicament she was in – and how much he might stand to benefit from at least that.

'So,' Jack declared, deciding to go for the advantage of abruptness, 'what do you say, Miss Knight? Shall we make this happen?'

Frances looked at Jack, with his sharp whitened teeth and narrowed hazel eyes, leaning forward in his seat as if about to pounce on his prey.

'Please,' said Mimi, reaching across to lay her right hand gently on the older woman's forearm, 'please don't feel pressured. We're just very excited. There is no need to make a decision on the spot.'

Jack felt that old, irritating migraine starting up. Nothing would get done if it was left to these two.

'How long are you here for, in Chawton?' Frances asked hesitatingly.

Mimi quickly looked over at Jack before replying, 'Well,

we're staying in London while we look for a summer place, so we're not far, and we can always come back. In fact, I'd love to.'

'Then come back.' Frances smiled at Mimi. 'And we'll see.'

The words *we'll see* were, for Jack Leonard, the deal equivalent of tracing Scotch along a woman's collarbone, and he stood up confidently to shake Frances's hand just a little too vigorously.

Mimi stood up, too. 'Jack, do you mind if I just have a second alone here with Miss Knight? Girl talk,' she added with a wink.

He looked from one woman to the other. 'All right, honey. Just don't go giving the farm away. Oh, and Miss Knight, for all my fiancée's movie stardom, let's keep her identity just between us for now, hmm? The last thing I'm sure you Knights want is a bunch of news photographers showing up, hiding in the bushes.'

When he had left, Mimi sat back down again. 'I just have to tell you, whatever happens, how much of an honour this has been. To be welcomed into this house by you, and to have this time with you. I know Jack can be a little, ah, overwhelming at the best of times.'

'Not at all. He reminds me quite a bit of my father, but with much more energy and passion.'

'I understand your father is not well. I am so sorry.'

Frances nodded. 'It could be any day now.'

'Oh, I really am so very sorry.'

'It's all right. He has had a long and healthy life. He's nearly eighty-six, you know, in a family also famed for its longevity.'

'But still, the last thing you need right now are two Americans breathing down your neck to make a decision about something so incredibly personal.'

'I have nothing if not time to think, and no one really to consult with over any of this. I am the only one left, you see, of the direct descendants. My father is the great-great-grandson of Jane Austen's brother Edward Knight, and I feel very much both the privilege and the responsibility of that.'

Mimi shook her head in astonishment as she quickly did some maths, knowing that Jane's older brother Admiral Francis Austen had lived well into the 1860s. 'Your father would have known Jane Austen's brother, as a young boy, then. How amazing!'

Frances nodded as her features finally fully relaxed. 'The family would celebrate Christmas here at the house, in the dining room, all sitting about the long table with this very Wedgwood china, and here in this room, by this fire, they would have sung carols and drunk mulled wine and roasted chestnuts.'

'Just like any other family.'

'Exactly. It's a family, you see. My family. And yet for everyone else, it's some of the greatest writing the world has ever known.'

'And you? Do you love her books, too?'

'You're not going to want to hear this' – Frances smiled – 'but my favourites are the Brontës.'

Mimi laughed. 'That is so perfect.'

'But don't tell anyone.'

'No, don't worry, no one. Especially not Jack. He might try and knock down the price as a result.'

Frances saw that Mimi understood her fiancé well enough, and this made her marginally less concerned for the woman than Frances had been at first. For if Jack did remind her of her father, she could imagine enough of the years ahead to have her share of worries for Mimi Harrison.

Mimi stood back up and Frances rose, too.

'Do come again. With or without Jack.'

Mimi smiled gratefully at the woman. 'I have so many questions, I hope you won't regret the very kind offer.'

'I am sure I won't,' Frances smiled in return.

Watching through the window as Mimi and Jack headed back down the drive together, Frances felt as if she had passed some kind of cosmic test in resisting the charms of these two. In combination, Mimi and Jack had all the power of a high-explosive bomb being dropped in a sneak attack on their small, inconsequential village – a veritable Mary and Henry Crawford twosome run amok. Frances wondered to whom, if anyone, she should mention their visit. Wondered if other people she knew – Evie or Charlotte, Dr Gray, even Andrew Forrester – would recognise Mimi's name if Frances shared it.

The January sun was setting fast, and she could hear Josephine walking about the lower level of the house, turning on the electric lights and setting the fire in the other rooms.

Evie suddenly rushed in with duster in hand and stopped short upon seeing the mistress of the house standing by the large drawing-room window.

'I'm sorry, miss, we thought you were back in your bedroom.'

'No apology necessary, Evie – it was a longer visit than anticipated. Please, resume what you were doing.' Frances was always overly polite with her staff – she was terrified of turnover when they were the one constant presence in her life besides the old house and its memories.

Evie gave the smallest curtsy but made no sign of actually resuming her chores. Ever since Christmas Eve, she had been desperate to tell the older woman about the society they had formed and their hopes for it. Dr Gray had asked her not to say anything until they could present a proper offer to Miss Frances for the cottage, but today's visit arranged by Sotheby's was concerning Evie, and her gut told her now was the time to speak up.

'Evie' – Frances started, taking her seat on the sofa – 'I've been meaning to ask, did you finish with that book I recommended?'

'Oh, yes, it was wonderful, just like you said.'

'Some people find it to be too strange and unrelentingly depressing, a little too much of the supernatural at times. But I think *Villette* is Charlotte Brontë's real masterpiece.'

'I didn't find it too otherworldly for me. I was sheer swept away.'

'Please do remember, you and Charlotte both, that you have complete run of the library here, always. Those books are just sitting there. Remember that.'

'Thank you, miss.' Evie still stood there, duster in hand. 'Miss?'

'Yes, Evie?'

The young girl came and stood across the sofa from her employer, until Frances motioned for her to take a seat. This was when Evie's young age showed itself, as all the excitement and plans for the society jumbled out of her in one long rapid-fire sentence.

Frances listened calmly, waiting for a break in Evie's speech to say something.

'Evie, do you happen to have some sense of who my visitors were just now? Because your timing is impeccable. They want to buy the cottage themselves – apparently the woman is a huge Jane Austen fan, just like yourself, it seems. No, don't panic – I haven't agreed to anything yet. Frankly, it's not my decision, and my father seems quite lost at present to make such a one himself. So nothing's being decided anytime soon, if that's any consolation.'

Evie breathed a visible sigh of relief. 'But you will join us, Miss Frances? The society is nothing without you.'

Frances was touched by the girl's enthusiasm. 'Evie, I knew you had enjoyed *Pride and Prejudice,* but I must say it's quite an undertaking to commit to something like this. Wouldn't you rather be out and about with people your own age? I know both Benjamin Gray and Andrew Forrester quite well from school – I think their own social heyday is long behind them, and it's probably best they have a new hobby of this sort to keep them out of trouble.' Frances smiled gently. 'I'm teasing of course – they are both very good and honourable men. And poor Mrs Grover is lovely. But Adam Berwick – I would never have guessed. And to think it was all his idea.'

'Is that a yes, miss?'

Frances nodded in the face of her house girl's persistence. It must have taken some nerve to ask about something as delicate as the disposition of part of her dying employer's property.

'But let's not say anything about the society to Mr Knight just yet, all right, Evie? As I'm sure you know, he is not the world's biggest Austen fan. We'll keep it our little secret for now.'

Evie gave a quick curtsy and hurried off, although Frances suspected not to her chores. She looked over at the clock on the mantel. It was now a little past four P.M. Although she was feeling quite tired from all the commotion of the afternoon, she was still expected to visit with her father before supper.

They had not had a good visit that morning, and she had been asked to leave the room when Andrew Forrester had arrived to discuss some estate matters. She hoped that after a long nap her father might be a little more even-tempered. But telling him about their American visitors would probably only muddle things. Or at least that was what Frances told herself as she slowly walked up the stairs to see him.

Chapter Eighteen

Chawton, Hampshire
10 January, 1946

Adeline Grover was walking along the main village road in the direction of the Great House, pulling her dark grey wool coat tighter against the sharp winter wind, surprised to see small batches of snowdrops randomly peeking out their heads along the roadside a full month ahead of schedule. She was still peering down at the flowers when she heard her name called out.

She looked up to see Liberty Pascal waving at her from a few yards away.

'Adeline, it's been so long – how are you?' the woman asked with the slightly exaggerated manner that Adeline recalled so well from their college days together as teacher and nurse trainees.

'Liberty, what on earth are you doing here, of all places?' Adeline stopped walking and they stepped to the side of the road together. She noticed that Liberty looked extremely well, her striking ginger hair enhanced by the shade of lipstick she had chosen to wear, which in turn matched the healthful flush of her cheeks.

'I just accepted a new position here!'

'Really? With whom?' Adeline hadn't heard of any new doctors opening practise in the village or even in nearby Alton.

'Dr Benjamin Gray.'

'Really,' Adeline said again. 'I didn't know.'

'You're a patient of his, right? Oh, I am so sorry, Adeline – about the baby. So awful. You must be beside yourself.'

More than one downside of this recent hire by Dr Gray was starting to quickly dawn on Adeline. 'Yes, I've been a patient of his for a long time now. Although recently I have been thinking of making a change.' This was not altogether true, but Adeline's mouth was sometimes faster than her thoughts, and she had learned to trust the gut instincts behind such outbursts.

'Oh, that's too bad. I know Dr Gray speaks so highly of you.'

The idea of Dr Gray and Liberty Pascal discussing Adeline behind her back, whether about her health or otherwise, was making her suddenly and distinctly uncomfortable.

'I can tell I am going to like it here,' Liberty was energetically babbling on. 'I had no idea it was so quaint. You never said, you cagey thing. Although you did choose to come back here to teach, so I guess that says something.'

'How is Dr Gray?' Adeline asked as casually as possible. 'I haven't seen him since the Christmas Eve service for the village, in the little parish church.'

'Oh, I know the one. Adorable. We pass it on our way to see Mr Knight. I was just there actually, giving him his bath. Sad old man, quite near the end. Starting to lose his wits, although he has no idea of course. Benjamin – I mean Dr Gray – seems to be the only one that can manage him. The daughter looks pretty useless, if you ask me.'

Adeline inwardly congratulated herself on remembering Liberty's loose tongue and remarkable lack of discretion and told herself this was as good a reason as any to try to find a new doctor. She found it interesting that, as with Harriet Peckham, Dr Gray persisted in hiring such outspoken and formidable women.

'Listen, Liberty, it's actually a good thing we ran into each other. Would you be so kind as to let Dr Gray know about my plans to make a change? Like I said, I've been meaning to tell him for a while now.'

'Of course, Adeline. Anything to help you out right now. Be well, okay, dear?' Liberty reached out and gave Adeline a big hug, then walked off in the opposite direction.

Adeline continued on her way home. Running into Liberty Pascal, of all people, had done nothing to improve her mood for the day, and she would be glad to get back to the solitude and privacy of her little house. She was not due to see Dr Gray again for a few more weeks, when the Jane Austen Society was scheduled to have its second meeting. She was glad of that – Liberty would tell him Adeline's plans shortly, and he might wonder about them, but hopefully this business would be all done and forgotten by the next time they met.

⌣

Adeline was crouching in her front garden a few hours later, digging up the ground to belatedly plant some tulip bulbs, clearing the dead fall brush to showcase her own little patches of snowdrops, when she heard the front oak gate swing open on its creaky, fallen hinges. She stood up to her full height as Dr Gray approached.

He had an unusual look of concern on his face – he was

usually good at hiding his feelings, so much so that she often found herself spending a large part of their time together just trying to make him crack.

'You are well?' he asked abruptly.

She leaned both hands on the old wooden handle of her shovel and looked directly at him in surprise. 'Yes, tolerably. Are you?'

He started to pace about the garden path, which divided just before her into a long oval before resuming its red-brick march to her red front door. She was standing within the oval-shaped patch of ground, which was surrounded by a low box hedge that Samuel had planted for her as a wedding present less than a year ago.

Dr Gray continued to pace about distractedly on the other side of the hedge, pulling dead twigs off some of the hawthorn bushes and then mindlessly throwing the sticks onto the ground.

'I see you've hired Liberty Pascal,' Adeline finally spoke up. 'She's an old classmate of mine, from college. A real force of nature, that one – she should have you whipped into shape in no time.'

'What on earth does that mean?' he asked with a jerk of his head.

'Nothing in particular. She's just hard to resist. French lineage and all that.'

Dr Gray took off his right glove and rubbed his jaw with the exposed hand. 'Adeline, why are you firing me as your doctor?'

'I'm not firing you.' She pushed the shovel deeper into the ground until it was standing upright on its own.

'Really. What do you call it then?'

'Does it matter?'

'Is this about the medicine?'

Adeline looked at him in pure shock. She had been honestly

struggling to figure out why he was so upset, and now the full implication of his words struck her hard.

'The medicine . . . that you gave me . . . that medicine?' Her words came out slowly, as she tried to process his obvious anger at her.

'Is it because I won't give you any more of it?'

'Dr Gray!' Her eyes lit up with such fury, he immediately regretted saying it. 'Are you honestly standing there accusing me of being an addict of some kind? Of switching doctors so I can get more drugs? You, of all people?'

Dr Gray removed his other glove and shoved both of them deep into his coat pockets in visible frustration. Looking about for somewhere to sit, he spied an overturned clay urn under a crab-apple tree and went and plonked himself down on it.

'Well?' Adeline persisted in her anger.

Dr Gray sat staring at the ground about him, at the dead leaves and dried seed heads of last summer's hydrangea and allium blossoms. He could see that keeping up with the garden must have come to a crashing standstill for Adeline amidst the terrible events of last autumn. He thought about the broken front gate, and all the yardwork to be done about them, and how only a widow could find herself with such a house and property to manage all on her own.

'You need someone to help you out around here,' he answered her instead, trying to regain some verbal command of the situation now spiralling out of his feeble control, as things so often seemed to do whenever he was near her.

'You're changing the subject.'

'Look, I'm very sorry if I guessed wrong just now – but I felt it incumbent upon me, as your physician, to make sure there was nothing going on. Nothing of that kind, at least.'

'Dr Gray, I had hoped you would know me well enough to know that I would never get out of control like that.'

He looked up at her. 'Unfortunately, it can happen to the best of us. I know that for a fact. Look, I am sorry, but I had to ask. I had to know that I had asked the question at least, no matter how much it upset you.'

'How brave you are.'

He could see her dry humour returning, which helped him ask the one question he had dreaded even more, ever since the loss of her baby.

'Adeline, is it anything else I've done?'

'Not at all. I just — it's a new year, you know? And we're going to be working together again, with the society, and it's probably a good idea to keep some things separate.'

Dr Gray wasn't sure he believed any of this. 'But I am Adam's doctor, as you well know, and Miss Knight's, too. I am a professional, after all . . .' But his words struck even him as strangely disingenuous, and he let his voice trail off.

'I know that. Look, really, it's nothing in particular. I just feel like it's . . . it's time for a change.' Adeline was grasping for a way to end this conversation. She had never seen Dr Gray angry or distrustful of her before, not even in the slightest. She was not liking it one little bit, nor how angry he was making her feel in return.

'Who will you go to then, for care?'

She hadn't thought this through yet — he had caught her so off-guard.

'Um, Dr Westlake — Howard Westlake — the surgeon who operated on me, over at the Alton Hospital.'

This answer seemed to only perturb Dr Gray even more. 'You put greater confidence in him then, is that it?'

'Not at all. I just think it might be easier, to start fresh with someone not from the village. Not so, um, intimately connected with my case.'

The image of her bloodstained white lace nightgown

suddenly flashed through Dr Gray's head. For the first time, he appreciated that they might have shared too much – that they might not be able to go back to what they were before.

'Yes, of course, fine then,' he finally relented. 'It's whatever you think best.' He got up to head back towards the front gate, then turned to her one last time. 'Do you think I could send Adam round, to fix that gate for you? I am not at all handy like that, as everyone well knows.'

She shrugged. 'Whatever you think best.'

He noted her choice of words, mimicking his own just now – as if to say that she could be just as disingenuous as him.

'I'll see you in a few weeks then, at the next society meeting, if not before?'

She shrugged again. She was still a little angry with him. She wondered just how lost he thought she must be, how much in need of saving. It would never have occurred to her that he might be projecting his own struggles onto her grief-stricken state. Would never have occurred to her that, between the two of them, he was the one most in need of salvation.

Chapter Nineteen

Chawton, Hampshire
15 January, 1946

$\mathcal{F}$rances sat on the faded chintz sofa in the Great Hall across from Andrew Forrester. Josephine, Evie and Charlotte stood behind the sofa, at Frances's request. She was hoping that her father had provided gifts in his will for the household staff in recognition of all their service, particularly during these last several difficult years.

Dr Gray was also in the room, standing with his back against the front window, just off to the right of Miss Knight. Andrew had confidentially asked him to attend the reading of the will as Mr Knight's personal physician.

Andrew cleared his throat. He could not look Frances directly in the eyes – for years now he rarely could. In her eyes he always saw not just the crushing disappointment, but the self-recrimination as well. The sense that she had, through her own passivity and weakness, allowed this life before her to happen. That it might not have been inevitable after all.

Andrew started to read. "'I, James Edward Knight, being

of sound mind and memory, do hereby, on this fifteenth day of November, in the year of our Lord 1945"' – Frances's head shot up from staring at her lap – '"declare this to be my last will and testament, and revoke all former wills and testaments made by me. I declare Andrew Forrester, Esquire, solicitor in the town of Alton, County of Hampshire, to act as executor of my estate, and hereby bequeath the totality of that estate, with exclusions set out hereafter, to my closest living male relative on the British continent."'

Andrew heard one of the younger servants standing behind Frances gasp, then be quickly swatted by someone, most likely the elderly cook, Josephine.

Frances simply continued to sit there, silent. Andrew could feel her eyes still on him as he read but forced himself not to look back at her. This was no time to start doing that.

'"The aforementioned exclusions include, firstly, the steward's cottage on Winchester Road in Chawton, and the adjoining triangular-shaped parcel of 2.3 acres of land contained by the red-brick wall and rear hornbeam hedge, as set out on the attached survey."'

'I'm surprised he didn't drag himself out there and measure it in feet himself,' muttered Josephine angrily.

'"This property shall be the residence of my only surviving child, Frances Elizabeth Knight, until the time of her death or any arm's-length disposition of the cottage, whichever should occur the earlier, at which time the right to residence shall revert back to the estate. I also bequeath to my daughter a living allowance of two thousand pounds annually, for so long as that amount can be generated by the estate without exceeding five per cent of its gross annual revenue. I have set out in the attached schedule the required rates in reduction of this allowance according to any year-over-year decline in the gross revenue of the estate."'

Andrew had always found these last two terms to be the most unnecessarily punitive and cruel in a particularly mean-spirited document. Two thousand pounds was just enough for Frances to enjoy some of the nicer comforts in life, but not one whit more. And none of it was guaranteed as long as the estate continued to lose money as it had been doing, and at an alarmingly increasing rate. It was anyone's guess as to how much the estate would be further decimated by the death taxes that would now be owing.

Andrew saw, out of the corner of his eye, the young house girl Evie make some kind of motion to Dr Gray, then go and lean against the mantel of the mammoth stone fireplace with her head bowed down.

'"Finally, in recognition of their support and care of me in my final years, I bequeath the following gifts: an annual stipend of fifty pounds to Miss Josephine Barrow, and annual stipends of twenty pounds each to Miss Evie Stone and Miss Charlotte Dewar."'

Andrew cleared his throat one last time and said, while folding the paper back up in his white-knuckled grasp, '"This document has been signed, sealed and delivered in the presence of the following witnesses and at my request, being Mr Andrew Forrester, Esquire, of Alton, Hampshire, and Miss Harriet Peckham of Chawton, Hampshire."'

There was a terrible, awkward silence in the room. Everyone knew that Miss Frances should be the first, if any, to talk, yet everyone knew that she would not say a word.

Finally, Dr Gray came over to stand next to Andrew, who remained sitting on the sofa. 'Miss Frances, Mr Forrester asked me to be here today for several reasons. You must have questions about your father's state of mind at the time of execution only two months past.'

Frances silently shook her head. After a few seconds, she

looked up at Dr Gray and smiled bitterly. 'To the end, my father knew exactly what he was doing.'

Everyone else in the room was taken aback. It was the most assertive and complete statement they had heard her make in years.

'He may have done, but there are grounds, just so you know. If you want to pursue—'

Frances stood up and put her right hand slightly out as if to stop him. 'No, I don't want to pursue anything. It is what it is. The care he received from the staff has been recognised. That is what I cared about most.'

After all the distress of the past two days, this was too much for old Josephine to bear. She could be heard behind them sniffling into her handkerchief, before hustling the two house girls out of the room alongside her.

'Frances – Miss Knight – wait,' Andrew finally said, and he stood up, too. 'As executor, in my experience it may take some time to determine the legitimate heir. During that time, you will be permitted to reside in the Great House and – who knows – perhaps beyond that. Should the courts not be able to determine the proper male heir within a reasonable time, you can petition to inherit on the grounds of being Mr Knight's immediate next of kin.'

Frances shook her head dejectedly. 'I really can't think about any of that right now. Just prepare a landlord notice to the tenants in the steward's cottage – I will take the first available flat at the least amount of inconvenience to any of them.'

Dr Gray stepped forward. 'I know that Louisa Hartley is planning to move to Bath soon, to be nearer her son once her recent surgery has healed.'

'Fine,' Frances said flatly. 'If Mr Forrester could please make the legal arrangements. And thank you, gentlemen, both of you, for delivering this news. It cannot have been easy.'

She left the room. Dr Gray went and shut the drawing-room door behind her, then he and Andrew both slumped back down onto the sofa.

'Good God,' sighed Dr Gray.

Andrew opened his lawyer's bag and shoved the will inside before angrily snapping the straps shut.

'She was always pathologically stoical,' Dr Gray added. 'Even as children – remember?'

'I hope *stoic* is the right word for it. I shudder to think what else one might call it at this point.'

Dr Gray had a sudden realization. 'So this is why you were so concerned about joining the society . . . I'd never have guessed. If it's any consolation, not once did you betray knowing any of this. Your legal advice, as always, was irreproachable. Still, it seems so ironic that the old man would tie up the cottage in this way, given our own recent plans for it. We haven't even had a chance yet to run that ad in *The Times*.'

Andrew got up and walked over to the sideboard, turning his back to Dr Gray. 'I'm not sure how coincidental any of this was.'

'How so?'

'Ben, why did you fire Miss Peckham in the end?'

Now it was Dr Gray's turn to squirm a bit. 'She was just too intrusive. I felt like I was under surveillance by an enemy camp. Always making suggestive remarks about the ladies.'

Andrew turned back to him and smiled ruefully. Dr Gray's status as the lonely widower was a mainstay of Chawton village life – Andrew suspected several local women to be pining after his old friend.

'I get that, Ben – but I'm afraid she might have done far worse. I fear she may have tipped the old man off to your and Adam's initial plans for the cottage. We all know how disinterested – even peevish – Mr Knight was about the whole Austen legacy. Having buses of tourists traipsing into town to check out a museum in her honour would have been the last thing he'd want. And now he's arranged it so perfectly, with Frances losing her one place to live if the cottage ever gets sold outside of the family.'

'She's certainly been boxed into a corner by the old man this time. Crikey, I need a drink,' growled Dr Gray.

Andrew started to pour out two whiskies from the drinks tray always set up on the sideboard. 'She's lived her whole life in that box, though. Literally and figuratively. When was the last time she even left the house? Evie had quite a time of it, I understand, getting her out on Christmas Eve.'

'Aren't you being a bit harsh, Andrew?'

'I don't think anyone's been harsh enough, to tell the truth. Maybe that's been the problem all these years. Remember her brother, Cecil, how wild he was? That whole shooting incident – let me just say this, the father liked the cruelty. He admired it. He stomped all over everyone else. And she let him. Surely she could have seen what he was really about – and instead she bent to his will and let him completely control her. Not once did she ever try and assert herself – yet anyone could see that's what he wanted. He hated that she was like this, so meek and yielding, so he punished her even more.'

'Andrew, really, it's not like anybody else ever stood up to the old man.'

Andrew gave a small frown, then returned to his seat and passed one of the glasses of whisky across to Dr Gray.

'I still think you're being far too hard on her,' continued Dr Gray. 'You're looking at it as a man. It's much different for women, these types of things. When we were in school with Frances, women couldn't even become bankers or accountants – and we wonder why old Mr Knight wouldn't trust his one daughter with his money. Until the war, what were their options – servants, teachers, nurses, actresses? I mean, Cambridge, where you went, still doesn't even award the girls degrees, right? You walk away from all of this and who knows where you'd end up.'

'Being married to a strong woman like Jennie was such a godsend to you, Ben.' Andrew sighed with envy. 'I see that so much at times like this.'

'I had a very smart wife. I learned a lot.'

'You still have a lot to learn, though – we both do.' Andrew took a large gulp of his whisky. 'Why are we men so proud, so obstinate? What exactly are we afraid of?'

Dr Gray laughed. 'Oh, let's not start going there. It's been a difficult enough year already. First Adeline Grover fires me as her doctor, and then—'

'Wait, what?'

Dr Gray shrugged. 'It happens, I guess.'

'Did she give a reason?'

'Not particularly.'

'Well, that's a first for you. Does anyone in this town *not* use you as their doctor? That's got to sting a bit, what with your ego.'

'Thanks, Andy, that's just what I needed to hear right now. It's probably all for the best anyway – her powers of observation are so acute sometimes. Nothing gets past her.'

'And that's for the best *why*?'

'What are you saying?'

Andrew downed the rest of his whisky. 'I'm not necessarily saying anything.'

'Spoken like a true lawyer. And I'm not necessarily saying anything about Miss Frances, either.'

They stared at each other, calling to mind many moments from their youth, when they had fought over Frances and a few other girls.

'There's something about growing up in a village,' Andrew finally said, 'being boys and girls together, it's so intimate – how would you ever know if you had found the right person? I mean, what are the odds that they'd be in your own backyard? I was training Samuel Grover, remember?'

'Oh, that's right. I always forget that.'

'He was called up, when, 1942? Forty-three? I remember very clearly the day he and Adeline got engaged. He was so excited – he had been proposing for years apparently. She seemed less so.'

'Why are you telling me all this?' Dr Gray got up nonchalantly to take Andrew's glass, then refilled both their glasses before sitting back down.

'Because I think Adeline Grover fired you for a reason. She wouldn't be the first woman patient to have done so.'

Dr Gray shook his head. 'No, you're wrong. It's nothing like that. Look at me, I'm far too old.'

Andrew laughed. 'Thanks, for the two of us.'

'What on earth makes you say that about her anyway?'

'Oh, it's nothing *she's* done. It's you.'

Dr Gray felt as if he'd received a blow to the stomach. No one had ever guessed any of his secrets, or at least that's what he had always believed. The thought that he had been transparent to anyone, even an old school chum like Andrew, terrified him.

'It's all right, Ben. It's only because I've seen you this head over heels before.'

Dr Gray stared at Andrew, denial on the edge of his tongue, yet he also strangely wanted to hear more.

'And anyway,' Andrew added, 'I don't think she knows, not really. Not yet.'

'There's nothing *to* know, because nothing would ever happen.'

'The one doesn't necessarily preclude the other. And besides, why are you so sure of that? It's not inconceivable – I mean, Adam Berwick's only two years younger than us, and I've been told he's sniffing around her often enough.'

Now Dr Gray's head was starting to hurt. 'How on earth did we end up talking about this? Yes, she's a very attractive young woman – a very attractive young *widow*. And I feel strangely responsible for her. I think that must be mixed up with the baby and the horror of all that, bearing witness and so utterly failing them both.'

'You didn't fail, Ben,' Andrew reproached him gently. 'You can't save everyone, for all your efforts. You're still the best doctor around here and you know it.'

'Apparently Howard Westlake is even better – or at least that's what Adeline seems to think, seeing as he's her new doctor.'

'Ah, some good old professional jealousy to boot. Oh, well, if you're sure that's all it is.'

'No less sure than you are about Frances.'

'Well, Ben,' Andrew said ruefully, 'then I feel for us both.'

Chapter Twenty

Chawton, Hampshire
17 January, 1946

The irony had not escaped Frances Knight that, being no longer entitled to dispose of any of the estate, she would finally learn its true and impressive value. Only a few days after the reading of the will, Evie had – in a fit of anger at Mr Knight for so wretchedly reducing his one child's circumstances – finally confessed to Frances what exactly she had been doing in the library for the past two years.

They were walking through the lime grove together and had stopped next to the old shepherd's hut that had long ago been used to supply shooting parties on the estate. Frances sat down on the bottom steps to the red-painted hut, which balanced on four large wheels like a Gypsy caravan, and looked up at Evie's youthful, shining face. Frances had always admired the girl's spirit, so unlike her own. As the words came tumbling out of Evie, Frances appreciated yet again the obvious energy and discipline that she brought to all her pursuits.

'And there I was thinking you just liked to dust the library. A lot.'

'Miss Knight, how can you stay so calm at a time like this?' Evie waved her arms about them. 'How can you face the prospect of leaving here?'

Frances smiled sadly. 'It's not really a home, though, Evie, wouldn't you say? Not like you and your brothers have. Not like most people.'

'Still, it's so unfair – to make your situation so much harder than it needs to be, when he had the means not to.'

'I know it looks that way – maybe it even is. But we each of us have our own reasons for doing things – and no one owes anyone anything. I got to make my own choices, too, even if it doesn't always look that way.'

Evie wasn't so sure they were still talking about the inheritance but thought it best not to press any further. She knew Miss Frances well enough to know that if she wanted to say something, she would – and otherwise no amount of effort would pry it out of her. In this, the two women were more similar than they knew.

'Anyway, I have a bit of a surprise for you – although I wish it were under happier circumstances. Do you remember my American visitors right after New Year's, who wanted to buy the little cottage? Well, the woman is lovely and due back for another visit today, this time alone. I didn't have the heart to put it off, given how far she has come. But I'm afraid I now need to tell her, too, about the entire estate being in escrow, and my loss of rights over its disposition.'

Evie was only half listening because through the trees she was watching a woman walk gingerly on extremely high heels up the front gravel drive.

'It's so strange,' Evie muttered under her breath. 'She looks just like . . . no, wait, it can't be . . .'

Frances smiled and stood up from the front steps of the shepherd's hut. 'Evie, would you like to meet her?'

Evie was still peering through the trees. The woman looked tall and willowy in her heels, but all Evie could see was the famous image of a barefoot housewife in a kitchen, trying to lock the door against a Nazi soldier, her face a mask of terror – and the Polynesian princess on a tropical beach, nursing a capsized British sailor back to health – and, Evie's favourite of all, the nineteenth-century Russian countess standing on the train platform, the steam from the engine billowing across her face, and then just the sound of the train wheels screeching to a horrific halt.

The woman was waving to them now by the front gate as they approached from the adjoining woodland. With her other hand, she was fiddling with something about her neck.

'Hello, Miss Frances!' she called out.

'I'm sorry,' Evie was still muttering, 'but that woman looks terribly like . . .'

Frances patted the young girl's shoulder as they reached the stranger. 'Evie, I'd like you to meet a new friend of mine, Miss Harrison. Or Mimi, as you might know her. Mimi, it's so lovely to see you again. This is Miss Evie Stone, who helps me with the house and is a great fan of Jane Austen, like yourself.'

Mimi held her hand out to the young girl, recognising well her state of shock. 'Hello, Evie, it's a pleasure to meet you. And if you love Jane Austen even half as much as I do, we shall have a lot to talk about.'

For the first and only time in her life, Evie Stone was speechless.

❧

'Oh, Frances, this is awful. I don't even know what to say.'

The three women were sitting upstairs in the oak-panelled room once known as the Ladies' Withdrawing Room and reached by the beautiful Jacobean staircase in the south-east corner of the house. Frances had invited Evie to stay with them for tea, and the young girl was given a stern look of warning from Josephine as she placed the silver tray down on the small round table between her mistress and the famous guest.

Frances waited discreetly until Josephine had left the room, then poured out Mimi's tea with both milk and sugar as she liked it ('I'm a child!' Mimi had said, laughing, the first time she gave her order). Frances passed the delicate cup and saucer to her before replying, 'I feel awful for you, and for Mr Leonard. I know how much you wanted the cottage.'

Mimi shook her head. 'Don't give it a second thought – I never felt comfortable about the whole thing anyway. Jack is just so damn – oh, excuse my language – but just so persistent. It's almost impossible to say no to him.'

Frances nodded in agreement. 'I fully understand that. I probably would've cut him a lock of my own hair if he'd asked for it.'

Evie was sitting between the two women, looking back and forth as they each spoke in turn, her head following silently as if at a tennis match.

'What will you do now?' Mimi asked before taking a sip of her tea.

'One of the tenants has agreed to give notice for the end of March, as she was planning to leave soon anyway. Our lawyer, Andrew Forrester, is arranging everything for me. I hope to move out of here by the spring.'

Mimi scratched the side of her forehead, and Evie's mouth fell open in a gape of astonishment, as it was the exact same gesture she had seen the woman do several times in *Home & Glory*, Evie's all-time favourite film.

'But why the rush? My father was an estates lawyer before he became a judge, and I know a little bit about the American laws at least. You might end up declared the sole heir if no one

else pops up in time – why not wait until you have to leave?
Will Mr Forrester, as executor, not let you stay?'

'Mr Forrester would let Miss Frances do anything,' Evie
piped up.

The two women turned in unison to look at her.

'It looks like Miss Stone has found her voice,' Frances said
in an attempt at a quick distraction.

'So, Evie.' Mimi smiled at the girl in as friendly a manner as
possible to help further steady her nerves. 'Jane Austen. How
did it start for you?'

Evie had been picking at a piece of glazed lemon cake on her
china plate, and she placed the plate back down as she braced
herself to finally speak to one of the biggest movie stars in the
world.

'I had a teacher – Adeline Lewis – Miss Frances knows her.
She knows Jane Austen inside and out, can quote entire pas-
sages by heart, and she lent me her copy of *Pride and Prejudice*
when I was still in school, and that was it. I was a goner.'

'But you're not in school any longer? May I ask how old
you are?'

'Sixteen.'

'When did you leave school then?'

'Fourteen.'

'That's so young. Do you miss it?'

'Terribly,' Evie replied quickly, then turned to Miss Knight.
'But I could not have found a better employer. And Miss Frances gives us full access to the library here, all of the servants,
and you won't see a better collection of books this side of London.'

'My father had an impressive library, too, although nothing
like the Knights', I am sure. He was the one who introduced
me to Austen. He would read her to me at night. I found him
once, in his study, sitting by the fire, laughing out loud – I was

pretty little, around eight or nine – and I asked him what was so funny, and he read me the scene where Elizabeth parries so successfully with Lady Catherine de Bourgh, who is warning her against any engagement to her nephew Mr Darcy.'

'"These are heavy misfortunes indeed – but the wife of Mr Darcy must have such extraordinary sources of happiness, that she could have no cause to repine,"' quoted Evie.

'"Obstinate, headstrong girl!"' Mimi quoted back with a laugh. 'Exactly! And I crawled onto his lap and he kept reading to me. And pretty soon he decided to start reading the book all over again, this time out loud, to me, and he did this for many nights and years after, with all the books. Except *Mansfield Park*. He didn't get Fanny Price. Thought her far too passive for all the connivers around her.'

'He must be very excited, then, about your plans to make a film of *Sense and Sensibility*,' Frances said.

'I don't know.' Mimi added another sugar cube to her cup of tea, then added simply, 'He killed himself. When I was twelve.'

Evie and Frances looked at each other.

'Mimi,' Frances started, 'I am so sorry. How awful, for all of you.'

'It was awful. It still is. The hardest part is wondering whether I could have done something, to help him – to stop him. The never knowing is what hurts the most. I try so hard to just remember our relationship, how we were together, and not think about his secret pain, because I can't do anything about that, and that's what haunts me.' Mimi looked at Frances carefully. 'Don't let any of this haunt you, Frances – your father's last days, and the new will. It has nothing to do with you. It was his life – *his* choices.'

'She knows that,' Evie piped up. 'Oh, I'm sorry, Miss Knight, I don't mean to speak for you.'

'It's all right, Evie, I know we were talking about this very thing in the grove just now.' Frances stood up and flattened her long, black, velvet skirt, then said to Evie, 'Should we show Miss Harrison the lower library before she goes?'

They headed downstairs and through the Great Hall until they entered the book-lined room next door.

'What will happen to all of this?' Mimi walked around the room and gently touched the spines of various leather-bound books. 'It's remarkable, really. Yardley has been watching the market for me, and I bet there are some real treasures in here.' She turned back to Evie. 'Yardley Sinclair works at Sotheby's in London – he is another great lover of Jane Austen, and he keeps me up-to-date on things. In fact, he's the one who introduced us to Miss Knight.'

'He is a most persistent man as well,' said Frances.

'Yes, I seem to be surrounded by those, both here and in Hollywood.'

Evie's eyes widened, as she thought about all the famous people that Mimi must know.

'Yardley wants to visit you, terribly,' Mimi was saying to Frances.

Frances absent-mindedly touched the back of one of the books nearest her. 'I've done a good job at putting that off. I always do. But I suppose we are going to need a valuation soon, especially under the circumstances.'

'Yardley can be trusted, I promise. He would keep any valuation confidential until you knew what you wanted to do. He considers himself another caretaker of Miss Austen. I know he very much wants to keep as much of her physical legacy here in England as possible, so he's very good to share with me what he does.'

'Miss Knight,' Evie half whispered, trying not to appear rude, 'would it be all right – I mean, are you all right – if I tell Miss Harrison about the society we've started up?'

'Of course, Evie, please do. I am sure Miss Harrison would love to hear about it.'

Evie explained to Mimi the recent formation of the Jane Austen Society, with Frances and herself being the newest members in addition to Adam Berwick, Dr Gray, Adeline Grover and Andrew Forrester – just two people short of the desired quorum of eight.

Mimi listened with increasing excitement, then exclaimed, 'I need to be part of this. I mean it. Please?'

The other two women stared at each other quickly in surprise, with Evie looking as if she was doing various quick calculations in her head.

'Are you sure?' Evie asked first. 'I mean, we're a bunch of people who never leave this village – you would be in a pretty bright spotlight when you needn't be.'

'No, I totally want to do this. And I know Yardley will want to join, too. So that gets you to eight, right?'

'But you're not a resident here,' Frances added.

'But I plan to be, for at least a good chunk of the year. Can you ask Mr Forrester for me, if that could pose a problem of any kind?'

'Of course, if you want. But give us time to prepare everyone. We have some rather romantic gentlemen in the group—'

'Three!' Evie piped up again, holding up as many fingers on her right hand.

'Yes, how amusing.' Frances smiled. 'Evie is right, they are all three of them terrible romantics.'

'Well, Yardley will love that,' Mimi tried to interject, but the comment went straight over the other two women's heads.

'They are also all inveterate filmgoers, as far as I know,' Frances was continuing. 'It might be a bit too much for them at first.'

Mimi thought it delightful that these two women were

being so protective of the group. She thought it said something, for both the society and the village of Chawton as a whole, that they all knew each other so well. She had left her near decade in Hollywood without any such understanding. In fact, the longer she had stayed there, the less she had understood of the people around her. That there might be a place where people were not constantly competing against each other for their very sustenance, but were instead helping each other survive through war and injury and poverty and pain, seemed as much something out of a Jane Austen novel as anything else she could have hoped to find.

Chapter Twenty-One

$\mathcal{A}$deline was a little annoyed to see Liberty Pascal answer the front door when she arrived at Dr Gray's house for the second meeting of the Jane Austen Society.

'Addy,' Liberty said, even though everyone who knew Adeline also knew how much she disliked that shortening of her name. 'You're early.'

Adeline noticed the ring of keys hanging from Liberty's belt and wondered just how much the young woman had already ingratiated herself into both the business and the personal life of Dr Gray.

'He's so particular about his things,' Liberty explained, catching Adeline's questioning glance. 'I'm the only one with access to the medicine cabinet during office hours. He doesn't want even one copy of the key left lying about.'

'That's quite a responsibility.' Adeline wondered why Dr Gray would be so strict about the keys that he wouldn't even keep a copy for himself. 'You must be here at all hours.'

Liberty nodded. 'I've taken a room at the boarding house

near the school. Your old stomping ground I understand. Dr Gray tells me you were quite the teacher in your day.'

'Does he? That's a little surprising, since he and the other trustees were always trying to get me fired.'

'Oh, Adeline!' Liberty laughed. 'You always were so dramatic!'

This struck Adeline as so ironic coming from the other girl that she could only step silently away at the sound of another knock at the front door. She started to wander down the hallway and realised she had never before been this far inside. Halfway down the corridor, a steep staircase led upstairs. Adeline's breath caught as she saw the sharp edge at the bottom that jutted out from the banister and had killed Jennie Gray.

At the end of the hall, there was a step down into the back kitchen, and this galley-shaped room was very different from the austere medical quarters in the front section of the house. Bright and cheery, the kitchen featured white-painted cabinetry, a row of windows that stretched the width of the back wall above the butler sink, and a maplewood butcher block in the middle of the tiled floor. Feminine touches were everywhere: from the delicate cream-and-rose-patterned curtains that covered the bottom halves of the windows, to the collection of Cornishware on the open shelving trimmed with Victorian lace edging.

She was picking up a little blue-and-white-striped pitcher from one of the shelves when she heard a cough behind her.

Turning around too quickly, she fumbled with the pitcher and just managed to hold on to it as she put it back in its place.

'I'm sorry, you startled me.'

Dr Gray came into the room. She noticed that he wasn't wearing his usual suit jacket and tie, just an open blue shirt beneath a brown tweed vest that matched his eyes. He looked like any regular husband, busying himself about the kitchen.

'The meeting's in the drawing room,' he said.

'I know that. Liberty's out there playing hostess, have no fear.'

He nodded at the kettle warming up on the stove set back inside a former inglenook fireplace. 'While you're in here snooping, why don't you help me with the tea?'

She nodded and got out of his way just as he reached for a matching creamer jug and sugar bowl from the bottom shelf nearest her.

'The spoons and napkins are in those drawers over there.' He gave another curt nod behind him, his back turned to her, and she went to count them out.

'We're seven, right? Or has Liberty developed a sudden appreciation for Jane Austen, too?'

'I'm not sure if Liberty actually reads.' His back was still turned to her. 'Anyway, I think we're eight. Miss Frances is bringing two guests now from the city.'

Adeline counted out the cutlery and napkins and brought them over to the tray he had set down on the butcher block. As she placed them down, he did the same with a stack of saucers, and their hands touched just so slightly, and she jumped back.

He didn't say anything, just looked down at the jumble of tea things in the middle of the tray for a second as if distracted, then turned back to get the teapot and tea leaves from a nearby tin canister.

The water in the kettle was starting to boil on the stove, and as he walked past her to get it, something in her stomach dropped. It felt as if they had done this kitchen routine a hundred times before, and she realised for the first time how very aware of each other's body they both were. They never brushed against each other, yet they never kept more than a foot apart.

The sound of the kettle whistle crashed into her thoughts, and he came over to pour the water into the teapot.

'Watch yourself,' he said as he passed by her again.

She took a step back and then realised to her astonishment that she didn't want to.

'Are you okay?' He poured the water into the large Brown Betty teapot. 'You're being remarkably silent for once.'

'I can't do two things at once,' she tried to say lightly, as she placed eight teacups down in a few separate stacks.

'I highly doubt that.'

'So,' she said, trying to change the subject, 'Miss Frances told you, about Mimi Harrison coming? I couldn't believe it when I heard. Samuel and I used to see her films together all the time.'

'Miss Frances seemed to think we men would need time to get used to the idea. Meanwhile, it's Liberty Pascal I've got running around town screaming her head off in excitement.'

'Oh, is that why she's here?' Adeline smiled. 'Films are definitely much more her thing, as I recall. Although she *can* read.'

Dr Gray put the kettle back down on the stove. 'That was probably a little unfair of me.'

'Just a little. Is everything going . . . well, though, with the two of you?'

He wiped his hands on a little flowered tea towel hanging from the oven door. 'Well enough. I do need someone around here to help out, with the housekeeping and the practise, and Liberty is very eager to do whatever I ask.'

'I'm sure she is.' Adeline quickly regretted her words as he raised an eyebrow at her. 'No, listen, it's great. She will keep things under control, as you said. And unlike Miss Peckham, Liberty doesn't know a soul in town to gossip with. At least not yet.'

Dr Gray leaned both his forearms down on either side of the tea tray, then looked up at Adeline, always a little surprised at how tall she was.

'Adeline, back at Christmas, when I came to your house . . .'

'With my present.'

'Yes, that, too. But your mother — she said Harriet had called first.'

Adeline shifted uneasily on her feet. She was starting to realise where the conversation might be heading, and it was something she had successfully blocked out of her mind until now.

'Yes, she called my mum to tell her you were on your way — or might be, I think.'

'I never told her any of that. I never told her where I was going. I had just taken your card from her, the Christmas card you sent me, but it wasn't return addressed. And I never said a word to her.'

'I see.' Adeline leaned back against the butler sink. 'Is that — was that — one of the reasons why you fired her?'

'It was one of them. Your mother . . .' He paused.

She felt her stomach drop again.

'Your mother seems to think . . .' He started again, then stopped.

'My mother respects you very much, Dr Gray. You saved my life.'

'No, I didn't. I lost your baby. I ruined everything for you.'

'Oh my God, no, of course not.' She came over to him and he looked away from her as his shoulders started to shake. 'Oh, God, is that what you've been thinking? Is that what you've been worried about all this time, from me?'

She hesitated, then put one hand on his shoulder, but he continued to look down, his arms still shaking.

'Dr Gray, not for one moment did I ever think anything

other than that you saved my life. Dr Westlake told me as much. He said that if you hadn't called the ambulance when you did, before heading over to the house, it would have been too late. I would have bled to death.'

'But you'd been bleeding a bit the night before and had the back pain, and I should have figured it all out right away, and then I could have saved both you and your baby from all of this.' He straightened himself up and backed away from the table. 'We'll never know what to believe.'

'But *I* know. Isn't that all that matters?'

He took a deep breath and picked up the tea tray. 'Maybe you believe only what you want to.'

'And why would I do that?'

'Because I'm your doctor – I'm everyone's doctor around here – and it's only natural that—'

'You're not my doctor any more, remember?'

'How can I forget? It's the first time I've ever been fired.'

'So it's an *ego* thing with you . . .'

'Look,' he said firmly, 'either way, you have been under my professional care for years, and it would only make sense that you would give me the benefit of the doubt.'

She was feeling confused again and even a little sick to her stomach. 'I'm not giving you the benefit of anything. I believe what I do not because you *were* my doctor, but in spite of it.'

Now it was his turn to feel confused, and he was just about to say something when Liberty appeared in the doorway to the kitchen.

'Everyone is here now, Dr Gray. Even ol' Miss Knight has been let loose – can you believe it?'

'Thank you, Liberty. You can head home now. It is a Saturday after all.'

But Liberty didn't look to be going anywhere. Instead she continued to stand in the doorway, her right hip leaning against the frame, looking from one slightly flushed face to the other. Something was going on between these two, she just knew it. She herself found Dr Benjamin Gray attractive, in a distinguished-older-man kind of way – plus he had that lonely widower thing down pat. She remembered from college how Adeline Lewis had had a crush on one of their professors, and even though she was practically engaged to a boy back home, they were all pretty sure that something had happened. Adeline always had a way about her, a confidence, that men seemed both intimidated by and attracted to. Liberty had even tried to model herself a bit on the other girl, although she would never have told her that.

Adeline Lewis was confident enough as it was.

Mimi Harrison and Yardley Sinclair had taken the noon train to Alton together from Victoria Station. She had spent the journey telling him all about Frances Knight, and the strange little servant girl Evie Stone, and the entail laying waste to everyone's plans for now. Mimi did not know much about the other four members, only that they were three local men of a 'romantic' inclination and a young war widow.

'I always find it interesting how Jane Austen's fans are always romantics to some degree – when I swear she wrote those books with a goose quill dipped in venom,' Yardley was saying over a paper cup of black coffee from the train station café.

Mimi laughed. 'You stole that line – I just saw it in Preminger's film *Laura*.'

'We steal in the auction business, don't you know?'

'*You* steal. And then you hold the rest of us hostage for the highest price. That's quite a system you've got going there.'

'Talking about holding hostage . . . how's that engagement going?'

Mimi made a face at Yardley, who she knew did not care for Jack, although not at all in a jealous way. Yardley preferred men, as he had made clear to her on their second meeting over lunch at Rules, when he had subtly flirted with the waiter in a way that she had not witnessed before outside of L.A.

'Jack is – and I know this is hard to believe – but he is actually a very loving and generous man.'

'To you.'

'Is it wrong of me to care most about that?'

'Mimi, you studied history at college, right? Did you learn nothing?'

She made another face at Yardley, but this time a little less confidently.

'You know he'll never change, though, right?' Yardley persisted with a sigh. 'Tell me that at least, or I will have given up all hope for you.'

'Yardley, this is becoming unfair. We always end up analyzing my relationships, and you get off scot-free.'

'But I don't have relationships. You know this about me.'

'Not through choice, though.'

He looked at her sitting across from him in the first-class cabin, her brilliant eyes set off by the plush purple velvet covering the high-back bench seat facing his. They had not discussed any of this before – but he hoped, and thought, that he could trust her.

'It's a little hard, when you can end up in jail for your efforts.'

'It's the same in the U.S. I know several actors who live together as room-mates in name only, or even as joint tenants. I know one who actually adopted his lover as his son on paper so that he can leave him his life insurance and his estate one day.'

'That's a pretty circular argument against all of these laws to begin with, wouldn't you say? When people have to – and can go to – lengths like that?'

'My father was a judge – did you know that? He always said, trust people to make the best decisions for their bedrooms and leave everything else to the law.'

Her words were such a relief to Yardley that he was uncharacteristically quiet for several seconds before asking, 'Mr Knight's will, by the way – how is Frances handling it? You've seen her a few times since then.'

'She's a remarkable woman. She has this almost eerie – I don't know, preternatural? – calm about her. Total acceptance.'

'Resignation you mean.'

'No, I used to think it was that. But I think she has a higher purpose in mind. I think she has a very different moral system from the rest of us.'

'Isn't that what you're always trying to argue about good ol' Fanny Price?'

'Maybe. I don't know. I just know that on some level she believes that everything is happening for a reason, and she just sort of swims in it, like a cork bobbing about in the ocean, not trying to find the current, just being.'

'Wow. Buddha.'

'Oh, look, we're here!' Mimi jumped up and grabbed her hat and purse. 'Yardley, get ready – you are going to love this place.'

～

Mimi was wearing flat brown riding-style boots for once, and Yardley, who was not particularly tall himself, could now see the top of her head as they walked along together. She had forsaken her usual towering heels so that she and Yardley could make the walk on foot from Alton to Chawton, with Mimi excitedly crowing 'just like Jane Austen would have done!' as they set off up the steep main road through town. But she had also wanted to be a little less physically conspicuous at her first meeting with the society, to the degree that was possible.

When they passed the village common at the triangular perimeter of the Alton town line, they could see ahead the opening up of vast farm fields bordered along the laneway by holly and blackthorn hedgerows. Sheep could be glimpsed through the greenery, and, in the distance, several Shropshire horses could be seen pulling at last year's desiccated fruit still hanging from an orchard grove. On the other side of the laneway was a long row of single dwellings, some of them little thatched cottages and terrace houses set right on the road, others more substantial homes – the old estates, manses and farmhouses of the past – set much farther back and preceded by stately long private drives.

'Well, you weren't kidding,' Yardley was saying as they walked closely together, arms linked. 'Some of these cottages are so small and self-contained, I feel like a bunch of munchkins could pop out at any minute.'

'I think *quaint* is the word you are looking for.' Mimi laughed. 'I love it.'

'I can imagine your face now, when Jack told you he'd bought you that cottage. You must have felt like you'd died and gone to heaven.'

She smiled in recalling the memory. 'That's *exactly* how I felt. So, if you look up ahead at the end of this road, you can see the fields starting up again. The village sits plop in the middle of what feels like one big farm.'

'You know, I never told you this before, but when I was a young lad, I actually dreamt of being a farmer.'

Mimi stopped to stare at Yardley. 'You *are* full of surprises.'

'No, seriously, sometimes I still do. A gentleman farmer though. Back-breaking work and way too dependent on the weather for a full-time vocation.'

Up ahead, they could see a fairly stocky blond man with a cap on his head leaving one of the little cottages on the right-hand side of the lane. Something about him struck Mimi as so familiar.

'Oh my God!' she exclaimed. 'I know that guy! I met him here, years ago, when I was just out of college.'

'Ah, yes, your first pilgrimage.' Yardley watched the man walk slowly up the lane in front of them, his head slightly bowed, two or three books held in the curve of his right arm. 'Very earthy-looking — very D. H. Lawrence. You do have an eye for these things, I'll give you that.'

She playfully whacked Yardley's side with the back of her hand. 'It was so sad — he'd lost both his brothers in the Great War. It was one of the reasons I made *Home & Glory* years later.'

'Oh, yeah, I forgot,' Yardley said facetiously, 'you're a movie star . . .'

Mimi ignored his playful dig. 'He helped me find the graves, remember, of Cassandra and their mother? He'd never read a word of Jane Austen himself, though. It's sad — he looks so, I don't know, lonely somehow. The way he's walking. He looked lonely then, too.'

'Where are we heading, by the way?'

'The first house on the corner of Wolf's Lane, with the rose bushes out front and the green door. A Dr Gray's house.'

They watched up ahead as the man in the cap walked a few more yards and then turned to cross the street at the intersection of Wolf's Lane and Winchester Road. He moved the books to his left arm, then knocked on the green front door of the rose-covered house with his right.

'Well, what do you know?' said Yardley. 'One of the romantics.'

They looked at each other and smiled.

Chapter Twenty-Two

$\mathcal{T}$he first order of business was to welcome Frances Knight, Evie Stone, Mimi Harrison and Yardley Sinclair to the Jane Austen Society and to approve both Frances Knight and Yardley Sinclair as the fourth and fifth trustees of the Jane Austen Memorial Trust. It had already been decided that Mimi should not take on the role and responsibilities of trusteeship, given her permanent residence in the States. And, as with Adam, Evie Stone would also be spared any of the possible legal, financial and administrative burdens of involvement with the trust.

In light of his other role as executor of the Knight estate, Andrew was quick to point out Miss Knight's potential interest in the cottage and the possibility of conflicts arising as a result. Accordingly, Miss Knight agreed to abstain from any vote on the use of trust funds to purchase the cottage or any other property to which she might still end up heir.

'So,' Dr Gray said to the room from his seat near the front

window, 'we have five trustees in place, and a mission statement in the minutes that reflects our goal of acquiring the
cottage as a future museum site in honour of Jane Austen. As
chairman, I move that, in addition to our December motion
to post a notice in the papers seeking public subscriptions, we
now pursue with haste the possibility of any necessary bank
loans.'

'Do we need to act so fast?' asked Evie.

'Yes, I'm afraid,' replied Andrew. 'Although we have no
reason yet to worry, a potential heir could launch a claim at
any point within the next twelvemonth. If they manage to
get a court order in their favour, they could then dispose of
the property, or any portion of it, in whatever manner they
choose. We want to be ready to make a quick offer should that
happen, in the hopes of staving off any other competitive bids.

'Of course, if the estate resolves itself as it should' – Andrew
looked pointedly in Frances's direction – 'Miss Knight could
then do whatever she wanted with the cottage, so long as it is
sold at market value or less. A trustee must not profit – or be
perceived as profiting – unduly from a sale of their own asset
back to the trust. Even at fair market, we'd still need a court
order to approve any such sale by a trustee, although I don't see
any real issue with that, given the charitable purposes of all of
this.'

'Exactly how much money do you need?' Mimi asked from
her seat on the sofa facing him.

Dr Gray glanced quickly at Andrew and gave a little cough.
'Five thousand pounds, give or take.'

'I'd like to help out then, if I may.' Mimi looked about the
room at the faces staring openly in astonishment at the movie
star in their midst. 'I'd like to pledge five thousand pounds to
get this all started.'

Adeline watched with amusement from her chair next to

Dr Gray as both he and Andrew started to chivalrously shake their heads at the offer.

'Miss Harrison, really, that is too generous of you,' Dr Gray spoke up. 'We simply cannot take such a sum from you. I'm afraid we must insist.'

'May I at least provide something of value as collateral then, should you borrow any monies?'

Adeline continued to watch as Dr Gray practically blushed under Mimi's persistence.

'In fact, I brought something here today that I could lend to the society.' She took a small velvet box from her purse on the floor next to her and held it open.

Inside sat the two topaz crosses.

'They were acquired for me recently at auction, ironically for exactly five thousand pounds.'

Andrew got up and came over, well aware of the two necklaces from the Sotheby's catalogue. 'May I?' He held the box up to the front window until the afternoon winter light caught the amber in its dwindling rays.

'They belonged to both Jane and her sister – gifts from their sailor brother,' Mimi was telling them all. 'They are the only known pieces of jewellery belonging to Austen, in addition to a bracelet and this ring. My engagement ring actually.'

A little self-consciously she now took the ring off and held it out before her, then watched as Adam, the farmer she had met years ago, came forward shyly. He held the ring in his hand and showed it to Adeline, who had joined him by his side.

'All these objects are only going to increase in value,' Yardley said, speaking up for the first time from his seat next to Mimi on the sofa. 'The more money we can raise – and fast – the better.'

'Then let's get drafting that advertisement, shall we?' Andrew asked the room.

As the rest of the meeting proceeded, Evie Stone remained in the far corner of the drawing room, sitting on a little piano stool that must have belonged to Dr Gray's late wife. Evie was indulging her always active imagination as she observed the five trustees before her. For months she had been watching the Knight family's lawyer *not* look at Miss Knight whenever he had the chance, and her do the same, and Josephine – as unromantic and tight-lipped as she was – had let something slip once about old Mr Knight wrecking Miss Frances's one chance at love with a smart village boy. On the other hand, Mimi and Yardley seemed to be chummy, but in a familiar, brother-sister kind of way.

But years of reading Jane Austen had made Evie alert to characters who, for whatever reason, can't see things right in front of their noses, and right now she was most intrigued by Adeline Grover and Dr Benjamin Gray.

Dr Gray was sitting on the right-hand side of Adeline, and as she took notes, he would occasionally lean over and point out a word or two that she had skipped or got wrong, and Adeline seemed to be vacillating between letting his hand redirect her pen and smacking it away. At one point, Evie had got up to serve more tea, and when she offered the cup and saucer to Dr Gray, he had immediately taken the pad of paper away from Adeline and leaned back so that the teacup could be passed to her instead. He had then tried to assume the note-taking himself, only for Adeline to reject the cup of tea and firmly take the pad of paper back from him. Dr Gray was known in the village for his chivalry, but his solicitousness towards Adeline at this moment was most noteworthy for her total rejection of it.

Some kind of battle was going on between these two, Evie was convinced. At the recent Christmas Eve gathering, Adeline had been in full mourning, pale and withholding, and uncharacteristically but understandably bitter. Dr Gray had been particularly solicitous towards her then as well, in a way that Evie had recognised as being something beyond mere sympathy for Adeline's situation – and something beyond Evie's own ken.

And there was another moment blazed on her flawless memory – from more than two years past – when Dr Gray had come by the schoolhouse one day, almost sheepishly, to speak to Miss Lewis about her class syllabus. They had been talking about Evie's own father, and the reading list Miss Lewis had given him for his long convalescence, and Dr Gray had smiled teasingly at the teacher and said, 'I'd like to see such a list sometime, if I may.' Dr Gray seemed to have always had more than a passing interest in Adeline, her preoccupations, and her pain, as if she were a mystery of some kind that he were trying to get to the bottom of.

Evie Stone, then all of fourteen years old, had picked up on the feeling that everything being said in the little schoolroom was not at all what was wanting to be said. She wasn't even sure the two grown-ups in front of her knew what that was. There just seemed to be a ton of thwarted energy in the room between Adeline and Dr Gray, as if they were somehow being held back by outside forces, or maybe even forces of their own making. After all, if Evie recalled correctly, Miss Lewis had just become engaged to her childhood sweetheart, and Dr Gray was quite a bit older and already the subject of much village gossip. If they were flirting, it was so subtle and indistinct as to appear undetectable even by them. Evie now wondered if that was how people ended up alone and adrift, like Miss Frances and Mr Forrester. Evie was determined never to become that way in life, for in that direction she saw a quiet but preventable tragedy, if only people could be brave enough to go after what they really wanted.

At times such as this, Evie was grateful to be only sixteen and focused solely on her secret ambitions. There would be time enough for romance one day, but for now it would only get in the way, however much Tom in the stables might circle her, or the much-older Adam Berwick might act so awkward and shy.

But Evie was indeed very young, and perhaps not quite as intelligent as she liked to think.

———

Adam Berwick sat in the opposite corner of the drawing room from Evie. But he was not watching her discreetly or amorously. He, too, had spent his young life in a fog of grief and singular focus, fed by his own world of books. His dreams and ambitions for higher education had been ripped out from under him by the unfortunate toll of the First World War on his family. He had gone to work every day merely to survive, saving for himself a few hours every night to disappear into fictional worlds of others' making. He was hoping to find some answers inside these books, answers for why he didn't care about some things and cared too much about others. He had always felt different from everyone else around him, different in a way that was so essential to his being that it practically blocked everything else out, it was so huge. It was as if a whole other world were inside him, so big that he couldn't see it without somehow getting completely out of his own way. But there was no one to help him do that, and try as he might, he couldn't do it on his own. Not with his innate temperament, the lack of family support, or the particular lessons he had been forced to learn so far in life.

When he first started reading Jane Austen, Adam had immediately identified with Mr Darcy in *Pride and Prejudice*. He had worried about Darcy, about how he could be in such obvious lust with the heroine Elizabeth Bennet and yet make such bewildering social missteps instead – missteps that Adam himself could relate to, despite not being an educated man of property, wealth and high rank.

Darcy just couldn't help himself, that much was clear to Adam – even if it wasn't clear to Darcy. The character would spend over one hundred pages rationalising all sorts of behaviour and reactions, grabbing on to straws, projecting onto Bingley the undesirability of marrying into the Bennet family, and rupturing his best friend's budding romance with the heroine's sister – all the while not understanding his own reasons for acting like this. To Adam's mind, Darcy fancied himself an appointed puppet master, pulling others' strings – the strings of those less able than him in some way, dependent on his intellect and judgement and financial largesse. For the first half of the book at least, Darcy seemed to be using Bingley as a strange sort of proxy for himself – trying to enact through Bingley's and Jane's break-up the extinction of his own feelings for Elizabeth.

Adam had slowly realised, the more he read, that he had made his social self a strange, sad proxy for his true self, too. It was as if he had decided early on not to process certain unspoken attractions, but to retreat instead, and his social person lived one sort of life while his inner self remained closed off even from himself. Now he was nearing forty-six years of age, and his mother was not well. One day soon, she, too, would be gone, and he would live all alone in that empty house until he might as well be gone, too.

Looking about the room, he finally understood that he had hatched the idea of the Jane Austen Society in part because of his loneliness. He had no essential family ties tethering him to any kind of legacy, no one that would miss a thing about him when he was dead. He was wrong about that, of course, as lonely people often are; everyone in the village had grown to rely on him for small chores about their properties, as well as the pleasant and reliable rumbling sound of his wagon heralding the changing of the seasons. The tip of his cap at the doors to the library. The cradling of a new puppy in his arms. The little hand-carved wooden rattles left on the doorstep whenever a baby was born.

He felt gratified, sitting there in Dr Gray's drawing room, that the society was finally taking shape. But he also felt apart from everyone except Evie, whose family circumstances and thirst for learning seemed to equal his own.

And he remained dumbstruck at the vision of Mimi Harrison, who, upon their introduction on the steps of Dr Gray's house, had immediately reminded Adam of their first time meeting over a dozen years ago. He considered it a strange twist of fate, how that one encounter in the parish churchyard had led them both here.

He was also relieved to see that Adeline Grover finally had a bit of her colour back – perhaps even too much of it. She was keeping herself busy taking notes of the meeting. Dr Gray now sat across from her (having moved at some point in a fluster of papers and pens and teacups and chairs), with Andrew Forrester on one side of him and Miss Frances on the other. All three of them as children had been two years ahead of Adam in the little village school, Mr Knight having been too cheap to arrange for his only daughter's education at home. Andrew and Dr Gray had been friendly rivals back then, and at one point were rumoured to have formed a little love triangle with Miss Frances, but Dr Gray had never stood a chance against Andrew Forrester, as far as Adam could tell. Miss Frances had been a noted beauty as a young woman, with her pale grey cat's eyes and long golden tresses kept half up and half loose about her neck, but over time everything had started a slow fade, until the eyes were now pale to the point of haunting, and the hair was greying and kept in a tight bun high up on the back of her head.

That left Yardley Sinclair, sitting next to Adeline, ever intent on her notes before her.

And – just like that – just like it always happens – Adam Berwick was in love.

⁓

Adam walked Adeline home in the darkness as far as her front gate. She was thinking of inviting him in for supper, but he seemed distracted and quite unlike his usual self. She wondered if the launch of the society had been a little too much for him, given how naturally shy he was. She did not recall him saying a single word at the meeting. That was a shame, because on his occasional visits during her recent illness and loss, they had taken to discovering their mutual love of Jane Austen, and she had found him to be an extremely insightful reader of the books.

On this walk home, they had been discussing Adam's favourite character, Elizabeth Bennet.

'I never thought it believable,' Adeline was saying, 'that someone as smart as Lizzie would fall for a cad like Wickham.'

'It was all Darcy's doing,' Adam replied, 'slighting her at that first ball. Gets her back up – makes her *want* to find reasons to dislike him.'

'"She is tolerable; but not handsome enough to tempt me." Ouch.' Adeline laughed. 'It would take some doing to get me back after words like that, I can tell you. But you're so right – she is vulnerable for once to a fake like Wickham because Darcy's hurt her, and it's getting in the way of her seeing things clearly.'

Something about all of this was starting to ring true for Adeline herself, but she quickly pushed the thought out of her head as she rested her gloved hands on top of the gate, feeling it sink a bit on its hinges under the weight.

'Dr Gray asked me today to fix that for you,' Adam remarked. 'I'll be round in the morning.'

'Dr Gray worries too much.'

'Does he?' Adam said quizzically. 'Always seems fine to me. Good chap.'

'Are you sure you won't come in, for some supper?'

Adam shook his head and started to turn back down the lane with a quick wave goodbye behind him. She noticed he was walking in the opposite direction from the small terrace house he shared with his mother. She wondered where else he could be going at this time of night.

She walked up the garden path in the moonlight, bending down frequently to pick up a stray leaf or twig, her compulsion for gardening having returned just in time for spring. As she felt for the front-door key in her coat pocket, she thought she heard a noise behind her and turned around.

Benjamin Gray was standing there in the moonlight, just a few steps from her front door, his hands in his coat pockets, his head bare.

'God, you startled me again. You have to stop doing that.' She turned to open the door, then realised something. 'Did you follow me here?'

He stepped up onto the porch until he was standing over her. 'What were you and Adam talking about?'

'Excuse me?'

'On your walk home together – what were the two of you talking about?'

'I'm not discussing this with you,' she said in irritation, and went to open the door again, but he firmly turned her back round to face him.

'Fine.' She sighed impatiently. 'We were talking about Jane Austen – what did you think we'd be talking about?'

'Are you in love with him?'

'You're nuts, do you know that?' she exclaimed. 'You practically let me get fired, you accuse me of being a drug addict, you do everything you can to push me away all these years . . .'

'What do you mean, pushed you away all these years?'

'My God,' she muttered, 'you even hired my archnemesis from college, a world-class *spy* . . .'

'Adeline, what on earth do you mean, pushed you away all these years?'

She dropped her head beneath his gaze to look down at her boots.

'I don't understand.' He sighed, looking up at the full moon and then down at the ground, too, his right hand across his brow.

'*You* don't understand? Well, then, I must understand too much.'

'Adeline, please, just listen to me.' He tried to take her hand, but she would have none of it.

'Listen to what? Listen to how lonely you are, when both my own husband and baby have been dead and buried less than a year? What incredible timing for you!' Her voice was rising in anger with every word.

'Adeline, please, just let me in, so we can talk about this.'

'No, stop, you're ridiculous – *this* is ridiculous – you have no right, do you hear me?' She turned the key in the lock, but her hands were shaking so hard, she had to retry a few times to open it, all the while muttering, 'You think you can finally wake up and just go and grab the first woman – the first young woman, I might add – who's free? Just because you're looking for someone – for some*thing* – to get you through the night? How dare you! How dare you presume that about me, of all people!'

She pushed the front door open and held it back against his reach.

'Adeline, I did not presume – I don't presume – anything. Surely you know that about me by now.'

'Please go,' she begged, tears starting to stream down her face. 'Can't you see how much you're hurting me?'

She slammed the door in his face, leaving him standing there alone in the darkness, listening to the sound of her sobbing from the inside. He couldn't have made things worse if he'd tried. He would be lucky if Adeline ever even spoke to him again, when he had come there tonight with completely opposite plans, fuelled by consuming jealousy over Adam Berwick and his little gifts to the ladies.

He waited for a few minutes until he heard her crying finally subside, then he marched down the garden path without looking back at the small house behind him, none of its lights on yet. This left him walking in near darkness, except for the moon. He felt as lonely as possible at that moment, with no one to guide him but that impersonal terrestrial orb high up in the sky, glowing for everyone and for no one at all. There was no one else watching over him, no one who cared about his well-being. He had been cheated of that years ago, and then the universe in its infinite unfairness had made a one-sided bargain with him: go back for more pain or get nothing in return.

So now here he was, with nothing in return. Except that he had also managed to get hurt all over again in the process, which took some doing by his count.

When he entered his own darkened house, the first thing he saw in the moonlight was the ring of keys to the medicine cabinet dangling just inside his office door. He could make himself feel better, so easily, and no one would ever know. But somehow Adeline would know – or, at least, he would move one step closer to the ridiculous mess she had just accused him of being, and he wasn't sure he could stand any further sinking in her own eyes or his.

Feeling this bad about himself usually had the opposite effect, usually made him cave in to the pain and the addiction. But after tonight, in a way, he had both nothing left to lose and everything to gain. He wasn't going to move one iota closer to what he wanted if he gave in now. Because if he submitted yet again, he would be continuing on the path he had set for himself several years ago, and that path had led up a garden and right bang into a locked front door, and it would keep doing so, in different ways, with different people, if he was even lucky enough to get another chance at any of that.

He wasn't living in his life, because his life *was* pain. He was living outside his real life instead, and he was using the drugs to help him do that. He had stayed away from the cabinet for several weeks now, ever since his vow to himself in the little church graveyard on Christmas Eve – hiring Liberty Pascal (that 'world-class spy', Adeline had just called her, and he couldn't help but grin right now at her words, despite his distress) had been a huge help in that regard, as the young woman missed nothing. He had been trying to make himself a better man, and right now the reason for that seemed to be slipping away, but that was the trap, after all. If he could resist the temptation at a time like this, when he had nothing left to hope for, then he could always resist it. It was a large cosmic test, and God knows he had failed so many of those before. But although Adeline might no longer be a reason for him to pass, she had conquered her own temptations in her darkest hour, and he would learn any lesson he could from her. She was still the smartest person he knew, and her rejection of him at this moment spoke to that, as much as it surely pained him to admit.

After all, he clearly had quite some way to go before becoming the type of man that deserved her.

Chapter Twenty-Three

Chawton, Hampshire
Midnight, 2 February, 1946

As the meeting was wrapping up, Miss Frances offered to give Mimi and Yardley rooms for the night. Mimi was thrilled at the idea of sleeping in a house once full of slumbering Austens – perhaps even Jane herself in the midst of nursing a feverish niece or nephew, despite living just a short distance away.

The three of them walked the length of the village together with Evie, leaving Andrew Forrester heading in the opposite direction towards Alton and Adam escorting Adeline home. The sun was already starting its descent at 4.30 P.M. on a brisk winter's day, and the shadow of the full moon was waiting patiently above to make its evening appearance. Yardley was peppering Frances with questions about Chawton and its history, and she was gamely answering everything, although she would often refer to Andrew Forrester as the best historian on the village that Yardley would find.

After a late supper in the dining room and drinks by the fire, Evie headed up to her small attic bedroom in the south wing, and Miss Frances to her suite in the opposite corner from Evie's. On the second floor below was her late father's bedroom, the door of which had remained sealed since his passing and burial two weeks earlier. Frances wondered when she would finally find the nerve, if ever, to re-enter the room and go through his papers as Andrew had so politely requested.

The guest bedrooms were in the north wing on the second floor, next door to each other on a separate landing reached by what Frances referred to as the Tapestry Gallery staircase. This was because the stairwell was draped in several medieval armorial tapestries from Flanders, which were making Yardley as quietly excited as Mimi had ever seen him. He was convinced their counterparts were hanging in the Metropolitan Museum of Art in New York, and he was already planning a long-distance call to one of the senior curators there to discuss the possible value.

Having said goodnight to Yardley in the long gallery hallway outside, Mimi entered the stunning Tudor bedroom suite she had been offered. After poking around among the different pieces of furniture, some Georgian, some Edwardian, and some practically medieval, she next took a warm bath in the tub that rested on a raised wooden platform in the far corner of the room, soaking and washing her thick mane of hair so that it would dry while she slept. Despite the coldness of the house in general, a fire raged in her fireplace, courtesy of Josephine, electric baseboard heaters were beneath the windows, and a hot-water bottle was wrapped in wool for the foot of her bed. An old white cotton nightgown had been left out for her as well, and with her sunglasses, powder compact and single red lipstick in her purse, she felt ready to face the outside world in the morning, whether she ended up recognised or not.

Climbing into bed, she immediately pushed her face into the goose-down pillows and tried not to think of Jack. She missed him the most at night, when his body seemed to enclose hers as they lay together, keeping her warm, keeping her bare shoulders covered with kisses, and as she looked about the stately old bedroom, with its canopied bed and wall tapestries, she wondered what he would have thought about all of this. She had telephoned him several times the past few weeks, after he had returned to L.A. following a few days' stopover in Scotland on business. Their month together in England had functioned as a honeymoon of sorts, even though their wedding date was set for April. When she had cabled to tell him of the Knight estate now being up for grabs by any living male heir, and the society being formed in honour of Jane Austen, he had made a crack about never getting her back stateside again. And on nights such as this, as she stared at the full moon through the row of casement windows made of leaded glass panels and diagonal glazing, wondering who else had once stared at the night sky from this very room, she could understand his underlying concern. Mimi had always been one for moving continuously forward, but now that Hollywood was losing interest in her, or, more specifically, her face, she felt this pull to England, and to the past, and to the lives lived in the books that she had spent her own life devouring.

She got out of bed and walked over to the black plastic phone on the vanity table, a modern instrument fully at odds with the rest of the room. Placing a collect call to Beverly Hills, she dragged the phone as far as it would go over to the windows.

'Hey, what time is it?' Jack's own voice sounded slightly groggy.

'Midnight — that puts you at what? Four P.M.? Cocktail hour.'

'Actually, I'm just about to head over to the studio to see Monte.'

She laughed. 'Say hi to him for me.'

'Actually, Mimi, I'm serious.'

'Oh?'

'Yeah, we're partnering in a new distribution company, trying to offset the risk from your *Scheherazade* with our upcoming *Sense and Sensibility*. Monte says the studio will put up fifty per cent in exchange for our covering their exposure to loss with your final film for them.'

'*Scheherazade* isn't going to lose any money,' she asserted, although she was becoming increasingly worried. She had learned the hard way that once money was at risk, few in Hollywood cared about anything else.

'Of course, baby, you and I know that – that's why it's such a great deal for us.'

'For you. A great deal for *you*.'

'Tell me about the book club meeting. Such a little ragtag group you've got there. Who cried the most?' he teased. 'Oh, who am I kidding – it was Yardley. It's always Yardley, that little fruit.'

'It was great,' Mimi cut in, ignoring him. 'I'm starting to think we might really pull this off. You know, there are few places left in England where you could still try and do this – the houses are usually long since demolished and gone, or otherwise unavailable. And that we could be bringing the home of Jane Austen, of all people, back to life—'

'So, Monte and I were talking.'

She heard him clear his throat on the other end of the line. If she didn't know him better, she would have thought he was nervous.

'So, okay, it's looking like the budget for *Sense* is going to approach one mil – but the good news is that we've got half of that now from your old studio.'

'As you just told me.' She found her throat becoming dry,

and cradling the handset under her left ear, she went and poured a glass of cool water from the pitcher left out for her on the bedside table.

'Yeah, well, look – this was never going to be easy to tell you. But the studio has some requests.'

'Of course. Fifty per cent worth of them, I should think.'

'Look, Mimi, this is still our baby, but the studio wants to go in another direction with Elinor.'

'You mean younger.'

'Not necessarily.'

'What the hell does *that* mean?'

'It's just . . . the energy, you know? We need a good complement to Angela Cummings as Marianne, and they feel the chem is a bit off with the age difference.'

'Goddammit, Jack, Greer Garson was a year older than me when she played Lizzie with Olivier – Jesus, she was even older than *Larry*—'

'But Garson had the muscle of MGM behind her and they wanted her in that role.'

'Oh my *God,* Jack – you're the one who told me to go free agent and screw the studio!'

'Honey, honey, calm down, would ya? You're gonna scare Frances Knight out of her frigid bed.'

Mimi took a deep breath. 'I can't believe you're caving in to Monte on all of this – you don't even technically need his cash from what I can tell.'

He was silent for once.

'Jack . . .'

'Look, I bought into a company in Scotland – nothing risky – but I used up some of my cash flow, and I need to cut corners a bit right now.'

'I don't believe you.'

'Listen, Mimi, it's all leverage, you know that. And the

more risk I minimise on this, the more risks I can take else-where. I won't allow myself to put too much on the line. You should know that about me by now.'

Something in his tone worried her more than his giving away the role of Elinor at Monte's request. She felt as if this was the Jack Leonard she should have been getting to know the past year. She had only herself to blame, because clearly he had been there all that time. Sometimes it was better to know the defects of one's partner after all.

'I can't do this right now,' she said into the handset, as she placed the base of the phone back onto the vanity. 'I have to go.'

She hung up and hit the wall with her slender right hand balled into a little fist. She half expected Yardley, sleeping next door, to smack the wall back at her, but there was no respond-ing sound. Everyone else in the house was surely fast asleep by now. It had been a long day.

She went over to the row of windows that looked out onto the expansive front drive and the adjoining woodland and fields of pasture beyond. The outside world, so dark and mys-terious, shimmered in a moonlit haze. She was furious at the other world, the one back home, the much more sadly pre-dictable one where Monte could assault her and then end up in bed with Jack all the same, and no one would ever say a word, would ever say anything that might lose them money and – most important of all – power. Because power was everything – you could get nothing done without it. The longer she stayed away from Hollywood, and the less negoti-ating power she had, the more she wondered if she might not be better off simply torching it all rather than enduring a slow but inevitable decline.

Jane Austen knew about money and power, too, Mimi reminded herself, in the specialness of her surroundings that night. Austen saw what lack of money meant for the women in her life, and this consuming fear was what was telegraphed most loudly in all her books, hidden behind the much more palatable workings of the marriage plot. Austen knew that no amount of charity or largesse from their male relatives could ever grant women real independence. Yet, through her genius – a genius that no amount of money or power could buy because it was all inside her head, completely her own – she had accrued some small degree of autonomy by the end. Enough to work, live and die on her own terms. It really was a most remarkable achievement, the legacy of those six books, revised and spurred on and cast solely by her own two hands, with no man with inevitably more power or money getting in the way.

Mimi realised that this was not altogether true – that perhaps Austen's life might have turned out differently, the canon might have been even more expansive, if some of the men in her family and in the world of publishing had made different decisions on her behalf. But all Mimi knew, standing there in the moonlight, a pawn between two moneymen without an original thought between them, was how much more satisfying and safe it was to be a creator of something that doesn't end with age, but only gets better. She accepted that this was her own Faustian bargain, going to Hollywood and forsaking the stage, where the crow's-feet and grey hairs weren't visible past the first few rows of the house. She had gotten rich and famous at an unheard-of clip, spurred on by her beauty and the fantasising that it generated. And, she suspected, she would lose it all just as fast.

She was about to turn from the window and climb back into bed when she thought she saw someone far off in the distance emerging from the woods. The little shepherd's hut stood on its wheels in the centre of the lime grove, awash in moonlight, and as she opened one of the windows slightly, she thought she could hear something, the shutting of a latch, the footfall of boots on a creaky wooden stepladder. It was probably just her imagination, which was almost as active as Evie's. But as Mimi climbed back into bed and dozed off just past midnight, her half-dreaming thoughts were a strange permutation of the eight members of the society into various couplings: Evie and Adam, Adam and Adeline, Dr Gray and Frances, Frances and Andrew . . .

Evie sat alone in the library. It was late and the rest of the Great House had long since gone to bed, but she found she could still function just fine on four hours of sleep, so she continued to complete her work in the smallest hours of the morning.

The catalogue was now complete. In a frenzy, she had worked through the final volumes the past few weeks and had, after two years, recorded everything of note about each and every book on the shelves. Two thousand, three hundred and seventy-five books to be exact. She had written down publication dates and edition numbers, then described in minute detail the binding and spine labels, the presence of any identifying seals, inscriptions or book plates, the condition of the boards, the presence and number of any illustrations or engravings or marginalia, the gilding of the pages.

Last autumn, she had started going to the Alton library on her days off and researching all the information that might be pertinent to her near-complete catalogue. She had then cross-referenced her findings with recent auction pamphlets and newspaper clippings found in the larger Winchester library on one of three day trips there, trying to learn about recent sales at auction and the condition and appraised value of similar texts.

She was excited to finish up tonight because sleeping just

above her was Yardley Sinclair. When she had attended the reading of James Knight's will and realised that a distant male relative could pop up at any minute and claim the contents of the library as his own, Evie had vowed to complete the cataloguing as soon as possible so that she could finally share with Miss Knight some accurate sense of its total value. When Evie had learned that one of the estate appraisers from Sotheby's would be joining the society – the very Mr Sinclair with whom she had many times ended up on the phone during his extended professional wooing of Miss Knight – Evie now had an equally pressing reason to complete her mission.

Because Evie had done the maths – and if she was even just half as bright as she thought she was, there were possibly tens of thousands of pounds sterling worth of books in this one room alone.

Evie had separated onto two neighbouring shelves the most important volumes, to her mind, which were also the most difficult to appraise. They included a first edition of the posthumous 1817 publication of *Persuasion* and *Northanger Abbey,* with the preface by Jane's brother Henry. There were also inscribed early editions of the books Austen had written and lived to see published, some of them still in fragile plain boards, which made them even rarer than the custom-bound versions more widely available on the market back then. There was the mysterious 1816 Philadelphia printing of *Emma* that had somehow made its way over the pond; first editions of Samuel Richardson's *Pamela* and Fanny Burney's *Camilla,* and *Corinne* by Madame de Staël; and an early edition in French of Dante's *Divine Comedy.* A Third Folio edition of the collected works of Shakespeare could not even be properly valued, so rarely had it ever come up for sale, according to the research Evie had done one Sunday afternoon at the British Museum. And, most amazing of all, there was the letter from Jane to Cassandra that

Evie had found last September tucked and hidden inside an old Germanic textbook. A letter that the world did not know existed. A letter that answered a few questions scholars had had for decades – and raised many more.

As Evie sat on her little stool, her completed catalogue open on her lap, she felt the ecstasy of discovery. The passion of learning. The pride of having achieved something no one else had done before. She was not quite seventeen, and the village boys might circle round for a few years more, but she could not imagine a feeling more complete, more satisfying, than what she was experiencing at this moment. She thought of the famous Arctic explorers crossing flat white lands of ice, and Captain Cook sailing to the Pacific, and the men who had started and fought wars over the centuries, and all that male energy going outward, seeking to conquer, seeking to own. And she had gone inward in a way, into the confines of a neglected old house, not even truly a home any more. She had seen the thing right under everyone's eyes, and she hadn't let it go or been subsumed by the rigours of daily life. She had made space for discovery in the midst of a most contained life – the life that the world seemed bent on handing her. She had watched Miss Frances float through that world like a ghost, and Adam Berwick sit alone atop his old hay wagon, and Dr Gray walk through town with that strange faraway look in his eyes, as if he were looking past reality, past pain, to a kinder, gentler world. But a world that did not exist. For the world that really existed demanded the pain, and the living with it, and would never let you go, even when everything else fell away.

Yet, even while immersed in that same world, Evie Stone had carved out something new and enlightening and earth-shattering, all on her own and on her own terms. No one could ever take that away from her.

'Evie, what on earth are you doing in here at this hour?'

She looked up to see Yardley Sinclair standing in the threshold of the doorway leading from the Great Hall next door. He was staring at the little notebook open on her lap, in which she had just been scribbling furiously. He looked behind him and then, firmly but quietly shutting the door, took a step towards her.

'I might ask you the same thing,' she replied, leaving him silently impressed by her temerity.

'I was given a little peek in here earlier by Miss Frances, but there wasn't time to see more. And then I found I couldn't get to sleep, so thought I'd come down and get something to read.'

He took another step towards her and she quickly closed the notebook before her.

'Evie, does Miss Frances know you are in here?'

She nodded but stayed sitting on her little stool in the corner.

'Does she know what you are doing?'

She nodded again, but this time more slowly. 'But only recently. After the will had been read.'

Yardley could tell that the young girl was going to stay firmly rooted in place, so he reached for a chair and pulled it out in front of her. 'Do you mind?' he asked, this time more gently than he had been addressing her so far.

She shook her head, and he sat down across from her and held out his hand. 'May I have a look?'

So many scenarios were suddenly playing themselves out in Evie's mind, and she was far too young and inexperienced in the world of business to know what might be at risk by disclosing everything now, before she had even had the chance to share it all with Miss Frances. She was also troubled by how Yardley seemed to be having his run of the place after hours, on his very first visit. Maybe he was just an insomniac, but she had watched him as closely as anyone at the meeting that afternoon, and he had a most inquisitive eye. Evie's self-appointed job, right now, was to protect Miss Frances and obtain as much value for her from the estate as Evie could – she just hoped that nothing she was about to do might derail any of that.

Evie also knew that Mimi wholeheartedly trusted Yardley, and Evie was in thrall to Mimi, both as a movie star and a fellow Austen scholar. So with some hesitation she held out the notebook and watched, quite gratified, as Yardley flipped through its pages with increasing astonishment.

'My God, Evie.' He looked at her, tears in his eyes.

She nodded happily.

Then he started to laugh, dabbing at his eyes with a mono-grammed handkerchief from his pocket, and she found herself laughing, too.

'My God.' He stood up and started running his fingers along the spines of all the books on the shelf right behind him. 'It's all in here, isn't it – everything she probably read – everything she read while she wrote those unbelievable books? And all these first editions. It's unbelievable. It's like a miracle.' He whirled around to look at Evie. 'And no one really paid attention to any of it before?'

She finally stood up, too, and he realised anew how tiny she was.

'According to Miss Frances, her father – the late Mr Knight – and his father before him, they neither of them had much time for Austen. Didn't get the fuss.'

Yardley was randomly pulling out different books now, flipping through them, realising just how minute and precise were the descriptions Evie had been allotting them in her little notebook.

'You know, Evie, you're too young to appreciate this, but Austen's books actually went out of print after her death. When Frances's father was born, back in – what was it she said earlier, 1860? – the books hadn't even approached their zenith in the Victorian era. It wasn't until the turn of the century that critical consensus really started to coalesce. I don't even think the first essay on Austen was until Bradley's at Oxford in 1911.'

'Oh, I know that.'

He laughed again. 'Yes, that was silly, of course you do.'

She had been saving the best for last. She went over to a shelf near him, took out the text on Germanic languages that was part of an imposing multivolume set and opened it up before him. Inside its pages, as if marking the place, was a folded-up piece of yellowing paper, covered in deeply slanted, familiar handwriting.

Yardley took a deep breath. 'Are you joking?'

'It's the only one, though – I'd really hoped to find others. But it's an important one. It explains a lot.'

'Can I open it?'

She nodded. 'It's not at all fragile – I think it's been in here for over a hundred years, untouched. And it was not finished, and it was never sent. She must have been interrupted and lost track of where she'd put it. Or' – and here Evie got quite emotional – 'she was getting quite sick, I think, at least enough to worry her. And perhaps she just forgot about it, or bigger things took over, and she stopped caring about what she had had to say.'

Yardley took the letter gingerly from the book and sat down to read it. When he was finished, he took a second to compose himself. It was the single greatest discovery of his career, and one of the most important finds yet in Austen scholarship.

'You realise the date here? August 6, 1816? The day she finished writing *Persuasion*.' And then he started to laugh again. 'Of course you do.'

Evie nodded and came over and sat back down across from him. 'Cassandra wasn't far, just a small trip away to some relatives, it sounds, and yet Austen wasn't going to wait one second longer to say what she had to say to her older sister. Imagine finishing those final, incredible chapters of *Persuasion* and then turning straight to writing this letter. That says something. It says some things that are pretty amazing about her—'

'—And also some that aren't,' Yardley cut in. 'And yet how alive, how real – how *human* – she seems now.'

He read through the letter again, which was cut off abruptly halfway down the back of the single page.

'So Cassandra intervened, then, after all, in the budding romance with the seaside stranger.'

'I don't have sisters – I have four very awful brothers – but that bond Cassandra and Jane had seems so intense. As if they were their own little family. Like Jane and Elizabeth Bennet, holding in the eye of the storm, everything to each other, leaving little room for anyone else. Easy enough for Cassandra, I suppose, having lost her fiancé so young, making her essentially a respectable widow of sorts. But where did it leave Jane?'

'You know,' Yardley mused aloud, 'I always thought it odd that the family of some random guy from a seaside town, a guy Austen presumably had met only that one holiday month, would have written to inform her of his death. Letters must have been going back and forth between the two of them. Or the family knew there was a relationship of some kind, even if just in its early days.' Yardley sat back and placed the open letter carefully on his lap. 'So she blamed Cassandra for the romance ending. For all those years.'

'The missing years. All those letters from the same time period gone, destroyed by Cassandra. We've always known that. But we never knew why.'

'Until now.'

'Until now,' agreed Evie, sitting there on her little stool, nodding happily at Yardley's enthusiasm for her discovery.

'So' – he passed the letter back into her waiting hands and stood up, too full of excitement to stay seated – 'so *Persuasion* was indeed her revising of her own life. Her working through the great disappointment. Her working through her residual anger at her sister.'

'By writing this, I think she tried to put a lid back on that anger for good. I think she knew she was not long for this world, and she wanted peace in her heart, full and total peace, and writing this marked the final forgiveness of her sister. And she needed to feel that, needed to be free of it.'

'You know, it's so strange, but I always wondered if someone like Jane Austen could have existed in the pages of her own books. If you think about it, if Cassandra hadn't interfered when Jane was – what, twenty-three years old? Twenty-four? – who knows what might have happened. We might never have got the three final books of genius if Austen had gotten her man in the end.'

'I think Austen knew that only too well,' Evie replied. 'Especially when you think about so many women at that time dying in childbirth, at least two of her very own sisters-in-law, and her fear about all of that, too. The letters that do survive say as much.'

'Evie, I know we don't know each other very well. . . .'

'Oh, no, I think we do.' She smiled at him. 'I think we are very alike.'

He laughed again. 'Yes, poor thing, we are. Is the catalogue complete then, well and done?'

'Yes, tonight. I finished it all tonight.'

He shook his head at her. 'Amazing. Truly. Listen, will you trust me with this, with the notebook?'

'Yes,' she answered slowly. 'I can't let you take the letter though. But I made a copy.'

'Of course you did. No, you are absolutely right, you cannot risk losing or disturbing any of the contents in here. Your estimations are right-on, by the way. We're looking at a hundred thousand pounds at least, if not hundreds. It would be one of the greatest estate-library sales in history, whoever inherits it. We have to do everything we can to keep this intact for now, *everything* – for Miss Frances, for the society, yes, but most importantly for our understanding of *her*.'

'I completely agree,' Evie said. 'I was hoping you would feel the same way.'

'We both love Jane Austen,' he replied with a wink. 'Why ever would we not?'

Chapter Twenty-Four

Alton, Hampshire
February 1946

*C*olin Knatchbull-Hugessen was an indiscreet and silly man of forty-two years of age. He had been living the bachelor life in a small row house on the outskirts of Birmingham. One day in February, as he was checking the racing times in the morning paper, his eye caught the following announcement in *The Times*:

> *Notice of the establishment on 22 December, 1945, of a society dedicated to the preservation, promotion and study of the life and works of Miss Jane Austen. The Jane Austen Society is working with the Jane Austen Memorial Trust, a charity founded to advance education under the Charities Act, to acquire Miss Austen's former home in Chawton as a future museum site. Subscriptions and donations of funds from interested members of the public, to advance this purpose, are welcome and may be remitted to the Jane Austen Memorial Trust, care of Andrew Forrester, Esq., High Road, Alton, Hampshire.*

At the very same moment that Colin was skipping quickly past this announcement, he received a telephone call from his late mother's solicitor with the news that James Edward Knight was dead.

The solicitor had learned of the death through remarkable diligence. Since being retained by Colin's mother decades earlier, he had had his clerk check the principal probate registry in London every three months to search for the surnames Knight, Knatchbull and Hugessen. He also sent his clerk every few months to Winchester to check the local Hampshire registry as well, knowing his late client had been a direct descendant of Fanny Austen Knight Knatchbull, the eldest of the eleven children of Edward and Elizabeth Knight. The lawyer was worried that a will might enter probate and Colin's chance to claim an inheritance from such a vast and landed family could be missed within the twelve-month window provided for at law.

Colin was less concerned with his family tree than the lawyer. The news of James Knight's death moved him not at all. He had no real connection to the family, and little interest in genealogy or history in general. He liked to visit his local pub for a pint – or two – every afternoon, bet on the horses, go to football matches and occasionally bed the waitress at that same pub in exchange for small gifts of a varying nature.

Over the telephone, the lawyer carefully explained to Colin the potential windfall he could receive through the death of this distant relative connected to the world-famous writer Jane Austen. To Colin's mind, Austen was a romance novelist of some kind, although he had enjoyed the Laurence Olivier– Greer Garson adaptation of *Pride and Prejudice* a handful of years ago. He also knew that his most unsuccessful attempts to bed ladies of a certain age seemed proportionately connected to their love of this writer – which had probably contributed to a certain enmity he felt towards the authoress on his own behalf.

The lawyer urged Colin to appear in person at the Hampshire probate registry to file a claim under the Inheritance Act as promptly as possible. In the meantime, the lawyer would write to the executor on record for the estate, a Mr Andrew Forrester, explaining the entitlement of Colin Knatchbull-Hugessen, as the closest living male relative of James Knight, to the latter's entire estate, excluding the right to residence in the Chawton cottage held by Frances Elizabeth Knight and the living allowance, and the gifts in stipend for the servants.

This was the letter that Andrew Forrester read to Frances Knight two weeks before the next scheduled monthly meeting of the Jane Austen Society.

He had asked her to come to his offices in Alton. He suspected that she had not visited the town in several years, even though it provided all the major shopping, banking and commerce for the region. But since her father's death, Andrew had noticed a subtle change in Frances – whether it be attending the second society meeting at Dr Gray's, or inviting Mimi Harrison and her Sotheby's friend back to the Great House afterwards to stay the night. He wondered if Frances would walk the forty minutes to his offices, as she remained surprisingly healthful for all her time indoors, or take her late father's Rolls-Royce out for a drive. He knew that Tom had been given permission to drive the old car on occasion, having argued to James Knight that the car, like his horses, needed the exercise.

When Frances arrived at Andrew's offices on foot instead, he noticed that the tight bun in her once-golden hair had loosened somewhat, her cheeks were rosy from the winter wind and her pale grey eyes shone brightly from the exercise. Suddenly she looked so much like the young woman he had once loved that he caught himself staring at her as if at an old photo in a frame. Motioning for her to sit down before him, he went back to his own seat behind his large banker-style desk and gave his typical introductory cough.

'I received a letter this morning that I am obligated to share with you as executor of the estate.' Frances sat up even straighter in her chair. 'It is from the solicitor for a Mr Colin Knatchbull-Hugessen, who claims to be the third cousin, twice removed, of your late father. And I'm afraid it speaks to a very plausible claim against the entirety of your late father's estate.'

Frances listened carefully as Andrew read the letter, keeping his eyes down on the paper the entire time. When he had finished, he finally looked over at her.

'Well, that's it then,' she said calmly. 'He surely has standing for his claim, and I am no one to fight against reality, as you well know.'

It was the first time she had ever alluded, even subtly, to her submission to her father's will in the face of Andrew's secret proposal and engagement to her in 1917, when she had not yet turned of age and he was about to be called up to the navy.

'Miss Knight' – Andrew pushed the sheet of paper across the desk towards her – 'I still believe there is an argument to be made for your father's mental capacity at the time of the execution of the second will.'

Frances shook her head. 'Andrew, I am fine with all of this, really. The will gives me a roof over my head for life, and money enough for the few things I need.'

'It's not about what you need. It's about your father honouring your lifetime of sacrifice to the family. Give all the money away at the end, if you want. You will surely – from the sounds of it – dispense with it more charitably than this Colin Knatchbull.'

'I don't see how any of that will be possible. And I see no

value in focusing on the impossible right now. I have enough for a good life, which is more than many others can say.'

Frances rarely asked for anything and just as rarely complained. Andrew could see that she needed to be heeded in this matter – that she must know what was best for herself now, no matter the mistakes he believed her to have made in the past. Perhaps he was even pushing the issue to make up for his own mistakes with regard to their shared history. For when she had written that final letter to him at sea, breaking off their engagement, he had vowed never to speak to her again if he was lucky enough to survive the war. Instead he had returned a naval hero, resumed his law studies at Cambridge and built up the most successful practise in the greater county. Then, one day in 1932, James Knight had walked through Andrew's office door to retain him in the investigation of his son Cecil's death from what the police were calling a shooting accident. Even then, as Andrew Henry Forrester became increasingly relied upon by the fading patriarch in all his legal and financial matters, he had hewed as closely as possible to his secret vow to never again say another word to Frances Elizabeth Knight.

While away at war, Andrew had been surprised that Benjamin Gray had not tried to scoop Frances up for himself. But, in 1918, Benjamin had fallen head over heels in love with a beautiful young scientist at King's College London, near the end of the medical studies that had prevented his own conscription. Andrew understood Ben well, knew him to be brilliant and caring but flawed like any man, with a propensity for a saviour complex. Andrew's propensity, like Frances's, was to be a martyr instead, and for years the two of them had resisted any interaction, while never building a life with anyone else. Yet recently, as her father's health increasingly failed, Frances and Andrew had found themselves living a type of proxy version of married life, occasionally breaking bread together, walking the Great House's landscape to discuss various improvements to come out of the estate, and administering to Mr Knight's every whim.

So Andrew listened carefully to Frances when she told him that she did not want to fight the will. A small reserved corner of his heart wondered if this decision was ironically part and parcel of her greater independence now that Mr Knight was gone. To Benjamin, Andrew had accused Frances of letting herself be boxed in by her father, but the woman before him did not seem trapped. She had a calm about her instead, as if she finally knew what, and whom, she could count on. For it was never as much as any of us like to hope – the key was to know whom one could trust to be there and when, in good times and in bad. As the only daughter of Mr Knight, she had been required to accord him his deference and his due, all the while suspecting deep down how he really felt about her. At least she no longer had to pretend. There was liberation in that, however emotionally cruel to endure.

'Well, if you are sure then, I shall write the lawyer back and agree to this visit that Mr Knatchbull-Hugessen would like to make to the estate. The claim will be filed anon, I am confident of that. And he can kick you out of this house once the court has approved him as the sole beneficiary. He has a most diligent and shrewd lawyer – I suspect any such approval will be obtained in record time.'

'That's all right. Evie and I have already started packing. She is intent on rescuing certain volumes from the library for me, and the balance for the Austen Society. Do you anticipate any issues there?'

'Not necessarily, but you should get a valuation done as soon as possible – the trustees can then vote to make an offer to Mr Knatchbull-Hugessen for the contents of the library and, hopefully, for the steward's cottage as well. But leave me out of any assessment, all right? I will abstain, as discussed, from any society meeting or voting to acquire, and the offer can then be made by the trust directly to the declared heir.'

'How soon might he visit?'

'I suppose anytime.' Andrew looked at her with one eyebrow raised expectantly.

'Perhaps ' – she looked back at him, equally expectantly – 'perhaps we should call an emergency meeting of the society? To advise them of Mr Knatchbull's claim, and to vote on making an offer for the books and the cottage, just in case he is inclined to dispose of anything fast himself?'

Andrew nodded in agreement. 'But you'll want that valuation done first – Yardley might be able to help, although I worry about any impact on his professional reputation if it's not done strictly to the letter.'

'I have good news then.' Frances had a surprising smile on her face. 'Evie's already done one and handed it over to Yardley for his appraisal.'

'You're joking.'

She shook her head happily. 'Not at all. It's really quite impressive. She's been at it for two whole—'

Andrew put his hand up to silence her and she bit her lip in acquiescence. Then he stood up, shuffled the papers about on his desk and looked straight at Frances Knight for once.

'But just so you know, just between the two of us, I am hoping, as executor of the estate *and* as a friend, to be completely taken advantage of by the young Evie Stone and her rapacious eye.'

Chapter Twenty-Five

Chawton, Hampshire
19 February, 1946
Emergency Meeting of the Jane Austen Society

The meeting was quickly held, at seven the following evening, in the front parlour of Dr Gray's house. Five members of the Jane Austen Society were in attendance: Dr Gray, Adeline, Adam, Mimi, and Evie.

Andrew and Frances had abstained from attending both the discussion and the vote. Yardley was unable to get down from London with Mimi on time, which at first worked out well since Andrew feared that Yardley's reputation and employment at Sotheby's could be jeopardised by any involvement in an amateur appraisal with such significant financial repercussions for the parties involved.

That left only Adeline and Dr Gray for a vote by the trustees of the Jane Austen Memorial Trust. Three votes – a majority of the five trustees – would be necessary to establish the majority required according to the law of meetings in parliamentary procedure. After some to and fro between Andrew

Forrester and Yardley over the phone, Mimi was designated Yardley's proxy for the vote. The reasoning of both gentlemen was threefold: Sotheby's had no legal or financial interest, or anticipated interest, in the Knight estate at the time of voting; Yardley would not be personally or professionally profiting from his vote, and he was willing to sign an affidavit to that effect; and – finally – as a director, Yardley was permitted to use his expertise in cultural and literary valuation for the good of the trust's charitable objectives.

After the meeting was called to order and the imminent vesting of the Knight estate in Mr Knatchbull-Hugessen of Greater Birmingham was announced, Dr Gray called for a vote on presenting an offer to the heir of the estate for the contents of the Chawton House library and the leasehold interest of the steward's cottage.

The vote was swiftly carried.

'We next need to vote on an appropriate purchase price for the library, as it has no present market value. Evie,' announced Dr Gray.

The young girl stood up from her regular perch on the little stool by the piano. She held in her hands the notebook that contained a cataloguing of all two thousand, three hundred and seventy-five books in the library, plus one loose-leaf letter. The notebook was passed around to each of the other four attendants.

'So you're saying, from what I can tell, that some of these particular editions have not appeared in a public notice of sale before?' began Dr Gray as he flipped through the notebook in astonishment.

Evie nodded.

'Has Mr Sinclair seen this?' Adeline asked.

'Yes, when he stayed over the night of our first meeting. He came in rather late to the library and caught me at work. I showed him some of the volumes, and he took the notebook away for a bit to study.'

'And?' asked Dr Gray eagerly.

Mimi spoke up now. 'I looked it over with him earlier today in London, before my train, and brought it back with me. It's a good thing you're all sitting down – he thinks, based on the public records he has access to, that we are talking anywhere from one hundred thousand pounds upwards.'

'How far upwards?' asked Adam.

Mimi looked at Adam, who was now standing with Adeline behind Dr Gray, both of them examining the notebook over his shoulders. 'Well, the Third Folio of Shakespeare alone is potentially worth ten thousand pounds or more. There are also dozens of first editions of critical eighteenth-century texts, both fiction and non-fiction. *The First Book of Urizen* by William Blake and the first edition of *Don Quixote* each figure into the tens of thousands of pounds as well.'

'This is absolutely astonishing,' exclaimed Dr Gray. 'Evie, my God, do you know what you have here?'

Evie had the look of pride of scholarship and achievement written all over her face. 'Yes, of course – that's why I did it.'

The last item in the notebook was not a book entry at all, but the letter from Jane Austen to Cassandra Austen, dated 6 August, 1816.

'That's the month she finished writing *Persuasion*!' exclaimed Adeline.

'Why . . .' Dr Gray looked up at Evie and Mimi. 'My God. It can't be.'

Evie and Mimi smiled at each other. 'We would have told you sooner, but Miss Frances needed to keep this all extremely confidential, for obvious reasons,' Evie explained. 'She and I were the only people in the world to know, until Yardley, and then Mimi here this afternoon.'

Dr Gray started to read the copy that Evie had diligently made of the letter, the original still hiding safely within the flap of one of the two thousand, three hundred and seventy-five books in the lower library. Evie informed them all as he read that she had checked out Jane Austen's deeply slanted handwriting in the *Persuasion* manuscript on display at the British Museum during one of Evie's Sunday outings there, to make sure that her 'translation' was competent and complete.

Dr Gray fell back in his chair and wordlessly held the copy up for Adeline to take next. She carried it over to the light near the piano and read it standing next to Adam.

Everyone in the room was speechless.

Finally Adeline said, 'Do we have any idea on the value, at all?'

'Not really,' replied Mimi. 'Yardley checked everywhere – so few have ever come up for auction. One letter sold in 1930 at Sotheby's, but only for a thousand pounds.'

'It's not the value, though,' spoke up Dr Gray.

'It's what we learn,' added Adam, and everyone in the room turned to look at him.

'Yes,' Evie stated proudly. 'There is no price on that.'

'But it's still in its rightful place, correct?' questioned Dr Gray. 'We can't afford to be accused of hiding or stealing any-thing.'

'No worries at all. I only moved the books about as I dusted,' Evie replied. 'If Mr Knatchbull-what's-his-face wants to take stock of what's in there, he is welcome to it.'

'Well, then, what do we think?' Dr Gray asked the room.

'Forty thousand pounds,' said Mimi without hesitation. 'I have been tracking Jane Austen sales through Sotheby's and Christie's for several years now, and with the war, things stayed pretty flat until recently. If we average out each book at twenty pounds, that will look completely reasonable to any-one inclined to sell quickly.'

'But where on earth will we get that much money?' Adeline asked.

Mimi looked about the room. 'From me.' She stood up. 'I know you all have been hesitant to take any money from me, but, as I understand it from Andrew, public funds are only slowly trickling in from the notice we posted in *The Times*. Look, it's fine, it's a movie or two – without sounding arro-gant, I mean. I have more than enough anyway. And God knows my fiancé does, too. Then, once the books unrelated to Jane Austen are sold off at the appropriate time and place, the trust will have tens of thousands of pounds to purchase the cottage and as many Austen artefacts as it chooses, as well as to generate enough interest on the capital for future endeavours.'

Adeline and Dr Gray looked at each other, then back at Mimi.

'You will allow us to pay you back, though, once the trust realises such profits from the sale?'

'If you insist.' Mimi smiled. 'I have the utmost faith in both Yardley and Evie here that the library's sale will enrich the trust by that amount many times over.'

'Well, then,' announced Dr Gray, 'let's put this to a vote.'

By the time the meeting was over, it was too late for Mimi to get to Alton and catch the London train back to her hotel. Adeline offered her one of her two spare bedrooms, to save the mile walk back to the Great House, and Mimi acquiesced, so exhausted by the exciting events of the night that she was will-ing to forgo another night's sleep in a place steeped in Austen history.

As they approached Adeline's front garden in the moon-light, Mimi looked back down the quaint village lane behind them. 'Dr Gray seemed in a better mood tonight than at the last meeting.'

'I guess earth-shattering historical discoveries will do that to a man,' Adeline replied.

'The two of you seemed to be getting along better, too. That last meeting, I swear I thought you were going to tear a strip off him. If you don't mind me asking, I always wondered, what was going on there?'

'Just a misunderstanding, I think.' Adeline held the gate open to let Mimi pass, still a little intimidated by the famous actress, through no fault of her own. Adeline was increasingly impressed by the glamorous actress's education and acute un-derstanding of Austen, as well as her very real and down-to-earth manner. Adeline didn't think it was just an act, either – Mimi seemed to be completely lacking in competitive edge and wholly focused on her own tasks before her. Adeline was the same way – it was, she felt sure, what made her such an easy target for women such as Liberty Pascal, who spread their ten-tacles far and wide in a constant overswoop, intent on a range of victims.

'Really – a misunderstanding? Dr Gray doesn't strike me as the kind of man who gets things wrong.'

'I think he thought there was something going on between Adam and me. Which is obviously completely ridiculous.'

'Obviously.'

The two women looked at each other for a second, eye-brows raised suggestively, each waiting for the other to speak.

'Is it usual for a doctor to take such an interest in the roman-tic life of his patient?'

'He has become somewhat protective of me since the baby,

I think. Since what happened. I worry – I know – that he blames himself.'

Mimi put her arm around the other woman's waist as they headed towards the front door. 'Oh, Adeline, I was so very sorry to hear of your loss. I should have said something sooner.'

'Please don't worry. Dr Gray really shouldn't worry either. Especially now that he technically isn't my doctor any more.'

Now Mimi raised an eyebrow at Adeline in interest. 'Really? When did that happen?'

'Just . . . a month ago? Maybe more?'

Adeline unlocked the front door and Mimi followed her in.

'So, like I said, there's plenty of room upstairs, now that my mum has seen fit to move back home and leave me alone again. In fact, when we hopefully acquire that library full of books, we can store them here – I will surely still have space for them. Yours will be the second room on the right.' Adeline glanced at the grandfather clock at the end of the hall. 'It's not quite ten yet – would you like anything to drink before you head up?'

'I'd love that – mind if I go and poke around while you're at it?'

Adeline smiled and headed back to the kitchen, while Mimi entered the front drawing room to the right. She found a table lamp and switched it on, and immediately noticed the improvised window seat, now almost sinking under the weight of all the books. Asleep on a pile of cushions was an adorable kitten with a brown-and-ginger coat. It reminded Mimi of the tabby she saw wandering around the gardens of the steward's cottage whenever she took a peek over its old brick wall.

Perusing through the stacks, she retrieved a particularly tattered-looking book, then found another lamp next to the sofa. She switched the light on and, taking a seat, kicked off her heels to casually pull her feet up onto the cushion.

When Adeline came back, she brought with her two tiny glasses of sherry.

'Thank you, that's so nice. I always have a nightcap with Jack when he's in town. My fiancé.' Almost as soon as the words left her mouth, Mimi caught sight of the wedding photo on the mantel, looking still brand-new in its shiny silver frame. She couldn't even begin to fathom the amount of loss Adeline had endured in just that past year. 'How are you doing, Adeline? I mean really?' she asked quietly.

Adeline sat down on the sofa facing Mimi. 'I'm not sure. I'm not sure there's even a word for how I'm doing. I do think that's what Dr Gray is worried about the most.' As Adeline spoke, she looked increasingly sad and confused. 'No matter what, until now, Dr Gray and I have always at least respected each other, even though we are different in so many ways. Being a man and a woman thrown together on opposite sides at work can be trying.'

Mimi laughed. 'Yes, I know – I am about to pledge myself for life to someone who would cast Lassie in a movie over me if it would make him more money.'

Adeline laughed, too. 'He sounds like a real charmer.'

'Oh, he *is* that. He's this fascinating mix of little-boy vulnerability and fearless energy. He really makes me up my game. And I am no wallflower, as you could probably guess from my choice of career. But back to Dr Gray and you – you said the word *respect* . . .'

Adeline looked down at the amber liquid in her sherry glass and swirled it about. 'I think he is disappointed in me. In how I've been coping with everything.'

'Oh, Adeline, really, I can't imagine that. I can't imagine he would judge – a widower of all people.'

'But that's just it – he, too, has suffered, and yet he keeps on going and listens to everyone else's much smaller problems, and does it all with such wisdom and calm, almost too much calm if you ask me.'

'Not all the problems are smaller. And one never really knows what others do to cope – you'd be surprised. There's coping and then there's just getting through the night.' She saw Adeline look up quickly at this last remark, as if something was dawning on her, but Mimi now knew better than to press when it came to Adeline and Benjamin Gray. 'And anyway, as far as I can tell, I think Dr Gray feels nothing but the utmost respect for you. Even, perhaps, a little too much. Well, except for maybe your note-keeping.'

Adeline laughed again. 'He's just much more thorough. He and Andrew both. Thank goodness for them or our meetings would devolve into hours-long comparisons of who is the bigger cad: Henry Crawford or Willoughby.'

'With Adam taking up the charge. You know, it's funny, I've never really thought about it, but I'm not sure that respect is what attracts Jack to me. Or me to him, for that matter.'

'Respect in friendship is critical – and of course in marriage, too. But perhaps you share other qualities or attractions that are simply much more intense. Certainly you are both so successful in your work, and you would respect that.'

'Yes, I suppose that's so,' Mimi agreed, nodding thoughtfully. 'I mean, Darcy and Elizabeth surely respect each other, even though they are so different. And Anne Elliot and Captain Wentworth of course. Knightley with Emma, on the other hand, I am not so sure. Yet they share a deep affection and attraction to each other all the same.'

Adeline sipped her sherry contemplatively. 'Maybe Knightley would respect Emma more if he didn't see her so clearly – maybe what bonds them together is that very willingness to love her so clear-eyed. He can help her that way, help her steer towards the truth, and do the right thing, whenever her over-indulged spirits start to get in the way.'

'Wow, you really don't care for Emma, do you? I have to admit, she's my favourite.'

'Oh, I know – Adam told me.'

'He did?' Mimi laughed. 'How on earth does he know that?'

'You told him. Years ago. When you were first here. He really wanted to like her, too. But Adam and I are all about Lizzie. Dr Gray on the other hand is a huge fan of Emma, like you – he loves how she just owns what she wants, no apologies, and sustains strong relationships without any compromise. He finds her so charismatic, how others just bend to her will.'

Mimi was watching Adeline carefully. 'My dear, that sounds a little bit like you.'

'Oh, no, not at all. I might be direct, but I have no problem with compromising, when it's called for.'

Like Evie, Mimi had been watching Adeline and Dr Gray with her professionally honed powers of observation, and compromise seemed to be the last thing these two were capable of.

'I compromised with Samuel all the time,' Adeline was saying. 'We weren't married long at all, but we grew up together, and so many times he had wanted to get married, and I wasn't ready – I'm still not even sure why – it just all felt too comfortable, you know? But then he got drafted, and suddenly certain things no longer seemed that important.'

'Forgive me for saying this, Adeline, but agreeing to marry someone should never feel like a compromise.'

Adeline nodded. 'I know. I think I was just too weighted down by our history together to ever feel like I was actually making a choice. Maybe *compromise* was the wrong word. Maybe it was just—'

'—Resignation? Oh, believe me, my dear, we have all been there.'

'All I know is that I really loved him, I really did, deeply. And now I have no one. And everyone wants me to just go on. It's been a year, they'll say, it's time to get out. Take walks. Long walks. Go to the cinema. Just get out there again and live.'

Mimi shook her head sadly at the young widow. 'Adeline, my father killed himself when I was very young, and it impacts me even as we sit here. It is a part of me, that awful, irrevocable act. And I am never going to be quite whole again because of it. You are not the problem: the loss is.'

Adeline looked up at Mimi with tears streaming down her cheeks. It was the first time she had let herself cry since that awful night outside in the garden with Dr Gray.

'And, yes, sadly, no one else can ever understand your loss. It belongs to you. It impacts only *you*. And guess what? They don't need to understand.' Mimi paused. 'But you do. You need to fully appreciate how this has changed you, so that you can indeed move on and live, but as this changed person, who might now want different things. Who might now want different people about them. And, yes, God forbid, different people to love again. You are still so young – you've been given all those decades to come for a reason. And it's not to waste them.'

Adeline was really crying now. It was what she had dreaded hearing.

And it was exactly what she had needed to hear.

Chapter Twenty-Six

Chawton, Hampshire
21 February, 1946

Colin Knatchbull-Hugessen was walking about the main-floor reception room of the Great House, randomly picking up various objects, first from the wooden fireplace mantel with the witches' marks carved nearby, and then from the sideboard along the oak-panelled wall.

'That dish is from the family china set,' Frances offered from her seat on the edge of the chintz sofa. 'Picked out by Edward Austen with Jane herself at his side. See the little family crest on the rim?'

Colin put the Wedgwood oval serving dish back down. 'Never cared much for her books. Do you keep many servants around here?'

'Just a handful, I'm afraid. The estate can't financially bear much more than that. But they are all long-term employees except for the two house girls, and they will keep things running for you.'

He looked back at her with some interest. 'House girls, huh?'

Frances felt herself become uneasy under his gaze. 'And Josephine, whom you just met at the door. Then there's Tom Edgewaite, who runs the stables and the gardens, such as they are. We also employ a local farmer, Adam Berwick, to manage the fields and pastures.'

Colin was now wandering into the library next door, and Frances got up to follow him.

'Wow' – he whistled – 'that there's a lot of books. You read all these?'

'Not really. I have my favourites – Evie's collected them, over there, on the lower two shelves. The rest have been in the family for ages.'

'This could make a nice room for a telly.' He turned about in the centre of the room. 'You got one?'

'No, I'm afraid, just the radio in the sitting room and the one in the kitchen.'

'Television's where it's at. I hear the BBC's finally opening again soon, now that the war's over. Hundreds of pounds though for a set, they tell me. Best sell some of this lot off, for what it's worth.' He randomly picked up one of the older-looking books. 'Must be enough in here for two tellies, at that.'

Frances had to bite her lip to keep from saying anything. It was not in her nature to be even remotely disingenuous. But she had the voices of a lot of other people in her head – Dr Gray, and Evie, and even Yardley Sinclair – and they had all been most strict with her, that she did not owe this 'boob', as Evie called him, anything. That she was completely free to walk away from the house with no obligation at all to help Colin Knatchbull-Hugessen profit off it any more than he was already going to.

Bored with the library, Colin headed for the dining room next, Frances reluctantly following him.

The dining room had always been one of her favourite

rooms, with its regal long table, deep-set window seats and the grand piano in the corner. Colin sat down immediately at the instrument.

'I am actually quite the musician, you know – watch this.' He grinned and started banging out 'Chopsticks' on the keys.

Frances wasn't sure she could stand much more. It was hard to believe she shared even an ounce of blood with this man. Such a thought would normally have made her feel quite snobby, but Colin was so unlikeable, he made it easy not to care about that at all.

She showed him the rest of the main floor, then they headed towards the north staircase. Colin noticed the boxes at the bottom of the landing and, in a rare moment of humanity, asked, 'Must be hard, giving all this up. You all right?'

'Oh, yes. It's important the estate be held intact and passed down as far as it is able. We're all just caretakers here, in a way. Now it's simply your turn.'

'Well, that's what I call a fine attitude. Yes, indeed. A fine attitude.'

He motioned for her to walk ahead, and she led the way upstairs. When they reached the second-floor study, which also contained several shelves of books (the most valuable of which Evie had discreetly been moving downstairs during her dusting), he gave another loud whistle.

'Bloody hell, here we go again.' He turned about in the middle of the room, and Frances steeled herself to say what she had been coached to by her fellow society members just two days before.

'It'll take some time and money, to get everything in the house appraised, I suppose,' she said as casually as possible.

Colin looked back at her with concern. 'Well, I don't want to waste a second – or a shilling – more on any of *that* than I have to.'

Frances nodded solemnly. 'Time is money after all.'

'Precisely,' he agreed, starting to think the old bird was perhaps not quite as out of it as she seemed.

'I am in a position, you see, to make you an offer on the books.'

'How's that?'

'We have a little society here, only – oh – seven or eight people, local villagers mostly, and we've raised money to buy things connected to Jane Austen.'

He cocked his eyebrow at her. 'Really? How funny.'

'Yes,' Frances said with an almost embarrassed smile, 'it's just our little pet hobby, you see. Village life doesn't necessarily provide the most exciting pursuits.'

Colin was listening to her carefully, the world of horse racing and football matches and willing waitresses seeming to slip away with her every word.

'Anyway, our society would be happy to take some of these books off your hands. Those shelves there, for example. And the two lower ones downstairs, that I was hoping I could take myself. And a few other books from the downstairs library.' She kept talking for as long as she could, while Colin pondered the life he was getting into.

'But, of course, if you would like to bring someone in, to value all of this . . .' She watched the glazed look starting on his usually overly animated face. 'After all, between the two rooms there are nearly three thousand books—'

'Three thousand . . .'

'Yes, give or take a few hundred. A full cataloguing and valuation would take months, perhaps even a year. Especially if one takes the time to go through each book carefully, page by page.'

But Colin Knatchbull-Hugessen did not have a year. He never did. He lived between games and races and betting-parlour hours of operation. He wanted his money, and he wanted it now.

'How much?' he interrupted.

'The society would be prepared to offer forty thousand pounds for the contents of the library.'

Frances thought back to everyone's faces at the third meeting of the society, held in a rush two nights before, and the moment when Mimi had stood up and pledged the money right away.

Colin composed himself and started to tap his right index finger on his chin.

'That would free up some cash for you, from the estate, while you decide what to do with it,' Frances said with an accommodating look. 'Right now, you see, sadly, any profits from the estate go straight back into the cost of operating it.'

Colin stopped tapping his chin. 'Come again?'

Frances was now recalling what Andrew had told her about the current state of the estate's financial ledgers. 'Well, as the executor has informed me and will do so with you, I am sure, the estate is actually running at a bit of a loss.'

'A loss? How so?'

'Well, you see, every time the estate has passed down, the death taxes would eat up such a big chunk of it that the new heir would have to sell things off to keep it going – a field or two of land here, a small barn or cottage there – and it worked, to a point. But really, all we have left now is this Great House and the little freehold cottage up the lane and the contents inside.'

'The little cottage where you are going to live.'

She nodded. 'And so, according to the executor, with the death taxes currently levied on the estate and the increasing running costs, we are in a bit of pickle. He suggests perhaps converting this house into flats as well and renting them out.

That will generate a bit more money to help keep things going, although not quite enough. Of course, you could always sell the cottage outright to realise more immediate funds.'

But Colin had no head for business. Just listening to Frances talk about the financial concerns ahead was giving him a headache. It was so much easier just plonking down some money on a counter and letting fate have its way. You win some, you lose some. No effort required. That was more his style.

'I'm going to have to think about all of this,' he said, with no intention at all of doing so. Unbeknownst to Frances Knight, he already had a potential buyer in mind for the estate. A golf course and hotel development company from Scotland had recently approached his lawyer upon hearing of the inheritance from one of their directors with a distant connection to Chawton. Always on the lookout for great estates about to be broken up and sold off due to a financial shortfall of some kind, the development company now had its eye on the estate of Chawton Park as a potential hotel and golf greens, and the little steward's cottage as a clubhouse and dining room for members' wives and their guests.

Getting rid of some musty old books was one thing – the bigger deal, to Colin's mind, was to keep the property as intact as possible and sell it all to one qualified and highly motivated buyer. Of course, if he did so, Frances Knight would lose her home for life – but surely some kind village soul would take pity on her. After all, he told himself, wasn't that what village life was all about?

'Of course.' Frances smiled as graciously as possible. 'Take all the time you need.'

Chapter Twenty-Seven

Chawton, Hampshire
That same afternoon

*W*hile Colin Knatchbull-Hugessen was counting his pennies over at the Great House, Dr Benjamin Gray was paying the one house call he had most dreaded ever having to make. He walked down Winchester Road in the direction of Alton, before turning into a small lane. Stopping in front of the first house at the end of a row of semi-detached terrace cottages, he looked quickly about himself, then gave a firm, hard knock on the door.

The door opened after a minute to reveal old Mrs Berwick, now well into her seventies.

'Has there been an accident?' were the first words out of her mouth, something Dr Gray was used to whenever he showed up unannounced at the most senior villagers' homes.

'No, everyone is fine — is Adam here?'

'He's making a delivery up at Wyards Farm.' She pushed her tiny reading glasses farther down her nose to peer at him closely. 'He'll be back by tea if you want to try again.'

'Actually, Mrs Berwick, it's you I came to see. May I come in?'

She pulled her shawl about her shoulders tightly and stepped back to let him in. The house had only four rooms: the parlour that they were standing in, the back kitchen, and the two upstairs bedrooms. Dr Gray remembered the acres-wide former Berwick farmstead a few miles out of town, now occupied by the struggling Stone family, and all the hardship that had been visited upon both families over the years. For the first time it struck him how ironic it all was – how Evie Stone and Adam Berwick had each grown up in that same old farmhouse, perhaps even slept in the same bedroom, then both ended up part of the Austen Society, despite such vast differences in temperament and ambition and age. He wondered what a less logical, more mystical man would have made of that.

Adam's mother pointed to a seat by the inglenook fireplace, which stretched the entire width of the room. Dr Gray sat down and spied several stacks of books on the floor next to him.

'Adam's been quite distracted ever since you lot started on all that Jane Austen nonsense.'

Dr Gray gave her an indulgent smile. He had learned well enough over the years never to unnecessarily contradict a woman like Edith Berwick – he was saving his energy for a very different battle ahead.

'I wonder if you know why I have come.'

She narrowed her eyes at him but said nothing. She was not going to give him an inch, he could tell.

'Edith – Mrs Berwick – I think it is time. To tell Adam. Things have changed for you both very dramatically and very suddenly this past week. You heard, of course, about Mr Knight's will?'

He saw her take a nervous gulp while she continued to stare. 'Yes, of course. What business does any of that have to do with me and Adam?'

'Adam's the closest heir,' Dr Gray said as quickly and forcefully as he could.

'He is no such thing.'

'Edith, please – you can't deprive him of all that, without his knowledge.' Dr Gray looked about the small dark room. 'He would own the old Berwick fields again, and the house and stables, and he could keep things or change them up as he saw fit – but knowing Adam, he would keep that old place going, keep it the centre of our village as in old times. God knows what will happen to it with anyone else.'

'There is someone else then?'

So she did know more than she was letting on.

'Yes, a Mr Knatchbull-Hugessen of Greater Birmingham. He's up at the house as we speak, being shown around by Miss Frances. Miss Frances, who we both know truly does not deserve any of what has happened. Not that the old man surprised anyone in his vindictiveness.'

Dr Gray wondered if his cause would be helped or hindered by criticizing her former employer Mr Knight.

She shook her head forcefully. 'I'm not telling him. You can't make me. You swore an oath.'

Dr Gray sighed audibly. 'Yes, I did. That's why this has been our secret now for well over twenty years. January 1919, correct? I won't forget. Not ever. I was back here to help old Dr Simpson, coping all on his own with the outbreak.'

'I'm not telling him,' she repeated, as if she hadn't heard a word he'd said.

'Who are you more worried about, you or Adam? Because as his doctor, I believe he is well enough to handle the news, if it means inheriting all that. I am not sure I would have said that in years past. But he is among friends now, good friends, and we will take care of him, just as you have done all these years alone.'

'He loved his father more than anything. He won't be able to abide it. I know.'

Dr Gray was watching her carefully. He knew her propensity for selfish gain, her overweening interest and delight in the failures of others. Her cynicism. Her self-loathing that manifested itself in all these other ways. He did not like her – he never had. She would not have known that – his steady gracious smile in the street, the respectful tip of the hat, the patient nodding while she spewed her venom against the other villagers, had always kept him in her good graces, as he knew he needed to be. That was how she exerted the minimal control over village life that she had, through terror tactics aided by a sharp and unforgiving tongue. No one ever wanted to get on the bad side of Edith Berwick, and he could only wonder at what toll this had over the years taken on poor Adam's health.

It was one reason why, ever since he had learned of the new will, he had been torn about saying anything. But his scruples had started many years earlier, during the Spanish flu epidemic that had ravaged Chawton and the world just as the Great War was ending, when Dr Gray was still just an intern. After only a few days of fever, Mr Berwick was starting to inexplicably haemorrhage and was rushed to the Alton Hospital. Here Dr Howard Westlake, recently returned from the war as a medic and local hero, had suggested immediate blood transfusion using techniques he had learned on the Western Front. Adam had eagerly donated blood, having been deemed the most likely to match his father's blood type, but still Mr Berwick could not be saved. Only Mrs Berwick would eventually be told the truth by Dr Gray: that based on cross-matching of their blood types, Adam could not possibly be his father's son.

Dr Gray had had to guess at the real story, for the old widow Berwick had been shell-shocked with grief at the time. Then years later, long after he had moved back to Chawton to take over Dr Simpson's practise, she had one day told Dr Gray everything, in a rare moment of trust and candour. He could not quite remember why – all he knew was that in the years since, instead of acting as if he had something on her, Mrs Berwick had acted as if she now had something to lord over him, such was the conniving brilliance of her power tactics. As if she was just waiting for him to betray his oath to her and crack.

He wondered how long she could resist doing the same when it came to her son. Wondered if the idea of the wealth waiting for Adam would triumph over her misgivings, for however faltering the estate was, it still yielded thousands of pounds in revenue a year. Dr Gray would be lying if he did not acknowledge, at least to himself, that he was extremely keen to see the entirety of the estate go to a man like Adam, with his commitment to Austen's legacy and to the village of Chawton in general, if it couldn't go to Frances.

Dr Gray shifted a bit in his seat. He had waited until today before saying anything because he had hoped all along that Frances would end up the heir.

'Why are you here now?' Mrs Berwick asked, as if she could read his mind.

'I just thought it was time.'

'But you've known for weeks. Adam told me you were at the reading of the will.' She stared at Dr Gray aggressively. 'Longer, even, I suspect, with the likes of Harriet Peckham working for you.'

'I can't speak to any of that. As a patient of mine yourself, I am sure you understand my need for discretion. But things have changed recently, and so dramatically, as I first said – and I always thought it best if you came to this decision on your own. I will respect what you decide to do, either way, I can assure you. But you are running out of time, now that Mr

Knatchbull has appeared. And I wanted to be absolutely clear with you on that.'

'My boy won't want any of it.'

'I think you are wrong.'

'I know I am right. Everyone will know, and it will be his shame as much as mine, and all the land and money in the world won't be worth it to him.'

'I know that is how you feel, otherwise you would have also told Mr Knight himself when you had the chance. You didn't tell him or Adam for a reason, even with Mr Berwick gone for so many years. But please, please think about what your reasons really are.'

With that, he got up while she remained seated, staring ahead. He left the cottage feeling some degree of relief. He had done what he could for Adam without breaching any patient confidentiality – otherwise his hands were tied. He was also relieved that the old woman had not pursued more of a connection between his speaking up now and the interest of the society in the little cottage down the lane. Dr Gray was aware of his own self-interest in all of this, and he had spent weeks trying to manage it. But he consoled himself with the fact that, in all the years he had known Adam Berwick, he had never seen him more engaged, or alive, or happy. Dr Gray knew that the Jane Austen Society was a huge reason why, and he knew that it had been Adam's dream first to try to acquire the cottage as a monument to his favourite author. And that as a result it was no longer Dr Gray's secret, or Mrs Berwick's, to keep. Adam deserved the truth, to make of it however much, or however little, he would.

⌒

Early the next morning Liberty Pascal, wearing an even brighter shade of lipstick than usual, appeared in the doorway to Dr Gray's office. She often had this funny way of leaning against the door frame, as if hankering for an invitation to come in and take a load off. He mused once again at the likelihood of his unknowingly hiring someone so connected to Adeline, as well as the misfortune of its being someone with such a competitive view of her.

'Yes, Miss Pascal?'

'Adam Berwick is here to see you. I didn't see his name in your appointments book.'

'That's all right. Please, send him in.'

Dr Gray rarely got emotional at his job – he prided himself on this. But he was suddenly overcome by the idea of Adam having to revisit the few certain and pleasant memories of his distant past, and having to integrate those memories with the reality of what had really been going on. No one ever wants to know that things were not as they seemed.

A few seconds later, Liberty reappeared, with Adam lingering behind her. He took off his cap as he entered the office, and Dr Gray noticed Liberty flash him an extra-wide smile and give the slightest curtsy before leaving the two men alone.

'Adam, come in, please.' Dr Gray got up and closed the door, then sat back down behind his desk.

'I don't want to talk much about it,' the bewildered man began.

'Of course, Adam, I fully understand. You must take care of yourself, and your mother. It had to have been extremely difficult for her to tell you. I can't imagine.'

Adam was gripping his cap so tightly in his hands that his knuckles were turning white. Dr Gray's heart was breaking a little for the poor man – he never could get a break. Yet there he was, trying to connect with people like Dr Gray and Adeline and Evie, trying to build something outside of his tiny world. It all took so much guts and nerve for a man like him. That terrible First War and its numbing degree of loss had deprived Adam Berwick of something essential years ago – an understanding of hope – an understanding of how sometimes it is all we have. But how hope can also sometimes be just enough.

'I didn't want you to know just so that the society could get the cottage. I need you to know that, Adam, as your physician and your friend. You are a strong man – look at what you have survived. You will survive this, too, and put it in its place, whatever you decide to do. But you are the one who should get to decide all that.'

'My father . . .'

Dr Gray could hear the pain in Adam's voice as it trailed off.

'I know – again, we don't have to talk about it. But as a doctor, let me just say this: for all the ties of blood and birth that I see about me, each and every day, and the babies delivered, and the tears of the parents, I only ever remember the love. You were loved, Adam – you are loved. Your father loved you, and you cherish his memory, and that is all that really counts. And you get to safeguard that memory however you choose.'

Adam wiped his nose with a handkerchief from his pocket. 'I keep coming back to the cottage, and all the books and things, and what if we lose it all? Let alone Miss Frances and the one home she has left?'

Dr Gray came around to lean against the back of his desk, facing Adam. 'That really doesn't need to be your concern right now. I just wanted – Mrs Berwick, too – we simply wanted you to have the information. But it's nobody else's business what you decide to do with it. And don't panic about Miss Frances just yet – after all, Mr Knatchbull may never sell any of it.'

Dr Gray was touched, though, by the man's visible conflict, the conflict Dr Gray himself had been enduring. If they were caretakers out here of something bigger than themselves, then they each had a responsibility beyond their own self-interest that was incredibly difficult to deny.

'I want someone to tell me what to do.'

Dr Gray gave his first genuine smile in days. 'Trust me, Adam, we all feel like that sometimes.'

'What would you do?'

'I honestly don't know. That's what's so trying about all of this. It's so completely, so thoroughly, unique to *you*. Like all of life. None of us can ever say for sure what we'd do without feeling all of someone else's slings and arrows along the way.'

Adam stuffed the handkerchief back inside his front jacket pocket. 'I want to take a vote.'

'Come again?' Dr Gray asked in surprise.

'The society. I want to tell them — I want *you* to tell them — and I want them all to vote. Miss Frances told me yesterday — I stopped in at the house on my way back from Wyards — she told me that this Mr Knatchbull is pretty focused on the money from the house. She thinks we might get the books — says it shouldn't be too difficult to pull off — but the rest of it all, and the cottage, who knows. So I want a vote, a proper official one, and soon. I trust everyone in the society.'

Dr Gray looked at him carefully. 'Adam, we don't know everyone that well — Mr Sinclair and Miss Harrison are pretty much strangers still, for all I like and respect them both.'

Adam shook his head firmly. 'No, it's fine. I trust them. I trust you.' He gave Dr Gray a pointed, emotional look. 'You knew all these years and you never said a word.'

Dr Gray put his right hand out to touch Adam's shoulder, an unusual display of the internal compassion he felt for all his patients but stoically concealed in the pursuit of his professional duties.

'Adam, it was important to do so, of course — but in some ways, if you think about it, it isn't important at all. It doesn't change anything – it doesn't change what you shared with your father. The rest of it, even your mother's role in all of this, is secondary, at least I think so. There's the centre of the life, and there's all the stuff that flies around on the periphery – and you, and only you, get to decide what you want to keep in place. Don't let anyone else move it about.'

Adam nodded.

'But I still want that vote.'

Chapter Twenty-Eight

Chawton, Hampshire
23 February, 1946
Second Emergency Meeting of the Jane Austen Society

*T*he agenda for tonight's meeting was enough to put Andrew Forrester over the edge.

'So we're here to hold a vote, one vote, on whether Adam should claim his inheritance of the Knight estate? A claim based on his alleged paternity by Mr Knight, a fact even Adam was unaware of until just a day or two ago?'

Dr Gray nodded. They were all assembled again in his front parlour. Everyone was there except Adam, which was more a relief than anything else, given the magnitude of the decision before them.

Mimi had met Yardley at the station that Saturday afternoon, having never returned to London after the first emergency meeting four nights earlier. She had stayed with Adeline the first night, then moved into the guest bedroom at the Great House. The country air was doing her good – she had never looked lovelier.

'But you knew about this? For how long?' Andrew asked Dr Gray.

'I can't get into that, Andy, as you well know,' Dr Gray replied. 'But I have here written permission from both Adam and his mother to disclose the nature of the claim to the current members of the society. These are for your solicitor files, as executor of the estate, to be locked away with the utmost confidentiality.' Dr Gray passed the papers over to Andrew, then sat back down.

'Poor Adam,' Adeline spoke up. 'He loses almost his whole family, and then this. How is he doing?'

Dr Gray rested both his hands on the arms of his wingback chair closest to the fire and stared down at the floor. 'I can't say much, of course, as he is still my patient as well, but he has asked us all here today to vote on his next steps because he is too emotionally torn, I believe, to make the decision without our help. Our vote is not at all determinative or binding on him in any way. It's purely to help him decide.'

'It must not have been an easy decision for you either, to say anything,' remarked Adeline.

Dr Gray looked up in surprise at her understanding tone. It felt like many months since she had treated him with anything akin to compassion. It might not have seemed like much to the others, but to Dr Gray her words offered both comfort and hope – the very sense of hope that he, like Adam, had long ago lost.

Andrew read through the two affidavits before him. 'So it's a potentially valid claim, then, no question about that?'

Dr Gray nodded.

'And besides you, Adam and his mother are the only other people who know – Mr Knight never knew, correct?'

'Yes, which makes the wording of the will – "closest living male relative" – so important. Without the word *legitimate*, correct me if I'm wrong, anyone related by blood can make the claim.'

'Yes, correct, that is the law of the land,' Andrew replied. 'Well, then, let's discuss as a group and call a vote, obviously with Miss Frances and myself abstaining along with Mr Berwick. That means, according to the law of meetings in parliamentary procedure, that a majority of all eight society members – five – must vote aye for any resolution to pass. That leaves the five of you who are allowed to vote in a pretty tight spot.'

'Well, I for one am not sure what there is to discuss,' Adeline spoke up again. She was sitting on the small love seat next to Evie. Mimi and Yardley were on the sofa across from her. Andrew had pulled another wingback chair over between the sofas to face the fireplace, in front of which Dr Gray and Frances sat on opposite sides.

'I mean, clearly Adam is conflicted by the news, rightly so, and must be so upset,' Adeline continued. 'And I don't see how letting the whole village know the history behind all of this will make a shy man like Adam anything but even less secure than he already is.'

'I'm not sure Adam is insecure, so much as he is just quiet,' said Yardley.

'But you don't know him the way we do,' Adeline retorted. 'Village life is extremely intense in a way – no one misses a thing. There is no anonymity, you can't hide yourself on a bad day the way you can in the city. Your neighbours force you to own up, by their sheer proximity.'

'You make it sound so enticing,' said Dr Gray, letting his old teasing tone with her return.

'My neighbours knowing everything I am up to, every house I visit, or don't, is not why I stay here.'

'It certainly does make decisions much more loaded when you know there'll be a constant chorus of approval or disapproval either way,' Frances offered.

'I can see that,' said Mimi. 'In a way it's like Hollywood.'

They all turned to look at her.

'Yes' – Evie laughed outright – 'that's exactly what they say about Chawton.'

Mimi smiled self-effacingly. 'I just mean, we are lucky if we get to live in places where so many people care – the trick is understanding *why* they care. Here, what I love, is that you care because you have a history together. You have known each other's parents and grandparents, and all the siblings running amok in each other's yards, and when times are hard, you help each other through. In Hollywood, it's quite the opposite. Everyone comes there to start new and makes up a history – even makes up their own name. Mine's Mary Anne, by the way, not Mimi.'

'You're joking!' exclaimed Evie. 'You're about to film *Sense and Sensibility* as Elinor and your real name is Mary Anne?'

'Yep. Ironic, huh? Although even that right now is up in the air – they suddenly want a younger actress for Elinor, to go with the even younger actress playing Marianne.'

Adeline and Frances looked at each other.

'Will Mr Leonard let that happen?' Frances asked.

'I suspect it's his idea,' replied Mimi archly, causing Adeline and Frances to glance quickly at each other again. 'Anyway, in a town where no one even knows your real name, let alone where you come from, what is tethering you to anything? What is there to keep you on the ground?'

'Oh, we do plenty of that around here, let me assure you,' answered Adeline. 'No one in Chawton is eager for anyone to rise above their station. Don't even get me started on the education system. There's a reason Evie was self-teaching in the library all those years. Not that you didn't love every minute of it,' she said with a smile at the girl.

Dr Gray and Andrew looked over at each other, aware that they were fast losing control of their limited agenda.

'So, Adeline,' Andrew intervened, 'you think the stakes are too high for Adam, both emotionally and reputation-wise. Evie and Yardley, what about the two of you?'

Evie hesitated. Yardley was facing her on the sofa, and for a few seconds they stared at each other knowingly, both recalling that night in the library when she had revealed its many secrets to him. They were indeed very alike, and they had sworn that night to keep the library and the collection of Austen-related artefacts throughout the house as intact as possible.

'May I speak first?' asked Yardley. 'I know I am very new to you all, but I really do think Adam can handle whatever happens. That he feels wonderfully supported by all of you, and by the society and what we're trying to do. And, speaking professionally, the risk of losing all of these items, let alone the house itself, is very significant. Once you lose it, you might never even get an Austen family salt shaker back one day. We haven't even scratched the surface of the rest of the house, the paintings and furniture and who knows what else. I hadn't mentioned this yet, but Miss Frances showed me a mahogany writing desk in her father's bedroom earlier today, and it could very well be the biggest find of all. Sotheby's sold one for over ten thousand pounds last September, on the chance it was the one Jane Austen used while travelling. I think this is the real one instead. We might be looking at tens of thousands of pounds for that little desk alone.'

'Well, that is indeed ironic,' said Andrew, 'as that is the very desk the old man so wretchedly amended his will on.'

Everyone now turned to look at Andrew in surprise at his aggrieved tone.

'Evie,' he continued, ignoring all the looks, 'we haven't heard from you yet. You're the keeper of the catalogue. What do you think? Do you agree with Yardley?'

Evie was not used to being put on the spot like this. She glanced almost helplessly at Miss Frances, afraid to say something that would hurt her or Adam, then finally spoke.

'I am not a professional anybody, but I do think Yardley has a point. From all the research I've done, seeing what all's been wasted over the centuries, trying to find what's been lost . . . as hard as it might be on Adam, it could mean the possible destruction of one of the most culturally important collections out there. There's no escaping that fact.'

'Well, not its entire destruction,' countered Dr Gray. 'I mean, yes, she lived here for ten years and wrote the last three books here as well – but she lived a long time in Steventon, too, the longest, and almost as long in Bath. We know where some of her other homes were, and the Bath ones in particular are still standing. And even if Adam doesn't speak up for his rightful claim, we might still manage to buy the library out from under Colin, as I understand from Miss Frances that he has a bewildering lack of interest in the books. Maybe we could do the same with some of the other objects, like the writing desk. All would not be lost entirely, and over time perhaps another suitable location could be found.'

'Do you really mean that?' asked Adeline.

'I wouldn't say it if I didn't,' Dr Gray replied defensively.

Adeline shrugged. 'It just doesn't sound like you – you're usually so hell-bent on everything staying as it is.'

Dr Gray shifted uncomfortably in his chair as he felt Andrew watching him curiously.

'May I say something?' asked Mimi. 'It's probably too emotional of me, but then again I am an actress, so what else is to be expected? It's just, I know what it's like to have regrets, real regrets, about someone's life. I don't want to have those regrets about Adam, not for anything.'

She paused. Everyone in the room grew unusually quiet.

There was a reason Mimi commanded a twenty-foot-high screen in theatres around the world.

'And I also know what it's like to lose a father, and to have felt helpless in the face of it, and to have always wondered if you could have somehow saved him. Grief and regret puts a hole right through you that nothing can ever fill. And trust me, I've tried. And I suspect some of you have tried as well, with your own losses over the years. And the hard, crushing reality of it all is that the hole can never be filled. That you have to live with it, this absence that is not replaceable by money, or objects, or art – or even by another person, no matter how much you might learn to love and trust again.'

Mimi paused. She had the room and she knew it. She had never, as talented as she was, understood her audience better.

'So, it seems to me, we're being asked to vote on making a hole inside Adam's heart, and then hope somehow he can live with it. Well, I can't do that – I can't willingly do that. Because if we're wrong, he is the one who has to live with it every day – every second – of his life. And nothing is worth that.'

'I agree,' said Adeline. 'And, what's more, I think Jane Austen would agree, too.'

Dr Gray sat back in his chair. 'Shall we vote then? Wait, Frances, we haven't heard from you. What do you think, you who have the greatest interest of all?'

Frances was sitting there next to the fire, her hands clasped in her lap.

'I think I have a brother,' she cried, as tears fell down her cheeks.

It was all anyone needed to know.

Chapter Twenty-Nine

Chawton, Hampshire
April 1946

*M*imi's wedding day to Jack Leonard was fast approaching. He had not been thrilled by the recent pledging of a significant part of her dowry, as he jokingly liked to call it, to the Jane Austen Society so that it could buy a pile of books from a rotting old mansion. Forty thousand pounds amounted to her working fee for several films, and she wasn't even planning to do many of those any more.

It had been a year since they had first met by the pool, and Jack was now starting to feel a little antsy. He recognised this feeling well – the tan line about his ring finger had been hard-earned over time. This was one reason he had wanted a shorter engagement: he did not trust himself to stay interested enough to self-deprive for long. But Mimi wanted the wedding to be in the Chawton parish church, and this had taken some finessing with Reverend Powell after the leasehold sale of the cottage as a part-time residence had fallen through.

After that, never one to lose face in a deal, Jack started to see the estate of Chawton Park and the little cottage as less of a bolt-hole for his bride, and more of an investment opportunity. An avid golfer, he had recently acquired significant voting shares in a Scottish golf course development company called Alpha Investments Limited, and he was the one who first raised with its board the idea of buying the whole Knight estate for future development. He had been privy now for many weeks to Mimi's occasional evening updates on the Jane Austen Society, Miss Knight's financial predicament, and the recent legal declaration of a Mr Knatchbull as heir following a rather bizarre vote by the society on which Mimi had for once refused to detail him.

'But essentially you, the five of you, voted *not* to fight Mr Knatchbull's claim with information you had at your disposal?'

'Yes, pretty much,' she had replied over the phone.

His question that followed – 'Are you sure the society understands its own mandate?' – had not gone over well.

So, in light of this confidential information, the hefty death duties now owing, and the flat U.K. economic climate following the war, Jack saw an opportunity to buy the estate out from under the hapless Colin Knatchbull, and accordingly advised the board to make a lowball offer as soon as they could.

Regarding the contents of the library, as described to him in mind-numbing detail by an excited Mimi, Jack was less interested. Whatever the potential value of the books, which he was apt to estimate downwards, he doubted the current interest in Jane Austen would sustain itself for long. And the society itself sounded like a band of misfits with negligible expertise and no head for business: a country doctor, an old maid, a schoolmarm, a bachelor farmer, a fey auctioneer, a conflict-averse solicitor, a scullery maid and one Hollywood movie star.

The pre-war property valuation of the Great House, the surrounding fields, and the little cottage stood at one hundred thousand pounds. When Mimi told Jack about Miss Frances's offering Knatchbull almost half that amount just for a pile of books, Jack had practically fallen off his lounger. There was no way the shareholders of Alpha Investments would pay even a fraction of that, so Jack had sat back and let Mimi pledge the purchase price to the society. It made her excited – and he liked all his women in a state of excitement.

A week before the wedding and the fifth meeting of the Jane Austen Society, Colin Knatchbull's diligent lawyer drew up the paperwork to sell the contents of the library, sight unseen, to the Jane Austen Memorial Trust for forty thousand pounds. Adam Berwick had brought his hay wagon right up to the front gate of the Great House the very next day, and in a human chain of sorts, the eight members of the society and Frances's three long-term employees had carried out all two thousand, three hundred and seventy-five books. The move took most of the day, as the books had to be kept in strict shelf order, to comply with Evie Stone's catalogue – this would make it easier for any eventual official appraisal to be conducted. Then Adam's wagon had carried the books through town to Adeline Grover's house, as she had two spare bedrooms upstairs in which to store everything.

Now all the society could do was sit tight and hope that Knatchbull would also agree in time to sell the old steward's cottage as the most ideal location for the proposed Jane Austen Museum.

'Well, look at that,' Adeline's mother was calling from the front parlour window early the morning of the wedding. 'Mr Berwick has shown up in the Knight family Rolls. I wonder why?'

Mrs Lewis looked back and smiled suggestively at her daughter, who sat in the rocking chair by the fireplace, rereading a small pocket-size copy of *Pride and Prejudice*.

'Put the book away, my dear, you have a gentleman caller, arrived in style.' Mrs Lewis tidied up the window seat a bit. 'All these books, and now all those old ones upstairs, falling apart at the seams. I really can't imagine what has got into the lot of you.'

'Mum, could you get the door for me – I'm almost finished this chapter.'

Mrs Lewis shook her head. 'Nonsense, you've read that story a dozen times. You can greet your visitor yourself. And, Adeline, please, be nice.'

'Mother!' Adeline said with a sigh, shutting the book reluctantly. 'I resent that. I am always nice to Adam – he is a very sweet man. *Although*' – she raised her voice for emphasis – 'I don't mean that in any kind of romantic way.'

'Why does everyone always talk like that about Adam? He is a lovely man, very gentle, and quite pleasing to the eye in his way.'

'Well, for one thing, he's not interested in someone like me.'

'Ridiculous! Who else would catch his eye around here? Certainly not that little Evie Stone. Too suspicious and astute. Caught her rummaging through the bookcase on the upstairs landing on her last visit.'

'Mother, I told her she could. She's convinced some old volumes from the Knight family library have been dispersed over the years throughout the village and beyond, and she's always on the lookout for ones with the family seal.'

Mrs Lewis shook her head at her daughter. 'What you people are up to is beyond me.'

'And for *another* thing,' Adeline continued in exasperation, 'Adam's quite a bit older than me.'

'Rubbish! He is not. And anyway, older men often make much more mature and suitable mates. Besides, how much older can he be?'

'He's only a couple of years shy of Dr Gray, I think.' Adeline watched her mother closely for her reaction, recalling how difficult she had been to the village doctor during his check-in's last winter.

'Really? Well, the forties can still be a productive age, when one is not hampered by one's children.'

'Oh, Mum' – Adeline smiled at her – 'I do hope you know how much you have helped me, despite being hampered and all—'

There was a gentle knock on the front door.

'Only to be replaced by a pile of mouldy books,' replied Mrs Lewis, whose sense of humour was as sharp and direct as her daughter's, while Adeline went to get the door.

Adam and Adeline took a cup of tea with Mrs Lewis for a few minutes, then headed upstairs, as they had been doing most days that week. They would sit down in the spare bedroom, Adeline usually cross-legged on the floor and Adam on an upturned crate, and they each had a set of photographs that Yardley had had made from Evie's little catalogue. They were going through the wooden crates of books in almost quiet ecstasy, making sure the number on the crate corresponded with both its contents and the assigned section of the catalogue. They marked up any discrepancies with red ink pen right onto the photographs, pleased to have found just a handful of misplacements out of the hundreds of books so far. This was a particular relief, given how rushed the move of the entire library had been the previous week.

They were still at their task an hour later when Frances Knight surprised them by suddenly appearing in the doorway. Adam started to get up, but Frances motioned for him to stay sitting.

'The wedding is starting soon – shouldn't you two be getting ready? Although' – Frances smiled at Adam in his old-fashioned but well-fitted suit – 'I have to say, Mr Berwick – I mean, Adam – you already look very well this morning.'

Adam practically blushed – for all the years he had worked for and admired Miss Frances, she had never addressed him in such an informal and teasing manner. It gratified him that the recent news of his paternity had only increased her warmth towards him. Upon first hearing the news, he, too, had not immediately processed the one silver lining to his mother's deception: that he had a sibling again, and that his new sister was someone as wonderful as Frances. By taking a few chances, Adam was starting to see that life never completely gave up on you, if you didn't give up on it.

'We could say the same about you, Frances, what with the wedding breakfast being held at the Great House in just a few hours,' Adeline replied.

Frances waved both her hands as if in resignation. 'Josephine has it all shipshape and under control. And I'm afraid I have something rather pressing to tell you both that could not wait.'

Adeline and Adam stared at Frances in concern, especially as she was never one to exaggerate things.

'It's a good thing you're both sitting down already.' She pulled a letter out from the right pocket of her voluminous skirt. 'Andrew Forrester brought me this letter first thing this morning. He received it as my solicitor of record. The letter is to inform me that following the recent court order declaring Colin Knatchbull heir to my father's estate, the entire property has been sold outright to a golf course development company called Alpha Investments. The letter is also written notice that my rent-free accommodation at Chawton cottage is hereby terminated by Alpha. It gets worse – Mimi's fiancé Jack Leonard is on the board, so he must have had a hand in all of this. Andrew and I just walked here together to tell you – he's right behind me, he just wanted to stop in at the cottage along the way to warn the other tenants as soon as he could.'

Adeline stood up carefully among the books she had been perusing. Evie had everyone on a strict system of accountability, and they all lived in fear of accidentally disturbing her order of books inside the dozens of crates.

'Let me see that.' Adeline reached out for the letter tightly gripped in Miss Frances's hands. 'I don't understand . . . where are you supposed to live?' Adeline sat back down on one of the crates and looked at Frances glumly.

'What did Mr Forrester say?' asked Adam.

'He said that my father's will made it extremely clear that my rent-free accommodation was not legally binding upon any future owners after Colin. Andrew had hoped I might acquire some kind of easement over time instead, but unfortunately my not yet living there precludes any common law entitlement to reside.'

Adam and Adeline stared at Miss Frances, still confused by the complex legalities of her present situation.

'Basically,' she sighed, 'if I had been living there long enough, we might have been able to argue that I had a right to stay.' She gave what, to them, seemed the first overt look of displeasure with the whole debacle. 'I had wondered why Mr Knatchbull and his lawyer were so accommodating about my staying in the Great House until after the wedding.'

Adam looked down at the book in his lap, unable to face Frances as he said, 'It's all my fault. I just had to say the word.'

Frances put her hand out and touched his shoulder. 'Don't even think it, Adam, please? I know I'm not, and I'm not the only one – after all, that's why we held the vote.'

'Still, this is just terrible for you, Frances,' Adeline was saying.

Miss Frances took the letter from Adeline and folded it

back into the pocket of her skirt. 'It will somehow work out
– it always does. But I do feel for everyone in the society. I
think Evie in particular will be devastated. She's worked so
hard. And to find all this out on Mimi's wedding day no less.'

Adam looked at his watch. 'Mr Sinclair's at the station by
half past ten.' He stood up from the upturned crate and swept
the dust from the books off his knees.

Frances looked over at Adeline and explained, 'I'm lending
the Rolls to Adam today, to go and get Yardley in style.'

Adam reached down to help Adeline up from her own crate.
She stood looking glumly at Frances before reluctantly asking,
'So what do we do now? Do we wait, until after the wedding,
to say anything about the cottage? I know I had jitters enough
on my big day and my groom was a peach.'

Miss Frances sighed. 'Mimi is usually so smart. I think she
is at an interesting time in her career, and Jack Leonard presented a strange exit plan of sorts.'

'Well, I can certainly relate to that,' replied Adeline. 'Still,
it would take some nerve to tell anyone this just minutes before
their wedding. Besides, outside of all things Jane Austen, we
none of us know each other that well.'

'Perhaps,' replied Frances. 'But it's never the wrong time –
or too late – to show someone you care.'

They heard a cough from the doorway, and all three turned
to see Andrew Forrester standing there. 'I'm sorry to interrupt, but it's best we all get going to the church.'

Frances looked back at the room, filled with the books she
had grown up with.

'It must be hard,' Andrew added, 'seeing all this here.'

'No, not at all. In fact it's quite the opposite. They're so much
more appreciated right where they are. The important thing
is that they are being loved, and preserved, and taken note of.'

Adam saw Andrew give Frances a curious look, but decided

it was best to keep everyone moving. He turned to Adeline to ask, 'Do you want a pick-up when I get back from the station, to take you to the church?'

'No,' she said with an annoyed sigh. 'I got roped into walking over with Dr Gray and Liberty, God help me. She'll talk our heads off.'

'Dr Gray seems to like that,' Frances said, as the three of them joined Andrew on the upstairs landing and then headed downstairs together. 'The high spirits I mean.'

Adeline turned around when she reached the bottom of the staircase to stare back up at her. 'What are you saying?'

Frances gave an innocent smile. 'Benjamin Gray has been lonely long enough. I think Liberty could be quite a good match for him.'

'Liberty Pascal!' exclaimed Adeline so loudly that Adam, Andrew and Frances all looked at her in surprise.

'Liberty's mighty pretty,' added Adam with a wink.

'Don't you start.' Adeline gave him a playful swat. 'You never talk, and then you come out with *that*?'

Adam held the front door open to let Frances and Andrew pass, then turned back to Adeline, standing arms crossed in the hallway.

'Enjoy your walk,' he teased, as she slammed the door after him.

⌒

Dr Gray and Liberty were heading to the church together, with a quick stop at Adeline Grover's along the way. Dr Gray had taken extra care with his bath that morning, tousling up his hair and indulging in some of the eau de cologne that his late wife had bought him in Jermyn Street for what turned out to be their last Christmas together. When he'd dabbed a few drops along his jawline after his shave, he had looked at the bottle, and the memory of that Christmas morning had felt, strangely, at peace with his present life. Not pulling away at it, as his memories had so often done in the past; not draining anything from the moment, but completing it somehow. Reminding him of who he was, and what he wanted, and what he still deserved to have. He accepted that Jennie would have wanted him to keep living, and that doing so would not reflect on his love for her, which he knew to have been infinite and strong. He had no regrets there. And Jennie had loved him just as infinitely. She would want him to be happy and content again.

But he also knew that she would *not* want him to be with Liberty Pascal.

Liberty talked incessantly while taking his arm as they walked along. As usual, she was prattling on about Adeline Lewis Grover and her beaux. Her preoccupation with Adeline's love life struck Dr Gray as both strange and most unfortunate – ever since that night in the garden when he had lost his head, he had been avoiding Adeline, yet Liberty was always right there to remind him of what the young widow was up to.

'Oh, how I love weddings,' Liberty was saying. 'There's nothing like a wedding to stir up some romance, I always like to say, don't you think, Dr Gray?'

'I wouldn't know. I don't get to too many around here. It's a pretty small village.'

'Oh, but you must have gone to Adeline's, last – what was it – only a year ago last February? How sad that all was. And not so long ago at that. Did you?'

'Did I what?' asked Dr Gray absent-mindedly.

'Why, did you go to Adeline and Samuel's wedding?'

'Yes.' He nodded.

She gave him a hard look. It was like trying to draw blood from a stone.

'Well, I am sure it was a most romantic day. Childhood

sweethearts and all that. Although that Adeline, she's more complicated than she seems. I mean, away at college, we all wondered about the boy back home. He sounded an angel, to be sure, but – I don't know – it all seemed a little lopsided. On *his* side, I mean.'

Dr Gray was looking about him at the crowds of daffodils still filling the front gardens of the terrace houses along this stretch of the street.

'There was this professor, you see.' Liberty's tone was managing to sound both hushed and loud at the same time.

'Hmm?'

'Oh, well, perhaps it was just cold feet. But we all wondered whether Samuel was more an obligation of sorts, going off to war – didn't they get engaged right after he got conscripted?'

Dr Gray was barely listening, just recalling the image of Adeline standing at the altar in her cream-coloured frock, her hair down in waves about her shoulders, a little crown of cream roses setting off the perfect pink of her cheeks.

'In fact, there wasn't just the professor,' Liberty was droning on. 'Adeline has apparently always had a weakness for older men, throwing herself at lonely widowers and the like, confessed as much to me at college once. Said she—'

Liberty stopped talking. Dr Gray had stopped in his tracks, staring at her. Adeline's words in the garden that night – 'push me away all these years' – kept ringing through his head, like a long-suppressed clarion call.

'What did you just say?'

Liberty bit her lip. She was usually two steps ahead of Dr Gray, but today for once he was catching up, and way too fast at that.

'Well, look at me, talking your head off and we're already here. Let me go in and get Adeline, and you stay right there and relax, hmm?'

Liberty ran up the garden path to Adeline's house while Dr Gray tested the hinges on the front gate, swinging it easily to and fro. Adam Berwick had been by after all.

Just then he heard a honk and looked behind to see Adam himself at the wheel of the Knight family Rolls-Royce, Yardley Sinclair sitting in the front seat next to him.

'Dr Gray!' exclaimed Yardley, leaning over Adam to get closer to the driver's side window.

Dr Gray walked into the road to greet both men as the car slowed down, tipping his hat with a smile. 'Pleasant journey?' he called out over the noise of the engine as it sputtered to a stop.

'Adam here's a great driver,' Yardley called back.

Approaching the car, Dr Gray heard a strange noise coming from the back seat. Peering inside, he discovered a Border collie puppy sitting upright and panting. 'And who's this?'

'Dixon.' Yardley looked over at his driver with a smile. 'A gift for Adam, to cheer up the old chap.'

Adam, however, was positively beaming today, which was gratifying to Dr Gray as his doctor and friend, given all the stress the poor man had been through of late. It was wonderful to finally see him comfortable in his own skin. But Dr Gray also wondered if the arrival of spring was turning Adam's thoughts to more than mere fancy, and who in their tiny village could be the object of that.

'Looking forward to the weekend,' Yardley was saying. 'I've been itching to get my hands on those books all week.'

Dr Gray cocked his head back at the upstairs windows of Adeline's house just behind them. 'They're all up there. Two spare bedrooms filled to the rafters with crates and crates of books.'

'We're convening the society on Monday morning, before I return to town, correct?' Yardley smiled over at Adam behind the wheel. 'Hopefully that gives me enough time to make some headway with the physical appraisal. Wedding weekends can be full of distractions.'

'Well, I'm not busy,' said Dr Gray as Adeline and Liberty emerged down the garden path together.

Yardley gave a loud whistle. 'Come now, Benjamin, surely you can find a thing – or two – to get your hands on in between all the celebrations.'

Adam honked the horn again and Yardley gave a laugh as they sped off. Dr Gray took off his hat to rub at his temples – he was getting a serious migraine from all the doublespeak around him. How he was going to get through the wedding, he had no idea.

A half-hour before her noon wedding, Mimi sat in the guest bedroom wing of the Great House, where Frances had put her and Jack in separate rooms the night before. She was applying her make-up carefully, missing the days when she had just sat back in the chair and relaxed while a studio artist did all the work, and realising that she wasn't missing much else. She loved it here in Chawton – loved the talks at night with Evie and Frances by the fire in the Great Hall, loved the wagon rides with Adam Berwick and the long walks through the neighbouring fields towards Upper and Lower Farringdon, loved sitting in the little pub with Yardley on his visits down, laughing with the other villagers at all of her friend's snappy remarks.

Jack did not seem to love it quite so much. He could not get used to many things: the separate taps in the basin for hot and cold water ('I just want *warm*!' he would whine, as he scalded his hands), the rationing (Jack needed a certain daily supply of sugar and caffeine to keep him going), the drizzle that masked as rain, the pessimistic malaise that masked as dry wit. Jack could never reconcile himself to that latter aspect of the English character. He was a piston of energy and self-confidence himself, all go-go-go, and he needed a world that responded to what he was selling. Because he was always selling something.

Mimi knew that staying several months a year in England would be hard on Jack and was glad that Chawton was close enough to London to give him his occasional fill of luxury there. They had not yet found a little house to rent, supply and demand being pretty evenly matched in a village of only four hundred. ('At this point,' Frances had warned her, 'you are literally *waiting* for someone to die).' But Mimi had not yet given up hope and was willing to be patient until a piece of real estate became available. In the meantime, Jack had started hankering after the South of France instead – he had heard that in a few months over twenty countries would be presenting films at the Casino of Cannes for an inaugural world film festival to rival that of Venice. Jack was convinced that this was the time to buy real estate in Cannes, before it hit the world map, and his commercial instincts, at least, had yet to be proven wrong.

Mimi heard a knock on her bedroom door, and Frances popped her head in. 'We just got back from the Grovers'. Adeline and Adam were knee-deep in books.'

'I can't wait to get over there after the honeymoon. I call first dibs on any Burney.'

'You can have her.' Frances smiled and came over and sat on the edge of the bed. 'You know, I was almost married once.'

Mimi whipped around in her chair before the vanity table. 'No, I did not know. You never said a word.'

'Well, that's because it was a secret engagement, of sorts. Only our parents were told. And it lasted only as long as that.'

'Do I know him?' Mimi laughed, thinking the question was absurd.

'Actually, yes – it was Andrew Forrester.'

Mimi put down her Max Factor mascara stick. 'You're joking. No, wait, you're not joking, are you? Oh my goodness, it all makes so much sense now.'

Frances eyed her curiously. 'What does?'

'His solicitude for you. His worry. He's so risk-averse about everything to do with the society, always so concerned we'll breach a director's or fiduciary duty of some kind and all end up in jail, and yet he was out there pleading with you to fight Colin Knatchbull every step of the way on the will.'

'I really don't think that has anything to do with it.'

'Frances, please, he lives by the letter of the law. Yet I swear he would have burned that second will if he could have gotten away with it. What on earth happened?'

'It was so long ago, I hardly even recall. We got engaged, and my father would not consent, and I was persuaded to break it off.'

'That's a little ironic, don't you think?'

'Then he returned from the Great War and continued with his legal studies and became quite successful in town. His ability to spot risk ahead of time became legendary in the greater Hampshire County.'

'This has now moved beyond irony, Frances.'

'Trust me, I know,' she sighed resignedly.

'So, you might have provided an heir after all, if it hadn't been for your father, and then your father took your only home away from you because you never bore him an heir. It's the plot to a Bette Davis movie.'

Frances started to take out the letter sitting hidden in her right skirt pocket. 'A bad marriage, though, is worse than no marriage at all.'

'Yes, I suppose, although Charlotte Lucas would probably have had something to say about that . . .' Mimi was pinching the colour into her cheeks and then applying rouge as the make-up artists had taught her, to avoid overapplying for the daylight.

'Mimi, have you ever heard of a company called Alpha Investments Limited?'

'No, why?'

'Andrew was looking at their annual filings for some work matter. Jack is on the board.'

Mimi was now applying the rose-tinted lipstick she had bought at Chanel in Paris a few weekends ago.

'Oh, right, I know he has meetings in Scotland once in a while for some business up there. Golf, I think. I don't know. I never listen when he starts talking about golf.'

Frances held the letter out to Mimi. 'Andrew received this from the chairman of Alpha earlier today. It seems they – well, here, I should let you read this yourself.'

Mimi put the lipstick down and smacked her lips together, then blotted them lightly with a tissue from the sterling-silver Kleenex box on the vanity.

'Frances, really, on my wedding day.' Mimi took the letter and stood up while she read it, then sank down onto the edge of the bed next to her.

'So, wait a minute, you've lost everything? Even the cottage?'

Frances nodded.

'But where will you live? And where will we put all those books? What about the museum – and for *what*? A golf clubhouse?' She practically spat out the last two words as she angrily crunched up the paper in her hands. 'My God, he used me – he used us – he used all the information I'd been confiding in him . . .'

'I really debated about whether to tell you before the wedding. I mean, it really is just business, you know, and if you think about that for a moment, Colin could easily have sold to anyone, and Jack has every right—'

But Mimi was gone.

Frances looked about the room with a sigh, then lay back on the bed, her booted feet still on the floor. Something rustled in the heavy folds of her floor-length skirt as it fanned out beneath her. She sat up in surprise and retrieved from the left pocket a folded single sheet of paper with her name marked on the outside in a hurried scrawl. It had been so many years since she had seen that handwriting – decades even – that she first started to read the letter without any notion of its author.

Dear Frances,

This letter is so long overdue, that a wiser man would probably consider it ill-advised to ever send. But I find myself unable to leave the past alone. You must allow me to tell you how sorry I am for all the years that we did not speak, and for my misbegotten pride, and – more than anything – for not truly comprehending your unique and inimitable spirit. If I owed you anything, it surely was that.

Patience in love has not been my virtue, and yet in hurrying on, I ended up running a race with no destination, and with bitterness and hurt my sole companions. I can only hope that you have been wiser and kinder to yourself than I, in my neglect, have sadly failed to be.

I am writing this letter in the parlour of Chawton Cottage, where you have just left me, and I put it in your hands on this, Mimi's wedding day, in the spirit of the friendship I fervently hope we now and forever share.

Yours most admiringly,
Andrew

Frances folded the letter and slipped it back into her skirt pocket. She was most confused. The letter addressed the past, but asked for nothing more. This made it just one more tense occurrence to add to an already bewildering list: the recent discovery that she had a brother, the surreptitious sale of the library out from under Colin, today's letter terminating her tenancy of Chawton Cottage, and the consequent unburdening to Mimi of her own fiancé's role in that. It suddenly seemed to Frances that the more she inched forward, the more she grasped for connection, the muckier everything got.

It made a case for staying inside, if nothing else.

But Frances knew that she would have to get up off this bed in a matter of minutes, enter the church alone, advise all the guests that the wedding was off, and then face Andrew in particular with as much equanimity as she could muster.

She lay back on the bed with a final sigh and let her memories drift even further, to her childhood, and to all the famous people that had visited the Great House over the centuries and, just like Mimi Harrison, slept in this very bed. Even the Prince of Wales, when she was just a girl of four. He had pinched her little cheeks at dinner and asked to sit next to her, and she had never forgotten it. Many of the men who had visited seemed to have seen in her the lack of a father, a loving and affectionate one at least – one who truly comprehended her in that affection – and had often singled her out for innocent attention. In this she could have seen the entire arc of her life if she could have been handed a crystal ball – the very thing she hoped, just now, despite the sounds of yelling and vase-throwing from the bedroom next door, she had given Mimi.

Chapter Thirty

Chawton, Hampshire
20 April, 1946
The Wedding

he wedding had been called off.

Frances had come into the parish church just before noon, knocked on the front wooden doors held open in the warm spring air, and announced that Mimi Harrison had just received some difficult news from abroad and would not be getting married that day. The guests had all unwillingly dispersed, and the crowd that had gathered outside the church, including several London news photographers, had let out a collective groan for all their efforts.

The eight members of the society were now the only ones left behind. They sat together as a group in the front pew of the church, Reverend Powell busying himself in the sanctuary out of earshot.

Evie and Dr Gray were reviewing the letter from the chairman of Alpha Investments, having been ignorant of the whole debacle until Frances's ominous appearance in the doorway of the church. Mimi sat with her head on Yardley's shoulder, her eyes stained black by mascara. Across the aisle, Adeline was holding Mimi's bouquet of blush-pink peonies, roses and ranunculuses. Adam was sitting next to her; Frances and Andrew stood a little to the side of them all.

'I should thank you, Frances,' Mimi finally spoke, 'for being so honest with me. A lot of people would not have dared.'

'Well, Andrew,' Dr Gray spoke up, 'I suppose you'll tell us there's no hope now for even a roof over Miss Frances's head.'

'I wouldn't say that.' He gave Frances at his side a quick, indecipherable look.

'Can we counterbid, for the cottage?' asked Yardley. 'Make them an offer they can't refuse?'

'Even if a majority of the trustees agree,' Andrew replied, 'we could still run into trouble as a charity if we bid significantly above fair market value. We may think the cottage is worth whatever cost, and probably one day it will indeed be priceless, but right now it's worth about three thousand pounds and that's peanuts to a company like Alpha.'

'But surely we can try?' asked Evie.

'Forgive me, Mimi, but Jack's on the board, right?' Dr Gray asked.

She sat up a bit from her slumped position in the pew and nodded. 'I suspect my powers of persuasion over him are minimal, though, right now.'

'Mimi' — Andrew stepped forward — 'you said just now that Jack must have used the info you were sharing with him to make the deal with Colin, correct?'

She nodded again.

'Forgive me, too, my dear, but is there anything, anything at all, that you know about Jack and his dealings — business or otherwise — that could be used in turn? Seems only fair, under the circumstances.'

The entire row pivoted their heads to look at Andrew For-rester.

'Andrew Henry Forrester!' exclaimed Frances. 'Are you suggesting—'

He held up his hand. 'I'm not suggesting anything. I'm not suggesting the Austen *Society* do anything. Only Mimi knows in her heart what to do.' He looked about at all the faces star-ing at him and decided for the first time in his life to abandon restraint and go for broke. 'Frances, I think we do, too. Let me put that roof over your head, and my heart in your hands. No one ever deserved it more.'

And right then and there, before all seven other members of the Jane Austen Society, Frances Elizabeth Knight began to sob uncontrollably.

'Frances, please, don't cry,' Andrew was whispering to her gently, patting his jacket pockets to find a handkerchief to con-sole her.

She just kept crying. It was, by far, the most emotion any of them had ever witnessed in her.

'I have literally nothing, Andrew, you know that,' she fi-nally managed to say through her tears. 'You know that better than anyone.'

'Frances, darling, that didn't matter to either of us nearly thirty years ago – why on earth would it matter now?'

She wiped her eyes with the back of her hand and smiled at him lovingly for the first time in as long as that. 'Are you sure?'

'Frances, I just watched you have your whole world ripped out from under you, and you have borne it as no other woman in England would have. It would be my honour, truly, to be your husband.'

Yardley ran behind the altar to have a few words with Rev-erend Powell, who immediately agreed as a representative of the Church of England to conduct the ceremony and dispense with the need for a licence.

Adeline jumped up and, with a quick nod from Mimi, shoved the bouquet into Frances's shaking hands. Evie ran back to the Great House to grab Josephine and Charlotte, knowing they would never forgive her if they missed such a longed-for event.

Frances turned to Mimi. 'Are you all right, if we do this?'

'Oh, Frances, it's the only thing that would make any of this all right.'

With those words of blessing, Frances Elizabeth Knight let Andrew Henry Forrester take her hand and lead her to the altar.

⌒

Dr Gray was standing alone in the lime grove, listening to the bells peal three o'clock. The wedding had been over for a few hours, and the society had enjoyed Mimi's cancelled wedding breakfast in the courtyard, courtesy of Charlotte and Josephine. Immediately afterwards, Yardley had gone with Adam to Adeline's house to start going through all the books, Mimi had collapsed in the guest bedroom, Evie was helping Miss Frances pack quickly for her honeymoon, and Andrew had rushed back to Alton to wrap up some paperwork before catching the train to Brighton with his new bride.

Dr Gray looked about himself at the surrounding fields, the walled garden up on the hill, the ha-ha that ran alongside the lime grove to keep out the sheep. He remembered walking here in the rain with Adeline last summer, the many visits to old Mr Knight in his bedroom, the Christmas Eve service and the reading of the will shortly thereafter, an event which he now saw as the turn of the screw in all their lives. He allowed himself to think even further back, to the burial of his late wife in the parish graveyard, and his own wedding day decades earlier inside the little church, and the playing in the woodland with Frances and Andrew as little kids.

All of these memories, big and small, were equal in only one – but one very significant – way. They all belonged to the past, they were invisible matter, they could leave no trace or mark on the present. Only life in the moment could do that – only this second in the hour – only this one fraction of time that was gone before you could even complete the thought. It was all both that ephemeral, and that infinitely reliable.

If Dr Benjamin Gray could have strung even just a few seconds from the past into something permanent, it would have been the feel of Jennie's cheek against his neck. He missed that so much – missed her loving touch – missed being loved.

Instead he was reduced to being a lonely widower in need of salvation. Goodness knows where Liberty Pascal got some of this stuff, but when it came to Adeline Grover, Liberty never appeared to miss her mark. Dr Gray had not been able to stop thinking about her suggestive comments since their walk.

It made a lot of strange sense. He had always felt as if Adeline was trying to prod him back to life somehow, back when they had crossed paths the most, when she was teaching at the village school – as if she was daring him into some kind of action. He saw now that on some unconscious level he had been asking her to. He had assumed at the time that the friction between them had all been to do with the school – the syllabus, the other trustees, the collective resistance to her teaching style.

But now he also saw – he hoped – that it was not about any of that. It was about him.

And he knew that she had cared.

He turned from the lime grove and headed through the woodland, then up a small incline into the walled garden made up of two different 'rooms': a front enclosure full of symmetrically planted lilac trees, and behind that another even larger space full of rose bushes and vegetable patches and fruit trees, surrounded on all sides by towering red-brick walls. In each of the three outside walls was a dark-red wooden door, leading to where, he was not sure. He realised that in all the years he had visited the estate, he had never opened any of those doors.

When he entered the second enclosed garden space, he right away spotted Adeline sitting on a little bench against the farthest back wall, the small copy of *Pride and Prejudice* that he had given her at Christmas sitting open on her lap.

'Why, hullo. What are you doing here?' he asked in surprise.

'What are *you* doing here? Playing hide-and-seek with Liberty?'

'Just hiding.' He smiled and came over and sat down next to her on the bench. 'Well, all's well that ends well.'

'It was definitely like something out of Shakespeare, all those weddings at once.'

'Or Austen.'

She laughed. 'It's nice to see something work out, for once, even after all that time.'

'And they say you can never go back.'

'Do you believe that?'

'No, not now. Not after that.' He looked at her out of the corner of his eye. 'No one is more rigid and unyielding than Andrew Forrester.'

'No one, that is, except you,' Adeline countered.

'You're probably right,' he gave in with a grin.

They stayed there quietly for a few minutes, listening to the starlings and finches singing from the tops of the orchard trees.

'We haven't sat like this in a while,' Adeline finally spoke.

'Not since last summer, I think.'

She closed the little book on her lap. 'We were discussing *Emma* I believe.'

'The obtuseness of old men.'

'Knightley's not so old.'

'Old enough to know better,' Dr Gray said. 'Although perhaps age has nothing to do with it. Look at Evie. She's, what, all of sixteen, and she's got the entire British literary canon of the nineteenth century figured out.'

'What do you wish you had figured out?'

'You,' he said quietly, and she leaned her head against his shoulder, and he realised he wanted to capture this moment forever. Wanted – finally – to try to string these seconds into something permanent all over again, however ephemeral and futile and fleeting this moment, too, would always be.

'I was pretty obvious, you know. I practically handed you teacher's notes.'

He laughed. 'And I failed the catechism miserably.'

She looked up at him, at his sad, handsome face. 'I did love Samuel.'

'I know that, Adeline, I truly do.'

She started to cry, and he grabbed her hands in his.

'No one will understand,' she said through her tears.

'Is that important, to you?'

'No.' She wiped her eyes with the edge of her sleeve. 'But it would have been important to Samuel.'

'You do him a great disservice if you assume that about him. Mr Knight had that power over Frances, her whole life, and look at how he abused it. And anyway, what if you are wrong?'

She moved away from him a bit on the bench. 'I'll never know. That's what's so hard.'

'And I'll never know if I could have saved your baby. Or Jennie. Or, frankly, so many other lives. I did my best though,

I do know that. And when I couldn't, I at least punished only myself.'

She reached up and touched his cheek with her tear-stained hand. 'You're not doing that any more, though, right?'

'You knew?'

She kissed his cheek where her hand had been, hardly even able to look into his eyes. 'Only recently. Mimi said something so innocuous, but it made me think. And then there was Liberty and the medicine-cabinet keys. I thought you were so disappointed in me, in my weakness – and then I realised you were just trying to save me from what you might be doing to yourself.'

'I have stopped, I promise you. What else would make me hire a world-class spy like Miss Pascal?'

Adeline now had to laugh in spite of herself.

'But it will always be a struggle. It will always be in front of me, Adeline, never behind me. That's the Faustian nature of it. You invite it in, and it never leaves.'

She sat up straighter to face him. 'So, what do we do now?'

He pulled her onto his lap and buried his face against her neck, letting himself feel the softness of her cheek, letting himself fall into her essential loveliness, however ephemeral, however fleeting.

'Have you ever tried one of those back doors?' he finally said, looking up behind them from the bench.

She laughed through her tears. 'No, come to think of it.'

'Then I say, let's go and give Liberty Pascal her money's worth.'

'Benjamin Gray . . .' Adeline murmured happily, as his lips found hers.

Epilogue

Chawton, Hampshire
23 March, 1947
The First Annual Meeting of the Jane Austen Society

*T*he society now comprised forty-four members. They came from all walks of life, having seen the discrete advertisements in local Hampshire and London papers:

> *Notice of the first annual meeting of the Jane Austen Society, which is dedicated to the preservation, promotion and study of the life and works of Miss Jane Austen. In conjunction with the Jane Austen Memorial Trust, a charity founded to advance education under the Charities Act, the society has spent the past year working to acquire Miss Austen's former home in Chawton as a future museum site and is pleased to hereby announce the recent acquisition of Chawton Cottage for that purpose. New members of the society are welcome to the first annual meeting to be held at 7:00 p.m. on Sunday, 23 March, 1947, at Chawton Cottage, Winchester Road, Chawton.*

In addition to the three dozen newest members of the society, the original eight participants, including the five trustees of the Jane Austen Memorial Trust, would also be attending.

As an early agenda item at the meeting, the trustees would be announcing their unanimous decision to repay society member Mimi Harrison her original donation of forty thousand pounds, which had enabled the acquisition of the Chawton Great House Library. Last autumn, the sale of the library had realised a record four hundred thousand pounds over a dispersal of fifty days by Sotheby's, and this had enabled the trust to purchase the steward's cottage from Alpha Investments Limited for the reasonable sum of four thousand pounds. The trustees had also moved unanimously to gift fifty thousand pounds from the sale to Miss Frances Knight as the former and proper heir of the Knight estate, as well as in recognition of her successful efforts to secure the library and Chawton Cottage as a result.

Mimi Harrison was currently onstage at the New Theatre as Olivia in *Twelfth Night,* and so Sunday was chosen for the annual meeting as there was no evening performance that day. She would be bringing her new fiancé with her, a Harvard professor of American literature currently on sabbatical at Jesus College, Cambridge. She was also secretly planning to announce a gift to the society at the meeting: a turquoise-and-gold ring that had once belonged to Jane Austen and was considered priceless, along with two topaz crosses.

Dr Benjamin Gray, Chairman of the Jane Austen Society and the Jane Austen Memorial Trust, would be delivering the opening address. His wife, Adeline Lewis Grover Gray, was due to deliver their first child in a month's time, and the date of the annual meeting had also been selected with that important obligation in mind.

Mr and Mrs Andrew Henry Forrester, Esquire, had recently relocated to Chawton from Alton, where Mr Forrester's law offices had expanded to include two junior solicitors. He was now able to turn his attention to other endeavours, the most important of which was the small local hostel his wife had set up using her share of the estate sale. The hostel was intended for Jewish refugee children who had lost their families in the Holocaust and had no homes to return to after the war. That very month, official adoption papers were being finalised by the couple for two of these children; with Mr Forrester's full support, their last name would be Knight.

Evie Stone had just completed the Lent Term at the University of Cambridge and was working hard on the April launch of the first issue of its new student paper, *Varsity*. The society was very aware that Evie posed a significant flight risk as she had been able, with the financial support of Mr and Mrs Forrester, to finally complete her grammar schooling in 1946 under the accelerated tutelage of the new Mrs Dr Gray. Evie successfully gained admission to Cambridge in her eighteenth year in January 1947, as part of the post-war admission to full membership of women students in general.

Jack Leonard would not be attending the meeting. He was currently under indictment by the U.S. federal government for gunrunning during World War II, in violation of various domestic and international laws. He was also, following an anonymous tip, under continuing investigation by the Securities and Exchange Commission for insider trading.

Yardley Sinclair had been promoted to director of museum services for Sotheby's in recognition of his acquisition and sale of the Chawton Great House Library, which had yielded its record-breaking dispersal. The significant increase in his compensation had enabled the aspiring gentleman farmer to finally start looking for his long-dreamt-of bolt-hole for weekends out of the city.

Adam Berwick had lost his employment following the

redevelopment of Chawton Great House into a golf course, shortly on the heels of the death of his mother. Fortunately, he must have somehow inherited a significant amount of money, as he was soon able – in joint tenancy with Mr Sinclair – to acquire ownership of a lovely little farm on the perimeter of Chawton. On beautiful spring weekends, he and Yardley could be seen sitting atop the old hay wagon, their dog Dixon between them, riding about the village fields under the golden dappled sun.

Historical Note by the Author

The people and events described in this book are completely fictional and imaginary; the places are not.

In wanting to write about a group of people traumatised to varying degrees, who come together over their shared love of books and of Jane Austen in particular, I chose not to base the characters on anyone real in order to enjoy full artistic freedom and consulted historical Chawton census records available online to avoid using actual villager surnames. The only exceptions are the names Knight, Knatchbull and Hugessen, but again I completely fictionalised the branches, inheritance patterns and descendants of these families, as portrayed in this book, for my own dramatic purposes.

In reimagining the conception of the Jane Austen Society, I used as my jumping-off point one particular incident that did in fact occur: the finding of a piece of rubbish by the road that inspired Dorothy Darnell of Alton to found the real Jane Austen Society in 1940 and try to acquire the old steward's cottage for a museum. Unfortunately, funds were scarce due to the war, but in 1948 Thomas Edward Carpenter donated the cottage to the nation in memory of his son killed in action in World War II, a memorial trust was formed, and the Jane Austen's House Museum came to life. The objects that you can see in this museum, including the topaz crosses and the turquoise ring, were not acquired by a Hollywood star of the 1940s at a Sotheby's auction, but were brought home nonetheless under fascinating circumstances.

Finally, Chawton House remained under the care and ownership of the real-life Knight family until the early 1990s, when they were forced by inordinate estate taxes and repair costs to sell first to a golf course development company, which soon after defaulted, and then to philanthropist Sandy Lerner, cofounder of Cisco Systems, who restored the home and turned it into the world-class library and heritage site that it is today.

If you are lucky enough to one day visit Chawton House, you will find the Great House, the grounds and the walled garden, and even the shepherd's hut as described herein. The one major change is the location of the Knight family library, from a more removed corner of the ground floor to next to the Great Hall, thus enabling a host of fictional characters to run into each other and set my story into action.

Acknowledgements

$\mathcal{T}$his book would not have been possible without the stewardship of my agent, Mitchell Waters, who embraced my story and characters with his big heart from the very start and never let them go.

As a debut author, I have been spoiled by the kindness, hard work and confidence in my book that my publisher, St. Martin's Press, has shown every step of the way. I am especially indebted to Keith Kahla, Alice Pfeifer and Lisa Senz, who one December morning at 10.10 a.m. changed my life; to Marissa Sangiacomo, Dori Weintraub and Brant Janeway, who so ably shared the results far and wide; and to Michael Storrings and the creative team for so beautifully bringing my characters and story to life.

I am thrilled, as a British citizen by birth, to see my book published in the U.K. and other Commonwealth countries by Orion Books, and I have Victoria Oundjian to thank for making that dream come true.

My book has also benefited greatly from the enthusiasm

and expertise of everyone at Curtis Brown, Ltd., particularly Sarah Perillo and Steven Salpeter. Chocolates and tea will never be enough.

I will be forever grateful to my earliest readers, Jessica Watkins, Petra Rinas and Marlene Lachcik, whose responses to this story motivated me to seek representation one more time, after a ten-year break from trying to get published. And to Jessica's husband and fantastic media lawyer, Ian Cooper, for all his guidance and advice throughout the road to publication.

There may be no profession more affected by the efforts of its teachers than that of writer, and I am indebted to the years of support and encouragement I received as a student of the following: Nick Brune, Professor Emeritus Douglas Chambers, Nigel Marshall, Peter Skilleter, Dr Margaret Swayze, the late Norma Stewart and Professor Emeritus Cameron Tolton.

As the product of a very difficult time, this novel could also not have been written without the continuing support, guidance and compassionate care shown my family by the following medical specialists: Dr Ayeshah Chaudhry, Dr Eugene Downar, Dr Nathan Hambly, Dr David Schwartz, Dr Benjamin Raby and Dr John Yates.

Laurel Ann Nattress, a leading expert on Jane Austen and editor, writer and blogger in her own right, has been an indispensable champion of my book from her first read, and has so selflessly and enthusiastically worked to ensure it reaches as wide an audience as possible. I can never thank her enough. I am also grateful to Phyllis Richardson for her assistance with the epigraph for this book, and to the following authors and lecturers, whose expertise in the field of Jane Austen set the initial flame afire: Professor Lynn Festa, Susannah Fullerton, Professor Claire Harman, Caroline Knight, Professor Stephen Tardif, Whit Stillman, Professor Juliette Wells and Deborah Yaffe.

Words will never suffice to describe the awesomeness that is my daughter, Phoebe Josephine, who saved her father and me in our darkest hours, and whose spirit, humour and heart of gold inspire and motivate me every day.

On so many levels, this book would never have happened without my husband and first reader, Robert Nelson Leek. I could not have picked a better, more supportive, or more loving person to share in the ups and downs of a writing career, or of life.

Finally, I dedicate this book to Jane Austen, for all she has done for me in the past, present and future, for the centuries of enjoyment her books have given the world, and for the example she has set for us all in creating art in the face of uncertainty, illness and despair.